DEADLY AIM

A BAD KARMA SPECIAL OPS NOVEL

TRACY BRODY

Debbie
Great to meet you. I hope
you fall in love with my
Bad Karma team!
Tracy Brody

Deadly Aim

ISBN: 978-1-952187-03-2

First Edition

Also available as an ebook

ISBN: 978-1-952187-02-5

❀ Created with Vellum

To my awesome and supportive husband and family.

To our military members and their families. Thank you for all you sacrifice.

PRAISE FOR TRACY BRODY

"What do you get when you have a kickass female Black Hawk pilot, a sexy Bad Karma Special Ops elite soldier, and a deadly cartel out for revenge? You get toe curling romance, heart-stopping suspense, and a daring rescue that will keep you reading late into the night. Deadly Aim is a book you won't be able to put down." ~ Sandra Owens, author of the bestselling K2 Team and Aces & Eights series.

"What an incredible book. This book has all the feels. Romance, action, adventure and mystery all in one book. The ending was perfect!" ~ Christy (Goodreads review)

"Seat of the pants action with true military insight!" ~ Robin Perini, Publisher's Weekly Bestseller.

"I love Tracy's writing style and voice (and that her heroine is just as kick-ass as the hero!)" ~ Christina Hovland, author of the Mile High Matched series.

"Tracy weaves action and heart together with crisp writing

that kept me turning pages." ~ Colette Dixon, author of Love at Lincolnfield series.

"Mack and Kristie will have you glued to the pages in this action-packed story." ~ Merry (Goodreads Review)

"This is the first romance novel I've read where the characters felt like 100% authentic people. …. I absolutely loved both of them. This is what I want from romance novels. … Highly recommended." ~ Beckett (Goodreads review of *Desperate Choices.*)

"Wow, what an excellent debut for Bad Karma Special Ops series. A well written storyline that is fast paced, action packed with danger, suspense, romance and all around good feels. The characters are captivating and easy to fall in love with. Read this in one sitting, I couldn't put it down. Looking forward to reading more in this new series." ~ Maggi West (Goodreads review of *Desperate Choices.*)

ONE

Training mission, my ass.

Kristie Donovan banked her Army Black Hawk to the right and pushed the helicopter to max speed. It wasn't the time for an *I-knew-it* moment over her suspicions that there was more to this assignment than being sent to train Colombian Army pilots on the electronic instrument systems in their newer Sikorski UH-60 Black Hawks.

Command radioing new orders to pick up a "package with wounded" had Black Ops written all over it. Especially when the coordinates took them right into the heart of an area known for cocaine production. Army "need to know" at its best.

"How far to the LZ?" she asked her Colombian co-pilot trainee.

Josué checked the GPS. "Thirty klicks. If I am right, this is not what you call 'landing zone.'"

"Meaning ...?" Even with the tropical heat and full uniform, goosebumps erupted over her arms.

"Like sixty-meter clearing."

"You use it for practice?" She could hope.

"Never."

"But helicopters use it?"

"Small ones owned by cartel."

Josué might be a relatively inexperienced pilot, but he knew the players here, and his wide, unblinking stare told her more than she wanted to know about who used this clearing. And for what. Great. Let's use a drug lord's landing pad. I'm sure he won't mind. He might even send a welcoming committee—*a well-armed one.*

Sixty meters—if the jungle hadn't encroached. Drops of sweat trickled down her neck the closer in they flew.

She pulled back on the cyclic stick and slowed the helicopter. The blur of the jungle came into focus. She leaned forward, her gaze sweeping left to right through the windscreen at the terrain below. Nothing but trees, trees, and more trees. The thick veil of green hid anything, or anyone, on the ground.

"Do you see the LZ?" she asked her crew chief and gunner.

"Negative," they reported from their vantage points on either side of the aircraft.

"We're not giving anyone extra time to make us a target. Not in daylight." She keyed the radio mic to hail the package on the ground. "Ghost Rider One-Three to Bad Karma, come in." Energy drained from her limbs as she envisioned the scenario that would keep them from answering. "Ghost Rider One-Three to Bad Karma, come in."

Continued silence saturated the air. No, she wasn't too late. She refused to believe—

"Ghost Rider One-Three, this is Bad Karma Two-One. We have a visual on you. Popping smoke."

Thank God. She could breathe again.

The Bad Karma radioman's perfect English screamed American. No doubt now this mission was covert, classified, and maybe even suicidally dangerous.

"I see them." Josué pointed to where a thin smoke trail pinpointed their location.

Kristie banked left.

"Be advised, we have tangos inbound," the radioman reported, "and one friendly in their vicinity."

"You've got to be kidding me," she muttered. Her gunner couldn't deal with the tangos when they could hit one of their own. *Why the hell wasn't he with his team?*

She ground her teeth as the answer came. Someone *special* volunteered to do something incredibly brave—or incredibly stupid—to protect his team. Exactly the way Eric would have done. Had done.

Her throat constricted, and her eyes burned. She pressed against the seat. *Breathe, Kristie, don't go worst-case.* She couldn't change the past, but this time it was her responsibility to bring these soldiers back to their families. Alive. All of them.

Come on. Heroics time is over. Hightail your butt to the LZ, so I can get you and your buddies home.

A flash of light slashed through the dense wall of trees north of their position. "Was that movement at our twelve o'clock?" she asked Josué.

He studied the jungle in front of them. "I only see trees."

"Watch the area at my twelve," she ordered the gunner. She kept the location in her peripheral vision as she surveyed the area to her three o'clock, praying their friendly emerged from that direction.

They had to get down and back up faster than a Hellfire missile. She hovered the aircraft to evaluate the landing zone. Most combat missions on her tour in Afghanistan involved desert landings in open spaces. She could execute those in her sleep. Jungle landings required more precision—and time.

Time they didn't have.

"Heading down."

She pushed the stick, descending as rapidly as she dared.

Before the craft even touched the ground, men in U.S. Army camouflage raced from the jungle's cover toward the bird. Four men carted a stretcher between them. Behind them, a soldier held a slight figure with long, black hair in a fire-man's carry. His arm wrapped around a slender leg below the girl's blue plaid skirt.

Kristie maneuvered to give the soldiers a safe, straight-in approach to the aircraft's open side. When her crew chief jumped out, she scanned the clearing's perimeter. "Thirty seconds and we dust off."

Movement ahead yanked her attention to where an over-sized black SUV came to a hard stop just past the tree line. The doors burst open, and four men emerged, all taking aim with automatic weapons. *Shit!*

"Tangos at my one o'clock!" Her pulse pounded in her ears over the engine noise, but her hand remained steady on the stick. The American soldier holding the back of the stretcher stumbled as they neared the craft. A dark circle formed and spread over the sleeve of his arm, now dangling at his side.

Her gaze shot from her fellow soldiers to the cartel gunmen. She didn't dare rotate the aircraft, but there was no way her gunner could fire at the attackers from his position—and someone had to.

Adrenaline surged through her. She popped her safety harness buckle. "You have the controls," she ordered Josué.

"Wh—" Josué started, but she tugged out her communications line before he confirmed the order or called her *loca*.

Training took over, and she wrestled the M-4 from the mount beside her seat. Josué reached to stop her, but she ducked out, her elbow slipping through his grasp. She stuck close to the door for cover, raised the weapon's butt to her shoulder, and fired a burst of rounds at the vehicle.

Everything happened in slow motion: the tug on her arms and the bounce of the muzzle as she squeezed the trigger.

The slim, short-haired tango near the front passenger side of the vehicle jerked, then clutched a hand to his stomach. She made out the blood staining his light shirt and seeping over his fingers before he collapsed to his knees and fell forward.

A gunman in a plaid shirt and jeans came around the door and knelt at the injured man's side. He fired once more, then began pulling the wounded man behind the cover of the door. Another man darted around the back of the SUV, lifting the legs of the wounded man as they loaded him into the back seat.

From behind the relative safety of the hood, the driver stopped firing long enough to take in the men frantically motioning him inside. He shoved the rear door closed, then climbed in the driver's seat. With the passenger door wide open, the SUV snaked back into the forest.

Kristie's breath came in gasps as she held her position and aimed shots near where the vehicle disappeared. Her gaze swept the tree line. The soldier carrying the woman deposited his load to the ground. His broad back blocked most of Kristie's view of the young woman who scooted into the craft's belly as the soldiers crowded her in further.

The operators hoisted the stretcher inside. The soldier who'd been shot dove in, wincing in pain as he rolled out of the way. The remaining three operators spun to cover the area. Kristie climbed in, plunked down into her seat, and secured her weapon. A bullet hit the nose of the aircraft. She flinched, and Josué ducked to the side. *Son of a bitch.* These guys didn't quit. But neither did the operators, who unleashed a storm of return fire.

By the time she buckled in, there was only the sound of the Black Hawk's blades and engines. The operators switched to handguns. If they were out of ammo, it was time to get the hell out of Dodge. With shaking hands, she jammed in the plug for her headset, missing whatever Josué said.

The last of the operators scrambled aboard.

"All in?" she asked.

Josué jerked the controls, and they lifted into the sky. His rapid ascent tilted up the nose up before leveling and rotating for the gunner to lay down fire at any remaining enemy.

"Hold up!" The choked voice of her crew chief, McCotter, sent a chill through her body.

Kristie glanced into the body of the aircraft. The linebacker-sized operator leaned to speak directly into McCotter's headset.

"I still have a man down there. We are *not* leaving him behind." The deep, unmistakable voice of Ray Lundgren enunciated each word.

Oh, God, no. No!

"You said all in." Josué's voice hinted at panic. He didn't change course.

"We're going back."

"Bad idea." Josué shook his head. "Herrera very powerful. Has weapons to shoot us down. The cartel leaves no survivors."

She was *not* leaving a man behind. No way. Kristie reached for the stick. "I have the controls."

Josué maintained his grip rather than acknowledge the requested handoff. Kristie's pulse throbbed in her ears, dulling the roar of the turbine engines and the *thwack, thwack, thwack* of the blades slicing the air.

She checked her passengers. A shell-shocked teenage girl cowered between the soldiers flanking her. Their resolute faces locked on Kristie. The Special Ops team leader loomed over McCotter. She knew Lundgren, knew his family. If Eric had continued serving under Chief Lundgren, her husband would likely be alive today.

Save herself and others or leave a man to certain death? She didn't have to take orders from Ray.

In that second, she knew what she had to do. The price might be her career, but better to take the risk than live with the knowledge she'd left a man behind.

"Hang on, everyone." She leaned into Josué's field of vision and gripped the stick. "I. Have. The. Controls."

TWO

BARK CHIPS SPRAYED Mack's face as a second bullet thunked into a tree a foot away. Too close. He ducked behind the trunk, eyeing the jungle for denser cover. He gulped in air. So much for an easy retreat. Squawking birds and the nearby screech of monkeys drowned any noise made by the oncoming men.

Crouching, he dropped into the underbrush. The tang of damp earth filled his mouth and nose as he commando-crawled toward the base of two trees, which put him closer to the thugs on his tail.

The distinctive *thwap* of the Black Hawk blades reverberated through the jungle. He was out of time. Peering through his scope, Mack locked onto the lead cartel gunmen and took the shot.

It went wide to the right, just where he'd aimed. The group veered left, toward the claymore mine he'd set to buy his team time for the extraction. He kept his eye on his targets. *That's it. Go that way.* The lead unfriendly tripped the wire.

The ground shook as the explosion ripped through the underbrush. Dust, debris, and bodies flew.

Mack sprang to his feet and hauled ass, not turning to see how many tangos were on his six. Leaves whipped at his face. He vaulted bushes and darted around trees, hurtling toward the LZ.

The stuttered bursts of M-134 mini-gun fire joined the chaotic symphony of animal voices. Through a break in the foliage, he glimpsed the Black Hawk—above the treetops.

Across the clearing, men at the tree line fired on the departing craft.

That was my ride, you assholes.

Mack sank to a knee, steadied his rifle, and took the kill shots between heartbeats. Two men crumpled to the ground, and Mack scanned the area through the scope for more tangos. None. He pivoted. How many thugs were searching for him?

If he survived … No. Don't think that way. Images of his daughters, arms outstretched, running to hug him invaded his mind. He forced them aside to concentrate on the now— survive and come up with Plan C to get the hell out of a jungle crawling with men paid to kill him.

The Black Hawk grew louder. Closer? He scanned the sky. The beautiful, Army-green beast swooped in low over the trees and hovered. His teammates perched in the opening, weapons aimed. Hooah! A flood of relief coursed through his body.

If he'd missed a hostile, the crew above would have his back and every other angle. He dashed from the jungle's cover. They dropped a hoist line even before he signaled them not to land. The aircraft did a slow rotation while the Hawk's gunner chewed up the jungle with fire.

Mack hooked the line to his rigger belt. As soon as he waved his arms, the bird jerked him off the ground. A burst of gunfire erupted, sending bullets whipping past him. They pinged off the aircraft's underbelly. He tried to get a fix on the shooter, but his body twirled wildly as the Black Hawk rose, and his team and the gunner returned fire.

As Mack cleared the canopy, the helicopter surged forward. Treetops blurred past mere inches beneath his boots. The crew winched him up while the chopper gained altitude, flying them out of range.

When he reached the open door, Juan Dominguez grabbed his arm to pull him in. "Enjoy your ride?"

"Highlight of my day." Mack unhooked the line, his heart still hammering in his throat. He paused beside Hunter on the stretcher. "Hang in there, buddy," he said, even though his unconscious teammate wouldn't hear him. He met Ray's eyes. "Thanks."

He made his way to the rear of the aircraft and sank into a seat. His limbs were heavy, and his arms and hands trembled as he rested his head back and filled his lungs. He'd never been so thankful to breathe in jet fuel fumes.

Tony Vincenti sat across from him with a field dressing wrapped around his arm. "What the hell happened to you?" Mack asked.

"Got hit on the dash to the bird. Can you believe that shit? Just a through-and-through." Vincenti shrugged as though getting shot was no big deal. Maybe compared to Hunter—he might lose his mangled right leg after their truck hit that damned explosive when they fled Herrera's compound.

For the first time since the rescue, Mack got a good look at Judge Vallejo's daughter. Her eyes were red, glazed. She was alive and going home—but would she ever be the same?

Herrera, you better hope I never cross your path, you sonofabitch.

"Mission accomplished." Vincenti hoisted his water bottle in a mock toast.

"Mission accomplished," Mack repeated. But with a price.

"You buy me a case of beer, the good stuff, and I won't tell your ex you *volunteered* to charge *toward* a dozen cartel thugs to hold them off."

"Didn't seem like a stupid idea at the time."

"You shoulda let Dominguez do it. He doesn't have kids. Besides, I wouldn't miss him."

Dominguez flipped off Vincenti.

Mack cracked a grin. "Y'all needed the best shot. I hit them. I survived, and Rochelle doesn't get to put 'He had to play the hero' on my tombstone."

"True dat." Vincenti rolled his eyes.

Mack probably shouldn't have said that, but his *ex*-wife had called him selfish. More than a few dozen times, she'd accused him of risking his life for the rush. Rochelle couldn't be more wrong. He did it to protect the people he loved. How could the very thing he did to protect his family drive his wife away?

He closed his eyes and pictured Amber's blue eyes and Darcy's freckled nose and impish smile. If some drug lord kidnapped one of his girls as a get-my-son-out-of-jail-or-we-kill-your-daughter card, he'd want men like his Bad Karma team to make certain she got home alive. He'd done his job because it mattered.

Because of the pilot's composure under fire, he lived to fight another day. He owed the pilot a drink. Hell, a few.

The moment they touched down, the crew chief and

gunner unloaded the stretcher and handed Hunter to the waiting Colombian medics. Vincenti tagged along with them. Mack piled out last, in time to see Chief Lundgren walk the girl off the flight line. The chief supported her elbow as she tottered, her hair dancing in the draft from the Hawk's blades.

Two suited men carrying short-nosed, semi-automatic weapons waited beside an SUV with dark-tinted windows. The taller man opened the door and motioned the girl inside. He gave the chief a curt nod before he ducked in after her.

The rest of the Bad Karma team headed to their quarters, but Mack strode over to his boss.

"Hard to believe she's the same age as my daughter." Ray watched the vehicle kick up dust and gravel as it sped off. "She's been through a month of hell."

"She's gonna need counseling—and detox." Mack shook his head, praying Herrera would pay for what he put her through.

"You noticed, too?"

"Hard not to. Doesn't surprise me they'd get her hooked on their shit. Sending her to a boarding school abroad might be a good idea to keep her safe from someone like Baltazar Herrera."

The chief nodded in agreement, then looked him over. "You okay?"

"No bullet holes." His muscles ached, and his cheek stung. His fingers touched the crusted blood on his face. "Thought I was getting left behind."

"Yeah," Ray huffed. "A little miscommunication with the aircrew. They were supposed to get in the air for their gunner to cover since we were nearly out of ammo. Next thing I know, I about landed on my ass when the Colombian pilot took off like a bat out of hell."

"Right on par for this mission. Thanks for making him come back for me."

"I asked nicely." Ray didn't even crack a grin. "This mission was enough of a clusterfuck. I wasn't leaving a man behind, too. Especially not you."

"Appreciate it."

"Could've been a hell of a lot worse if the pilot hadn't engaged the group that hit Vincenti."

"Pilot? You kidding me?"

"Not the Colombian who dusted off, but our guy there, who also took over the controls to come back."

That pilot did have major cojones—thankfully.

The chief glanced toward the aircraft, then did a double take. "Donovan?" A gruff chuckle rumbled out. "Correction. It wasn't our *guy*." He broke into a smile.

Mack turned to see who Ray signaled. The pilot had removed her helmet. *Her* helmet. Sure, there was one or two female pilots in most regiments these days, but so few that it hadn't occurred to him a woman might be manning the controls.

"I'll be damned." He gave an appreciative nod and mouthed, "Thanks," to his rescuer.

"Yeah." The chief snorted. "I didn't realize Kristie was at the controls. I'm gonna say thanks before I write the after-action reports. Get cleaned up, then check on Hunter and report back to me. I want to know his and Vincenti's condition before I contact the colonel."

"Roger that. Might want to lead with the news we recovered the judge's daughter."

"What's that saying about poking the bear? Herrera isn't going to crawl into a cave and take a long nap."

Before heading off, Mack admired the pilot's profile.

Strands of golden-brown hair hung free from her braid to frame an attractive face with bright eyes and full lips. Her uniform didn't quite camouflage her curves. As daring as any man on the Bad Karma team *and* she looked like that? He really did need to buy her a drink.

THREE

INSIDE THE CANTINA, Kristie lined up at the counter with her fellow pilots to order. The sound system played an energetic Latin tune; ceiling fans spun overhead. Colombian soldiers in uniform filled half of the cantina's twenty or so wooden tables.

"Do you think the girl is an American?" Paul Wilson, her unit's lead instructor pilot, asked over the music before looking at the hand-painted menu above the order window.

"I don't know. I barely got a look at her." Though she expected her team would ask questions she couldn't answer, she had to come out with them tonight. Leave them with no doubt she could handle the job.

Paul gestured to a table in the back. "Those our Special Ops guys?"

Most in the group had hair longer than regulation. Some even sported beards. In their unofficial uniform of khaki cargo pants and collared shirts, they might pass for civilians, but she would peg them as Spec Ops, even if they hadn't flown with her today.

"Oh, yeah." She chuckled at seeing them positioned so

they had an unrestricted view of all the restaurant's entrances and windows. That seating arrangement had always been Eric's modus operandi, too. The memory ricocheted down, then around in the hollow space in her chest.

Damn. Ray Lundgren wasn't with them. Hopefully, he'd show up. She could ask one of the others about the condition of the injured men they'd extracted, but she needed to talk to Ray—this time without Josué around.

A few men glanced her way. Working with all men, she was used to that and ignored the stares.

The aroma of meat cooking made her mouth water. Josué had finished his after-action report in half the time it took her. Then he stalked from the briefing room, commenting he was thankful to be going home to his family after being duped by the Americans, and that he'd now have to watch his back for the rest of his life.

Not that she'd known the true nature of their mission, either. Who knew what the hell he wrote up about her exiting the craft and firing on Herrera's men. Probably not the brightest move on her part, but she couldn't sit there when she was in the best position to cover fellow soldiers. Josué's report probably blamed her for the premature departure, too.

Ray's guys were the best at what they did. *The* best. But they were low on ammo and leaving one of Ray's team with who knows how many thugs at Herrera's disposal ... No, she couldn't leave a man behind. Not with those odds. Going back had been the right thing.

They could have had rocket-propelled grenades and shot down her craft. A chill shook her whole body even though they'd dodged that possibility. But what if their wounded man lost his leg, or worse, died because of that delay? Thank God no one else got hit when she went back.

Command could question her judgment. If they didn't

trust her ability to make the right decisions in high-risk situations, she may never get a shot at a MEDEVAC position.

That couldn't happen. She needed to talk to Ray. Make sure his men were okay and explain the miscommunication and how what Josué knew about Herrera had him freaked out.

While she perused the menu, someone touched her arm, startling her.

"Whoa. I'm a friendly." The soldier Ray had spoken with on the flight line leaned back, his hands raised defensively.

"I didn't see you." Why was she letting Josué's warnings about Herrera get in her head? Herrera may not value the lives of his hired protection, but his top lieutenant wasn't stupid. It'd be suicidal to strike back without planning, especially on or close to a military base. By the time they regrouped from the fog of war, she'd be back home.

"Sorry." He pointed to the cashier. "I was going to tell him whatever you want, it's on me."

"That's not necessary. After nearly leaving you, I should buy *you* a drink."

"From what I heard, you weren't the one dusting off without me. Trust me, I owe you more than a meal. Thanks for coming back."

The lump lodged in her throat got pushed down by his calm demeanor. At least he didn't blame her. Still, as pilot-in-command, responsibility for today's mission was on her, despite any communication problems, and she'd owned up to it in her report.

The operator stepped back and waited to pay. He was tall, over six feet, and auburn highlights showed in his scruff and short hair. Blood crusted over a deep, fresh scratch that curved across his left cheek. Who knew a battle wound could amp up the sexy factor.

Her teammate, Paul, leaned close to her ear. "Use that

goodwill and see if you can find out who the girl was and what this is all about."

"I'm sure it's classified."

"Never hurts to ask."

She'd done her job. Saved lives—she hoped. Paul had a point, though. This was the perfect opportunity to get the information *she* needed. "How're your injured guys?" she asked the operator, praying the risk she'd taken had paid off.

"Hunter, the guy on the stretcher, is out of surgery. They saved his leg, and he's stable," he said. "They patched up Vincenti's arm and gave him pain meds, not that he would stay in the clinic. He's probably already in the gym doing one-armed chin-ups."

It sounded about right for these guys. The invisible band constricting her chest finally loosened. "I'm glad to hear it."

With that question answered, her attention shifted to the snug fit of the dark-blue polo shirt across the operator's chest. And his muscular arms. Her sex drive had been MIA for a while, but it was like this guy had performed a successful search-and-recover mission.

He stuck out his hand. "Sergeant First Class Mack Hanlon."

"Kristie Donovan."

Mack suited him. She reluctantly withdrew her hand from his warm grasp.

Even if his rank hadn't made him off-limits, today's heroics were all the reminder she needed of why getting involved with another man in Special Ops was never happening. No matter how handsome or dedicated to serving their country. If Eric had been a nine point five on the risk-taker scale, Mack was a thirteen. These operators might think they could beat the odds, but they weren't the ones who had to live with the consequences if they were wrong.

Paul picked up his beer and plate of nachos. He gave her the side-eye and mouthed, "Ask him," as he headed to a table.

"I'll have a mojito and the tamales," she told the cashier.

The young man turned to the bartender. *"Mojito para la dama."*

"I'll have another beer," Mack added. When he reached past her, his arm brushed hers. That simple touch made her want more contact. He handed colorful currency to the cashier.

Across the top of Mack's arm, she noticed faint black lines. "Are you using new mapping techniques to get around the jungle instead of GPS?"

"What?" He followed her gaze to his arm. "Oh," he chuckled. "My eight-year-old's class is learning about constellations. She's also a budding artist and decided I'm the perfect canvas to practice on. Except she used a permanent marker while she played connect the dots with my freckles."

The last photo Kristie had of her husband was of him holding a young girl about that age at the school in Afghanistan. "She's quite the artist." Maybe the catch in her voice gave her away because Mack studied her with narrowed eyes. He stepped over to where she waited for her order.

"Give her crayons, markers, sidewalk chalk, and she'll draw on paper, the street, my arm, my wi—*ex*-wife's new kitchen table." His voice went rough on those last words. "I don't get to see my girls as much as I'd like, so I couldn't bring myself to scrub it off."

He traced his fingers over the lines in a way even more appealing than his smile. It made her ache along with him.

They got their drinks, and she took a long, deep gulp of the cold, tangy mojito. "You're a good dad, letting your daughter turn you into a coloring book. Memories like that make you a hero in her eyes. I used to watch reruns of

M*A*S*H with my dad. My sister laughed that I wanted to fly the choppers that brought in the wounded rather than be a nurse, but Dad assured me I could be a pilot."

"*M*A*S*H*. A true classic. I still watch reruns. And your dad was right. You found your calling."

"Thanks for saying that." His response left her somewhat off-balance. Most men questioned her ability, her motivation. Even her femininity. It became hard to think coherently under the spell cast by Mack's vivid blue eyes. Eyes that she shouldn't be staring into with less-than-professional thoughts. She downed more mojito.

Meat sizzled on the grill. Men talked and laughed. Metal utensils clinked against glass plates. And for some reason, Mack stayed planted by her side.

"You should thank Chief Lundgren for making sure no man got left behind," she told him.

"How do you know the chief?"

"He, his wife, Stephanie, and I have been friends since we were all at Fort Lewis."

She provided minimal information, but this wasn't the time to explain how close they'd become when Eric served under Ray. They'd been there for Eric's funeral, and Stephanie kept in touch. "You're lucky to have him leading your team."

"Amen to that." Mack grinned in a manner that made her speculate what kind of missions they'd participated in before.

Today might be just another day at work for him. Would he remember it in a month or a year? She would. It was the closest she'd come to flying a real MEDEVAC mission. She'd helped save a life. Maybe more than one.

Before he had a chance to ask more questions, they served her tamales. She carried the plate to where Paul had joined the rest of their unit right next to Mack's teammates.

The operators all projected self-assured confidence. She saw it in the way they sat. The way they studied others in the cantina. The way they talked amongst themselves.

She'd spent enough time with Eric's Ranger buddies to recognize these qualities on a slightly lesser yet somewhat cockier scale. Not long ago, she'd been a part of the inner circle of a group like theirs. It hit her right in the chest how much she missed it.

The bond wasn't quite the same with the guys in her unit. Aviators moved around more, so they didn't form ties as close as the operators. Without Eric, she didn't fit in the same way at social get-togethers, especially being the sole female aviator in her company. The only place she felt normal was in the air.

While she ate, she listened to the conversation among the operators. No one mentioned Herrera, the girl, or the day's events. A testament to why they were referred to as 'quiet professionals.' Not that they were all quiet. The least imposing of the group spoke the loudest, jumping from major league baseball to his son's little league batting average.

Every risk she'd taken today was worth it to save lives. She couldn't bring Eric back, but these men's wives would not get a visit from a casualty notification officer. Would not have to break the news to their children and have their hearts broken.

When Mack bragged about one of his daughters, she snuck a peek in his direction. His face glowed with pride and love.

When the operator's attention shifted to the bar, she glanced over her shoulder. Ray stood at the counter. Finally. Time to get his assessment.

"How're you doing?" Ray asked when she reached his side.

She shrugged. "You tell me. You seemed pretty pissed off in my aircraft."

"Not much went down the way we planned. Been pissed off most of the day, but not at you."

Was he just saying that? "If I'd stayed inside, we wouldn't have left—"

"That's not on you. You were out there covering our asses. My men are sitting over there because of you. If I hadn't insisted on our own air support instead of relying on the Colombians, there's no telling how things would've turned out, how many casualties we might've racked up if you hadn't shown courage under fire. It was your Colombian buddy who took off before we could communicate we needed fire support and that he needed to stick around."

"Thanks."

"Sorry we had to use the training assignment cover rather than bring you in. Need-to-know basis. If word got out to Herrera, it would've blown the op. Brass wouldn't even use our regular aviation unit."

"I get that."

"Anything new with you?"

"I'm planning to transfer to a MEDEVAC position."

"We have those at Bragg," he hinted.

"I've heard."

"I can put in a word for you."

While she had family in North Carolina, Fort Bragg wasn't her first choice of locations. But with two MEDEVAC units recently selecting other pilots for open slots, her options were limited. She didn't want to get into that with Ray now. "I should hear something soon."

The cashier handed Ray a tray with a plate of steaming pork, rice, and beans. He stepped aside. "You ordering or coming back to the table?"

Rejoining her teammates and the operators would only stir up more memories. "No. I'm going to hit the rack." The mojito had given her a slight buzz, hopefully enough to slow her racing brain and let her sleep. "If you can, tell Stephanie you saw me, and I said hi."

"You should come up to Bragg. She and Alexis would love to see you."

"Why don't you bring them to Savannah and the beach instead?"

"I'll suggest it to Steph."

"Good. I hope to see you again soon on a social level— rather than another meetup like today." She winked at her friend.

A sly smile pulled at the corners of his mouth. "No promises."

FOUR

"EVERYTHING OKAY?" Mack asked Ray once he took a seat beside him at the table.

"Everything other than the after-action report being a bitch to write. Checked on Hunter, and Vincenti, too. He was in his room, sleeping off whatever they gave him. Got ahold of Colonel Mahinis and gave him the rundown for him to talk to Hunter's wife."

Mack let him finish rather than interrupt the Chief's narrative of what the rest of the team wanted to know. "I was referring to your friend and the way she ambushed you when you walked in."

"That? She wanted to apologize for nearly leaving you behind." Ray took a long pull of his beer. "She was concerned I might be pissed. Couldn't talk earlier with the Colombian pilot around."

"She friends with Stephanie? Old neighbors, or …?"

"Family Readiness Group. Her husband was one of my squad leaders in Second Battalion back when I was at Lewis," Ray continued as if aware Mack was digging for information.

"We've stayed in touch, though the last time we saw her was at her husband's funeral."

Mack winced. He'd noticed she wasn't wearing a wedding band, but he hadn't expected that to be why. "Was he your commanding officer?"

"No. Staff sergeant on my team. They were married before Kristie went to Warrant Officer Candidate School and through flight training," Ray explained. "Eric planned to go through Selection for Special Operations. He wanted to do a second deployment first. KIA halfway though, so he never got the chance. Damn shame. He'd have been a good fit. Her, too."

Not many women had what it took to be the wife of an operator—he'd learned that reality the hard way—but Ray's endorsement of Kristie said a lot about her. Maybe he'd find someone like that around Fort Bragg. Unfortunately, the single women who hung out at bars frequented by operators weren't the type he wanted to introduce to his daughters. Dominguez and Vincenti might enjoy picking up women this way, but to Mack, it was only a little more fun than digging a foxhole.

Dominguez wiggled fingers in Mack's face. "You still with us?"

Pulled back to reality, Mack knocked Dominguez's hand away. "Thinking about how today could've turned out differently on a lot of levels." No point in wondering about the pilot with distance and rank working against them. Too bad, since she was the first woman since his divorce who pressed all the right buttons.

The banter continued for a while, helping them all decompress. However, after a few long days and nights in the jungle with short stretches of sleep, tonight was not the time to close down the cantina. They'd had a couple of drinks when Ray pushed to his feet, and the rest of the Bad Karma team followed suit.

Outside, gravel crunched under Mack's feet as the cantina's music gave way to the call of tree frogs and insects. The bright sliver of the moon lit the way as the men walked the short distance to the housing building.

Mack eyed the building like it was a four-star hotel. A room to himself. A bed. No wild animals on the roam. Hopefully, little or no bugs. No worries about Herrera's gunmen on the base.

Inside the cinder-block structure, fluorescent lights buzzed. The men's footsteps echoed in the stairway, half the team peeling off on the second floor. At the third-floor landing, Mack followed AJ Rozanski and Kyle Lin down the dimly lit hall. The media lounge was dark, but light from the television screen flickered as they passed by.

Did he see who he thought on the screen?

"I'll see you in the morning," Mack told them, hanging back to investigate. On the television, Captain Benjamin "Hawkeye" Pierce wore an olive-green Army uniform and talked with a Korean woman.

Mack stepped into the room. Curled up and nearly hidden by the high back of the well-worn sectional sofa, Kristie watched *M*A*S*H*. Sleep could wait. He leaned over to make her aware of his presence. "What are you doing up?"

She glanced up at him. "Couldn't sleep."

"So, you decided to watch *M*A*S*H*?" He came around the corner of the sofa.

"One of the few options in English." She gave a sheepish shrug.

He could see shooting someone weighed on her. He understood trying to counter those feelings with something positive. "Which episode is this?"

"It just started, but Colonel Potter sent Hawkeye to care for a Korean villager and looks like he's falling for the daughter."

"I don't remember this one. Can I join you?"

"Sure." Kristie shifted as he took a seat near her on the couch, but her attention remained glued to the television.

It'd be too much to hope she set this up for them to hang out. It wasn't like she knew what floor he was on. He could make the most of the opportunity, though. "Trapper John or BJ Honeycutt?" he asked when the Spanish-language commercial came on.

She lowered the volume. "What?"

"Your favorite—Trapper or BJ?"

"Hmmm." She waggled her head and avoided direct eye contact as she debated. "As a girl, I had a crush on Trapper, but as a woman, I like BJ because he didn't cheat on his wife. Colonel Potter or Colonel Blake?" She hit the ball back into his court.

"I'd have to go with Colonel Potter. He knew when to break the rules but maintained discipline and respect. Frank Burns or Charles Emerson Winchester the Third?"

She chuckled at his attempt to add a refined Boston accent to the latter. "Neither. Frank Burns was a whiny cheater, and Winchester was a pompous, self-centered ass."

"Don't hold back," Mack teased, though he agreed with her. "Hate some characters, but you love the show?"

"Drama and comedy make for good TV. Don't get me started on Hot Lips. All Miss Uptight about the rules but is involved with a married man, then does a total turnaround when she gets engaged."

Everything that came out of this woman's mouth made her even more attractive. Maybe she wasn't a hundred-percent-by-the-book type.

"Radar or Klinger as company clerk?" she asked.

"Easy. Radar. He knew things before they happened. I'd want him on my team. He may have had a teddy bear and drank grape Nehi, but he never shirked his duty, whereas Klinger tried to get discharged by wearing a dress." He liked that she nodded in response to his reasoning.

The commercials ended, but they continued to make comments during the rest of the show. He hadn't felt this at ease with a woman since, hell, he couldn't remember. Maybe back in the early days with Rochelle. The last few years had been such hard work trying to make her happy that he'd forgotten it could be like this. *Should be* like this.

He angled his head to study Kristie discreetly. She was the kind of woman you could put on an Army recruiting poster. Not the fussy, glamorous type, but an alluring face with high cheekbones and lush lips. Long lashes set off captivating blue eyes. Her straight brown hair was tucked behind her ears and hung just past her shoulders.

She'd changed clothes since the cantina. Even in dark-blue sleep pants with a small star print and V-neck tee, she had a figure that would appeal to any man. Her looks were enough to attract attention, but the fact she served *and* supported a husband who'd been in Special Forces appealed to him even more.

It was tempting to brush his hand over hers. They were two thousand miles from home. No one would know if something happened between them. Better not to risk anything that could be construed as harassment, though.

"Should probably get to bed." He took a chance when the show ended and waited for her response. It was a struggle to keep his face impassive when she met his gaze. To not lean in.

She sighed. "You're probably right." She clicked off the TV and got to her feet. "You guys fly home tomorrow?"

"In the morning. Hunter'll have to stay a couple more days." He stood, too, right in her path to the door. She stared into his eyes with—what? Hope? Desire? Damn, he wished he could tell.

She broke eye contact and dipped her head. "Give your girls a big hug when you get home. And stay safe—for them." She tapped her finger to the drawing on his arm. "Good night."

She gave him a slight smile, but nothing else. Not the "good night" he'd begun to hope for, but somehow the past hour made up for it.

He couldn't let her slip away yet. Before she could maneuver around him, he laid a hand on her arm. She was close enough for her citrusy scent to tempt him; he breathed it in. "Thanks again for not leaving me behind.

"Of course. 'No man left behind,'" she spouted the Ranger motto, her voice cracking on the last word.

This time when she met his eyes, sadness clouded the other emotions, and he did know what she was thinking. About another man.

He lifted his hand from her arm. "Fly safe."

Too damn bad he wouldn't see her again.

FIVE

KRISTIE PADDED down the hall to her room. As she unlocked the door, she refused to check which room Mack went into. She didn't need the temptation.

Inside, she flicked on the light and closed the door behind her. She took a deep breath and looked over the sparsely furnished room.

She was doing better until Mack came and invaded her comfort zone. There'd been no way to politely tell him she wanted to be alone. He had no way of knowing *M*A*S*H* was one of the shows she and Eric watched together on their video dates when she was in flight school at Fort Rucker, and he was based at Fort Benning. After she graduated and they were stationed in Savannah, they'd watch, side by side on the couch, sharing a snack, holding hands, even making love.

Tonight, she'd hardly thought of Eric with Mack sitting beside her. She'd kept her arms crossed and hands to herself, but when he laughed, it ignited an ache in her chest and a longing for the companionship and love stolen from her. When Mack looked at her like he wanted to kiss her, *she* nearly made the first move. Right there where any of his team or hers could have walked in. But she couldn't afford to do something as stupid as getting caught in a lip-lock with a non-commissioned officer.

What was she thinking? She might have gotten a step closer to flying MEDEVAC, and here she was obsessing over a guy who could get her grounded—and not in a good way. Flying was all she had left. She loved flying, and most days, it was enough. Or almost enough.

She pressed her back to the door and rapped her head against it. It didn't help.

Get a grip, Donovan.

If she hadn't been able to sleep earlier, the past hour wasn't going to help. It'd been over a year and a half since Eric died. Nearly two years since they'd touched. Made love.

She couldn't hold onto him forever. She needed to find a new normal. One that didn't include a man who could jeopardize her career by merely going on a date. Even if he was engaging and daring and charming, and she was attracted to everything about him.

And so what if he reminded her of Eric? That was good and bad. She'd never get back what she'd shared with her husband, even with a man like him. Mack was in the same dangerous profession. With the same deadly risks. Exactly why she needed to put Mack out of her mind.

With an idea of how to do that, she pushed off the door and went to the dresser. She pulled out the single envelope, wishing she'd brought both death letters Eric left for her. But the 614 letter was back home in Savannah. Still unopened. Still waiting for the 614th day from his death. Eric counted on her being a rule follower, and she wouldn't disobey his last order.

This letter she could reread, though. And she needed it now. To remember Eric.

Slowly, she unfolded his letter and took a deep breath, then focused on every word as if reading them for the first time.

Hey darling,

You're not supposed to be reading this letter. We were supposed to drink champagne, burn our damn death letters, make love a few times to celebrate.

That had been a good plan. God, it had been so long … She shook the thought from her head.

You know, trying out some of the fantasies we came up with during our deployments. But if you're reading this, that isn't happening, and I'm sorry. So, so sorry. Because more than anything, I want to be there with you—making you smile and laugh and giving you everything you want in life.

Damn, this is hard to write, because I know if you're reading this, I'm gone, and you're sad, hurting, and probably even pissed off at me right now. Maybe if I hadn't been such a freaking awesome husband, this wouldn't be so hard for you.

A strangled laugh escaped every damn time she read that part. She touched a fingertip to the smiley face Eric had drawn after his statement. She took several breaths before continuing.

Thanks for understanding and supporting me in what

I had to do. And for loving me even in the hard times.
You made me a better man.

"And you made me a better woman," she said softly. She sniffed and dabbed at the tears blurring her vision.

I don't want you to stay mad. Kick some insurgent ass,
then I want you to move on. To keep living life.
Promise me you won't give up on your dreams. You
deserve to be happy and to have everything you want
in life—flying, kids, a guy who gets you. It would kill
me all over again if you gave up your dreams because
I'm not there. Stay the strong woman I loved.

Your loving and freaking awesome husband,
Eric

She wiped away the tear that ran down her cheek. With painstaking precision, she refolded the letter, placed it back in the envelope, and stashed it in the drawer.

Eric loved her as she was. Never treated her like she was one of the guys. Her desire to fly hadn't intimidated him. He'd encouraged her to go for her dream. He'd been the right man for her. *The One.* Though *he* never believed there was only one right person. How many times had he said any guy would want her as his wife, and he was the lucky one to have landed her?

Tonight, Mack's same respect for her career merely contributed to the emotional overload of the day. She turned off the light and climbed into bed. Pulling down a pillow, she cradled it to her chest. It was a poor substitute for being in a man's arms.

Tomorrow, Ray's team—including Mack—would go back

to Fayetteville. Out of sight and out of mind. And now that her unit had completed its real mission, this assignment would wrap up. Soon, she'd be back in Savannah. Back to status quo and routine flying without drug lord's thugs or insurgents shooting at her—until her next deployment. All would be good and safe in her world.

SIX

TWENTY-FOUR HOURS after dodging bullets in the jungle, Mack and the team sat in the air-conditioned comfort of the team room going through the debrief with Colonel Mahinis.

"You had no way of knowing Herrera had explosives planted on the roads leading to his compound. Guess he's taken a page from Al-Qaeda's playbook."

"Any updates on Hunter?" Ray asked.

"Upgraded to fair condition. They'll wait a few more days before transferring him stateside. It's questionable whether he'll be able to return to the team at all, much less when. We'll be assigning a new medic to your team. As for Judge Vallejo, he's thankful for the safe return of his daughter."

Tony Vincenti grunted. "We needed to get Herrera."

"Baltazar and Juan Pablo Herrera were not our mission." Colonel Mahinis gave the party line. "You put a dent in his operation and showed he's not invincible. Judge Vallejo won't back down."

"Except they have to get Herrera in custody," Ray pointed out.

"You did your job. Mission accomplished. The Herreras are the Colombians' problem. Not ours."

Mack wished that were true. What were the chances the Colombians would actually get Herrera and put him in jail or a grave? The Bad Karma team didn't put "a dent in his operation." They may have taken out a dozen or two of Herrera's protection force, but he'd recruit more poor suckers, lured in —maybe to their deaths—with enough *dinero*. Thank God Amber and Darcy were two thousand miles from Herrera. Not that they'd left any evidence to lead the drug lord back to the Bad Karma team.

"Missions will go to Alpha team until your new team medic is assigned and up to speed. Good job. Dismissed."

Groans echoed throughout the room at the colonel's declaration. Being sidelined sucked, but Vincenti needed to recover, and the newbie had to integrate into their well-oiled machine before they put their lives on the line in future deployments.

Outside the command post, Mack breathed in the cool night air. He needed to get the mission and the judge's daughter's haunted look out of his head. Stop picturing something like that happening to one of his girls.

Tony caught up with Mack before he reached his truck. "Dinner?" He motioned to his bandaged arm. "I deserve a nice steak."

Dinner with Tony beat going to an empty house with a frozen dinner or can of soup. "Need someone to cut your steak for you?"

"I can find someone better looking than you for that." Tony tossed him a grin before getting into his SUV. "Meet you at Logan's."

Mack checked the dashboard clock in his truck. Heading out of the lot, he tugged his phone from his pocket and tapped the top number on the screen.

"Hi, Dad," Amber answered his call in her usual subdued, pre-teen manner.

"Daddy?" Darcy piped in from the background. "It's my turn to talk first." The image of his youngest's excited face, wanting to talk to him, hit Mack right in the heart.

"Fine. Here," Amber said a moment before Darcy's greeting came over the line.

"Daddy, I miss you!"

"I miss you, too, monkey." The reminder he'd missed his mid-week dinner and nightly calls poked at him. Damn, after the past few days, he needed to see them. Now. Tonight. "Thought I'd come by and give you girls goodnight hugs and kisses." Tony would understand the change of plan.

"Mom! Dad's on the phone," Amber called out.

"I can show you a picture of me with the bunny Yao got for her birthday! He's so cute. I want a bunny, too, but Mommy said no." Darcy didn't stop for a breath.

"You're not getting a bunny." Rochelle's voice came through loud and clear. He could picture her face with the my-way-or-no-way expression that had become all too familiar in the past few years.

"I know." Darcy dragged out the words in a sad, singsong manner. "Daddy's coming over."

"What? Let me talk to him," Rochelle demanded.

Oh, crap.

"What's this about you coming over? It's bedtime. So, unless you'll be here in the next five minutes—"

"I can be there in twenty." If he hit the lights right and ignored the speed limit.

"They'll be in bed."

"Come on. I missed out on dinner this week."

"I had nothing to do with that. That would be because of your *job*." The condemnation in her voice scraped his nerves worse than the drill sergeants who'd screamed insults in his face.

His job. Everything circled back to that. What happened to the woman who promised to love, honor, and cherish? He clamped his jaw shut, so he didn't actually ask. "I'm not asking you to keep them up until midnight. We're talking ten minutes past their bedtime."

"Only you'll get them too riled up to sleep. I'm the one who has to deal with dragging them out of bed for school tomorrow."

"Let me take them tonight." He offered the perfect solution. "I'll get them in bed and to school in the morning. It'll give you a break." He preferred not to beg, but getting to spend time with his daughters was worth groveling to his ex.

"If I say yes, next time you go out of town or have special training, you'll want to trade your night again. It messes up our routine. Tomorrow, you get them for the whole weekend. That's good enough. You can make it up to them then."

Dammit. Couldn't she be reasonable? Give a little for once. He shouldn't be surprised. She was the one who gave him the Army-or-me ultimatum because she couldn't deal with being a Spec Ops wife any longer.

He was already in the elite 75th Ranger Regiment when they met and married. It appealed to her then. Her attitude changed as the conflicts in the Middle East dragged on and on, deployment after deployment. But they could have worked out a compromise. Instead, Rochelle seized every opportunity to punish *him* for their failed marriage.

"You should have asked me before you told the girls you were coming by." Rochelle broke the extended silence. "I don't appreciate you making me look like the bad guy. The custodial agreement is clear."

Pick your battles. Pick your battles. "Fine." Contempt leached into his voice. "I'd like to say goodnight to 'em." At least they'd know he had tried—*wanted*—to see them.

"Of course." Rochelle's martyred tone was akin to the warning sound of an incoming missile strike. "And *you* can break the news that you can't come over tonight after all. Darcy," she called.

Why not? Chalk up another instance of disappointing the girls.

"Hi, Daddy," Darcy greeted him again.

"Bad news, monkey. I, uh, didn't realize it was already your bedtime. *Sooo*, it's too late to come by tonight, but I'll see you tomorrow, and I promise we'll do something fun. You girls can pick, okay?"

"O-kay," she drawled. "Can we go to the pet store so I can pet the bunnies?"

"Sure. If that's what you want." Even though it'd likely piss off Rochelle, it might win him some points with the girls, and they were who mattered. He said his goodnights, telling Amber to think of something she wanted to do. He debated if her embarrassment of being seen with her dad would spare him from having to endure a trip to the mall. Mack could only hope.

SEVEN

BASED on the side-glances sent Kristie's way in the weekly briefing back in Savannah, speculation abounded the true nature of the assignment in Colombia. She got that. If it had been one of her teammates flying a covert mission, she'd have been hungry for details, too. Except she couldn't give them the details that they wanted.

She ignored the stares in favor of getting up to speed on the missions that lay before them. Routine flying. Routine training. The meeting didn't last long.

"Donovan, need you a minute." Major Sun singled her out after dismissing the rest of the pilots. He motioned for her to follow. Her rubber-soled boots hardly made a sound on the tile floor as she paced down the long, quiet hallway to his cubicle of an office.

The major took a seat and leaned over the desk. "I read over your report but wanted to tell you that Colonel Mahinis called me himself after the mission to tell me it'd been a success. Baltazar Herrera is head of the most brutal drug cartel. The Colombian government has been after him for years. Every time they get close, he gets tipped off. When they finally managed to pick up his son, Juan Pablo, using him to get his father didn't go as planned."

While she appreciated being filled in, albeit after the fact, why was the major telling her this now? The mission was called a success. Still, she didn't know what picture Josué's report painted.

"The cartel kidnapped the daughter of the judge who denied Juan Pablo bail. The Colombian government asked for U.S. intervention, but if Herrera learned we were there, he would have moved the girl—or killed her. Thus, the training mission cover. I figured we owed you that after reviewing the mission reports."

Good Lord, poor girl. Kristie had wondered how she was involved, but this was worse than she'd imagined.

"Job well done. Which brings me to the call I got this morning."

Call? She sat up straighter. Major Sun's expression made tingles race down her arms.

"Colonel Ball from the 82nd Aviation wants to see you."

"See me? About …?"

"About a position, I believe, tomorrow at thirteen hundred."

"Tomorrow? That's …" This was so sudden it had to be big. But Bragg. "Have you heard anything about openings at Fort Carson?"

He hesitated and ran a hand over his buzzed hair. "That's a no-go—for now. There's still Fort Drum and Hood. Though Bragg sounds like it could be a sure thing. Unless you've changed your mind about staying here."

She loved Savannah, but staying here, even for a MEDEVAC slot, wasn't starting fresh the way she needed. She didn't want to forget Eric, but there were too many reminders of him here. Favorite restaurants. Friends. Those things made it hard to move forward.

"I think I need to meet with the colonel." That didn't commit her. She'd have time to mull it over. What were the chances other opportunities would pop up like spring flowers?

KRISTIE ARRIVED in Fayetteville early enough to drive around the perimeter of Simmons Airfield, located across the highway from Fort Bragg. She pulled up to the security checkpoint to access the airfield, watching a pair of UH-72 Lakotas fly overhead. It gave her the feeling of home.

She didn't get the chance to sit after giving her name to the colonel's aide before she was escorted to his office.

"Chief Donovan, I appreciate you making it on such short notice." Colonel Ball stood to shake her hand. "Have a seat."

He sported the standard, almost civilian looking, aviator haircut, as opposed to the traditional Army buzz. There were hints of silver at his temples and lines at the corners of his friendly eyes. "A friend of mine sent over a mission report he knew I'd be interested in as I'd originally wanted it assigned to us." He motioned to a clipped stack of papers with thick black lines obscuring the first half of the top page.

Colombia. Had Ray sent it?

"I recognized your name. You've put in for a MEDEVAC position."

"Yes, sir." Anticipation nearly lifted her from the seat.

The colonel's mouth pursed, and for several seconds, his gaze settled on a folder bearing her name before returning to study her.

"Walk me through your decision-making process for the events on your end of Operation Sparrow."

Wouldn't he have this in a copy of her report? He obviously had security clearance since he knew the name of the mission when even she didn't. She drew in a full breath and clung to her waning confidence.

She stuck to the facts, and Colonel Ball nodded to signal his awareness of the instrument-system-training cover they'd been fed. She explained why she'd felt it necessary to exit the aircraft to cover the men they were extracting. Though she preferred to forget that she'd fired on, wounded, and maybe even killed a man, she kept the emotion from her voice and projected a strong, professional detachment.

He listened as she recounted the details around them dusting off without Sergeant Hanlon. "Can you explain why you returned to the landing zone when you had a critically wounded man on your aircraft and risked taking more fire?"

"Chief Lundgren requested it. He had more intel on the situation."

"You know Chief Lundgren?"

"Yes, sir."

The colonel's mouth shifted, and he took his time before asking, "Would you have gone back if it weren't Chief Lundgren giving the order?"

"He didn't give an order. *I* made the decision."

"Based on?"

She hadn't come here for an inquisition. If he needed proof she could make life-and-death decisions under pressure, she'd justify her reasoning and show him why he should give her the MEDEVAC slot.

"Josué Varga indicated Herrera's men could have heavy weapons; however, at that point, we'd only encountered small arms fire. The injuries I saw didn't appear life-threatening. I weighed the risks of leaving a man behind—in daylight and possibly low on ammunition—and determined there was a greater chance of ending up with a casualty if we didn't return for him."

"I agree. I flew MEDEVAC for seven years, starting back in Operation Iraqi Freedom. Did two more tours in Afghanistan. It can be brutal emotionally. You get an up-close look at the carnage that happens in war. Even when you get there within minutes, it's not always enough. Do you think your personal history could have played a part and pushed you to take the risk?"

Unable to deny it, she held his gaze. "I think it was the right call."

"Are you familiar with Complicated Bereavement?"

Those two words sucked the air from her lungs and hope from her soul. "My psychologist and I discussed it in counseling before my last deployment." She disagreed with Dr. Wynter's concerns that flying MEDEVAC would extend her period of grieving for Eric well beyond the normal time frame.

Apparently, it had still gone in her personnel file. The reason other commanders passed on giving her a shot in MEDEVAC became crystal clear. Wasn't that freaking fantastic. And totally unfair. "I *joined* the Army because I wanted to fly MEDEVAC. I don't want to fly MEDEVAC *because* I lost him. I know I can't bring him back."

Colonel Ball leaned back in his chair, studying her. "I'm no psychologist, but I have to agree with Dr. Wynter. I can't take the chance you're not ready, nor prolong your cycle of grief. I'm not going to offer you a MEDEVAC slot today."

Then why the hell did he rush her here and dangle this hope in front of her? Fine! She didn't want Bragg anyway.

"But I want you to fly for me," he continued.

What? "I—I don't understand." Did he want her to go through another psych eval to prove she was moving on? That sounded like bureaucratic bullshit. How did they expect her to show them she was moving on while denying her the chance to do it?

"You have an exemplary record. The instincts, decision-making, and knack for teaching make for an excellent instructor pilot—which I need. I was about to offer the slot to someone else when I received a copy of the Operation Sparrow mission report. I wanted to talk to you first."

"I'm already an instructor pilot." Did he expect her to get excited about a lateral move after yanking the MEDEVAC carrot out of reach?

"You've had a taste of flying missions for the most elite soldiers in the U.S. Army. We're not the 160th SOAR, but we're close. It's a step up."

She didn't have the right anatomy to fly with the 160th— until that all-boys club joined the twenty-first century. There were women in the Rangers now. Except that wasn't her dream. The idea of inserting men like Eric and Ray and their friends into dangerous situations was the *opposite* of her mission plan. "I appreciate it, but I want to be responsible for *saving* lives."

"There's more than one way to do that." He picked up the report. "I need the best pilots to ensure we bring our guys back alive."

She couldn't think of a single word to say as the room rocked like her craft in gale-force winds.

"Other commanders may see Dr. Wynter's note as a red flag. But with more time, signs of grief recovery, another psych eval, you may get a MEDEVAC slot. I'm offering you something *now.* You fly for me, show me you're moving forward in your career and life, and you still want to switch to MEDEVAC, I'll make it happen."

"I'd like some time to think about it, sir."

"That's fair, but I'm on a tight schedule. My current instructor pilot leaves for his new post next week. This past weekend, his intended replacement broke his wrist and suffered a concussion doing BMX bike stunts." He rolled his eyes. "With summer coming, I needed to fill this slot yesterday. Can you let me know by Friday? If you take it, I'd like you to start ASAP."

This was not the Army way. Usually, she'd have months before a permanent change of station. Her head spun. "I can give you an answer by then."

EIGHT

KRISTIE GOT CAUGHT in the end-of-day exodus from Fort Bragg, and she was a few minutes late when she rolled into the restaurant parking lot. She was off-balance when she'd left her meeting with Colonel Ball. Her housing inquiry hadn't gone any better. Was this the best move? According to what she'd just learned, waiting for another option might be an exercise in futility. She hoped talking it out with Ray would give her some perspective.

The special on margaritas must have been a draw since customers were already waiting for tables inside the packed restaurant. Spying Ray and Stephanie, Kristie bypassed the hostess stand and headed toward their table.

Seeing Mack sitting beside them, she almost stopped dead in her tracks. What the …? Great. This put a kink in her plans to get counsel from her friends. Mack popped into her thoughts once or twice a day since the mission last week, so he wouldn't help her think clearly, either.

Before she reached them, Stephanie sprang to her feet to pull her into a long, hard hug that whispered "Welcome home," giving Kristie the familiarity and connection she needed.

"I'm so glad you called." Stephanie released her, and Ray slipped in for a quick one. "Kristie, this is Mack Hanlon, from Ray's team."

"Nice to see you again." Mack held her hand longer than necessary. There was enough recognition in his steady gaze to spark desire low in her belly.

"Again?" Stephanie skewered them with a gaze worthy of any trained interrogator.

Kristie gave a helpless shrug. "I just gave their team a scenic tour." During which she shot a man. She couldn't shake the memory.

"Today?" Stephanie pressed as they sat.

"No, uh …" Kristie shot Ray a help-me look. Neither man said a word. She shouldn't have said anything. After what Major Sun had told her, she didn't want to think about Colombia.

"I'm not getting details, am I?"

Ray just shook his head at his wife; Mack chuckled.

"What brings you to Fort Bragg then?" Stephanie took a sip of her margarita.

"I had a meeting." Kristie picked up the menu. She could catch up now and go back to Ray and Stephanie's after dinner to talk. "How's Alexis?"

"Sixteen going on twenty-two and giving me gray hairs," Ray remarked dryly.

Stephanie rolled her eyes and laughed. "He doesn't like the idea of boys calling and asking her on dates."

"I know what those boys are thinking."

"He's threatened to meet them at the door armed like Rambo."

Ray shrugged. "Came all the way up here for a meeting? Did it go well?"

"I haven't decided yet. Are the burritos good?"

"They're okay, but the fish tacos are the best. Who were you meeting with?" Ray didn't give in to her deflection.

She presumed Major Sun was responsible for Colonel Ball's decision to interview her. But could Ray have played a role? Would he even know the colonel? "Colonel Ball with the 82nd Aviation."

Ray didn't flinch or even raise an eyebrow.

"Would you two quit talking in circles?" Stephanie demanded. "Why *exactly* are you here?"

Her relationship with Stephanie straddled friend and family ever since Stephanie headed up the Family Readiness Group when they were at Fort Lewis together. Sometimes Stephanie filled the role of second mother. Sometimes older sister. Sometimes favorite aunt. Always trusted friend. Was there a way to dodge her questions through dinner? Kristie shifted her attention to Mack.

"Well?" Stephanie said, not taking the hint.

"He wanted to speak with me about a position in a unit here."

"Really?" Stephanie gasped. "I'd love that."

"I'm not sure it's going to happen."

Stephanie's smile wilted. "Why not?"

"Because I want a MEDEVAC position, and he offered me a spot as an instructor pilot. It'd be more of a lateral move to a slightly more elite unit."

"If they know you want MEDEVAC, why would he offer you a lateral move?" Ray sounded indignant on her behalf.

"Apparently, he was given a redacted version of a recent mission report and thought I'd be a better fit in the 82nd."

"If that's the reason, then that would make you a good, or an even better fit for MEDEVAC," Ray commented.

Kristie didn't want to get into this here. Or now. Or ever, really, but if Ray had been the one to give the report and recommend her to Colonel Ball, she'd better explain. "Because of how Eric died, there's concern whether I should fly MEDEVAC."

"That's not fair." Stephanie laid her hand on Kristie's arm.

No, it wasn't fair that one damned bullet killed her husband and shattered her dreams of a family. Or that the same damned bullet now threatened to steal the one dream she had left.

"Why should that matter?" Mack asked.

A glance at Mack confirmed he had no clue. Kristie stared at the ugly white acoustic ceiling tiles. She swallowed and blinked away the burning in her eyes.

"Are you ready to order?" The waiter appeared in time to give her a reprieve.

"I could use a frozen strawberry margarita." Though a generous shot of whiskey might give her more fortitude. "Y'all order, that'll give me a sec." Her gaze roved erratically over the menu.

"Give us a few more minutes," Ray took command.

The waiter backed off, and an awkward silence ensued.

"Forget I asked." Mack shifted in his seat. "It's none of my business. You weren't expecting me here tonight, and clearly, you wanted to discuss things with your friends. I should go and let you all, um …"

Great. Letting everyone keep tiptoeing around what happened didn't help. If she was going to convince Colonel Ball, a shrink, even herself, that Eric's death didn't define her, she needed to embrace the suck and slog through it. It wasn't like she hadn't shared this story before. "No. Don't go."

Mack perched hesitantly on the edge of his chair.

"Eric's Ranger unit helped rebuild schools in Nangarhar province. He was part of the group that delivered the supplies the FRG collected to stock the school. I heard the kids were all excited about the school opening and came to help," she rambled. "Only some backward-thinking assholes, who weren't happy about kids getting educated, attacked. In the firefight, Eric and another Ranger were hit protecting the kids."

She paused. Even though his buddies hadn't given her all the details of what went down that day, she pictured Eric grabbing kids to get them to safety. "The area was deemed too hot for a MEDEVAC to land right away. Eric bled out while waiting."

"I'm sorry."

The sympathy in Mack's tone, in his eyes, was genuine. Anyone who'd served for even one deployment had lost friends.

"Sounds like the kind of soldier I would have liked to serve with," he continued.

That made her smile. "Thank you." Mack hadn't said something like, *"He died a hero."* He understood. Probably because he and Eric were cut from the same camouflage cloth.

"Does the colonel know you wanted to fly MEDEVAC even before that—not because of that?" Ray asked.

At this point, she might as well tell them everything. "In addition to the fear I might take unnecessary risks, the psychologist I had to see before I could deploy put a note in my file that indicated flying MEDEVAC missions might serve as a constant reminder of Eric's death. Therefore, I would keep grieving instead of moving on to a mentally healthy place."

"That's ridiculous to base decisions on a psych eval from over a year and a deployment ago," Ray groused. "You may, uh"—he glanced at Stephanie, then leaned closer to Kristie and Mack—"not be afraid to take risks, but you weren't reckless. I'd vouch for your abilities."

"Me, too," Mack said.

"You two may be a little biased. Colonel Ball said if I took the slot in the 82nd, and after time and another psych eval, if I still want MEDEVAC, he'll make it happen."

The waiter approached with her margarita, and they ordered rather than send the guy away again.

"I was going to say don't take it, but I want you here, and if you could get transferred, then maybe you should accept," Stephanie said.

"I'm waiting to hear about transferring to MEDEVAC at Fort Hood or Fort Drum, but that may not happen thanks to the note in my file." Kristie took a sip of her drink. "Colonel Ball needs my decision by the end of the week."

"That's hardly standard Army operating procedure," Ray remarked.

"No, but the replacement he had lined up got hurt, and with vacations starting up, he needs someone ASAP. Like next week."

"Between Fort Hood, Drum, and here, where do you want to be?" Mack asked.

"Well, I'd love to be going to Schofield Barracks in Hawaii or Germany, but it appears those aren't options. Of my current options, here," she admitted.

"Do you have any doubts about your ability to convince him you deserve a MEDEVAC slot?"

"No."

"Didn't think so. Take the position here." Mack sounded exactly like Eric with his confidence in her and his reasoning.

Though he couldn't be a factor in her decision, she couldn't deny that her attraction to him didn't help. But no dating Special Ops guys for her.

"Colonel Ball's timeline doesn't give me time to find a place to live, and there's no temporary housing available on base or at the Landmark Inn. I'm not comfortable signing a lease off post just to have a place immediately."

"I know where you can get temporary housing," Stephanie said adamantly, looking to Ray. He nodded. "The Lundgren Bed and Breakfast will give you plenty of time to find something permanent."

"I can't impose like that."

"You're not. You're invited. We have a spare room, and I'd enjoy the company."

"That's sweet, but, uh …" Kristie grasped for a solid excuse.

"You'd be doing us a favor," Ray said.

"How's that?"

"You could house- and pet-sit when we go to the beach."

She laughed. "That's a stretch."

"Yeah, well, now you're out of excuses. Don't force me to make it an order. My wife likes to get her way."

Stephanie leaned in and covered Kristie's hand. "Look, it's time for a fresh start. Here you'd be near family and friends."

"True," Kristie agreed. The senior pilot in C Company was a friend from her Fort Lewis days prior to flight school. "I'll think about it."

The waiter arrived with their appetizer in time to save her any more pressure—temporarily. Her eyes locked on Mack's muscled arm when he spooned queso onto a small plate. She had to order herself to look away.

With the airfield on the opposite side of post from the

Special Operations training grounds, it was conceivable she'd never cross paths with Mack. Sure, there were elite units at most bases, full of alpha males—the type she was drawn to—but Fort Bragg was the largest military installation in the world. While Fort Carson had a Green Berets unit based there and Drum had 10th Mountain, Fort Bragg had their type in spades and clubs and diamonds. The 82nd Airborne. The Green Berets. Special Forces Operational Detachment-Delta.

Could she really avoid three or four thousand best-of-the-best combat soldiers? No. No. And no. If—*if*—she came here, she'd definitely have to stick to her guns and avoid theirs.

NINE

Two days later, and one day left to make her decision, she stared at the envelope on the kitchen table. *Kristie,* in Eric's familiar hand, was written across the front of the "Do Not Open for 614 Days" letter. She'd almost gotten up last night and opened it after midnight, except she might not have slept after that, and she had to fly today.

Waiting had been torture, but it was finally time.

She filled a mug with coffee. Why was she stalling? Because she didn't want to face the finality. The last words from her husband. An ache spread through her chest. She carried the letter to the living room to sit in his favorite spot on the couch.

Reminders of Eric filled the room. The huge high-definition television for watching football. The pictures atop the fireplace mantle—one from their wedding, and one of them on their honeymoon. The scenic paintings they'd bought and hung. A tradition they'd started on each anniversary trip. There were so many places they planned to go that would have filled the blank spaces on these walls.

She drew air into her lungs, and with Eric's pocketknife, slit open the last letter from her husband.

This one was longer than the first. His handwriting not quite as neat.

Hey Darling,
How are you doing?

She paused, letting the words wrap around her as if hearing Eric's smooth voice. Warmth began to radiate from deep inside, thawing the chill that made her hands icy.

I know it's been a while now. You did wait to open this letter, didn't you? I started to say wait one year. Maybe I was thinking of something I read requiring a widow to mourn and wear black for a year—then I thought, well, that's stupid, and they don't make black camouflage uniforms. It's not like you hit some magic date and things magically get better. The anniversary might be hard anyway, so I started thinking further out, sometime after your deployment.
By now, you might be married again.

Not hardly.

Could even have kids.

I wish. Kinda hard without the husband. Without you.

I'm okay with that. I hope you haven't dodged your promise. I know you'll never forget me, and you'll never find anyone exactly like me, but what we had together, you can have again.

No. You were my one.

*I don't want you to be alone—to think flying is
enough. I want you to do the things you love. Fly,
dance, travel, laugh. Don't sit around missing me.
Yeah, I'm telling you this because you can be kind of
stubborn sometimes—but I've proved I'm more bull-
headed. Don't bother fighting me.*

A light laugh escaped. On the rare occasion they
disagreed, he usually won because he was almost always
right. His analytical nature consistently beat her emotional
one. What she wouldn't give to have him here to fight with—
though his being here would negate any need to have *this*
"fight." Even if he was wrong this time.

*Don't settle, either. Not for someone who doesn't get
you. Who doesn't make you smile or give you a reason
to stay on the ground. I want you to be happy.*

*I love you,
Eric*

*P.S. Remember when I invited you to go home with me
for the 4th of July after we started dating? I called my
folks to let them know you were coming, and my mom
asked if things were serious between us. I told her I
was going to marry you. Surprised myself when I said
it. And that I meant it. I never told you this, but I'll
never forget that day. It was June 14. (614)*

He hadn't told her because she wouldn't have believed
he'd say that.

She read the letter again, laughing at some of the things he wrote. Typical Eric. She found the humor that first attracted her to him in this letter, serving as his last gift.

She missed the hell out of him, but she wasn't sitting around mourning. She went out and did things. If she hadn't spent a year in Afghanistan, she might have taken a trip with friends. She didn't depend on a man to entertain or provide for her. She was okay on her own.

A certain kind of attention from a man on occasion would be nice. Other than Mack, no man had piqued her interest, but she was happy and living her life. She had flying and …

and …

She. Had. Flying.

She sighed in surrender. Had she volunteered for the Colombia assignment to let her teammates stay home with their families? Or was it because she didn't have anything to keep her here?

Crud. Eric knew her too well. He was calling her out from beyond the grave. She finished off her cup of coffee and went to the kitchen for a refill. Okay, so there were a few areas where she held back, but it sucked to lose the man you loved and planned to spend life with. No one should expect her to snap her fingers and be over it. It might help if she went on the adventures she and Eric planned on doing together. Start small. Like a paddleboarding lesson or join a kayaking group.

Or go big and move to Fort Bragg.

Even though moving closer to them would sway her family's input on the decision, she picked up the phone and typed the number. After a beat, her mother's familiar voice greeted her.

"Hi, Mom. Is Dad home, too?"

TEN

MACK ROLLED his shoulder until it popped. Damn Vincenti and his grueling workouts. They all took turns leading morning PT, but the days Vincenti led were nicknamed Groan Day for a reason. His buddy was a workout fanatic, and even though he was limited in participating while his arm healed, he hadn't gone easy on the team.

After changing into their uniforms, Mack and the guys filed into the team room per orders. Still no sign of Ray to find out if Kristie decided to take the position here. He wouldn't ask in front of everyone.

A few minutes of shooting the bull passed before the door swung open, and the chief entered. The mood in the room shifted as the men studied the camouflage-clad stranger who followed Chief Lundgren.

The soldier's dark-blond hair stood at attention from styling products. His movie-star-pretty face was clean-shaven, and his straight teeth gleamed in the bright room. His name patch read *Grant*, and Mack pegged him as a West Point grad lieutenant until he noted the rank chevron on his chest.

Grant didn't speak or take a seat but remained at Lundgren's side as the chief launched into the morning debrief.

"The report I received this morning is that Hunter's stable enough to be transported back stateside."

"Good. Especially with Herrera still crawling on the face of the planet," Vincenti grumbled and rubbed his arm.

Mack didn't disagree aloud. He wasn't scared of Herrera's need for vengeance, but he wouldn't mind getting an eye on the cartel boss—through the scope of his sniper rifle. Time to put Herrera out of his mind and focus on what lay ahead.

"However, due to his injuries, Hunter's return to the team is uncertain. We need a medic to make us deployable. This is Staff Sergeant Devin Grant. Grant, this is B Company." Ray pointed a finger to Mack. "Sergeant First Class Mack Hanlon, weapons and team sniper. Sergeant First Class Tony Vincenti, operations and best undercover man in all of Delta."

"Only As he got in high school were in Spanish—because he was already fluent in Italian—and drama. He's an ac-*tor*." Juan Dominguez gave a flourish of his hand in Tony's direction.

Tony flipped him off. "You're an ass, Dominguez."

Ray rolled his eyes and shook his head. "Colonel Mahinis told you that you were joining one of the most *elite* teams under SOCOM, right?" Sarcasm laced Ray's deep voice.

"He did."

Grant didn't appear to doubt it, despite the two men clashing. Mack kept his mouth shut. Tony *could* act. He was a quick, creative thinker, and with his dark, Italian looks and hooked nose from a few breaks, he could pass for a half-dozen ethnicities with stage makeup and the right accent.

"Staff Sergeants Walt Shuler, operations. Lincoln Porter, engineer. AJ Rozanski, communications. Kyle Lin, intel, and

Juan Dominguez, also weapons." Ray pointed to each man in turn.

"He joining us on a trial basis?" Juan asked. "If he doesn't pass muster, we get to send him back to doing cover shoots for GQ?"

Without hesitation, Grant flipped off Juan.

Vincenti busted out laughing. "I like the kid already."

Grant's middle finger curled down, and his flash of snark morphed back to the boy-next-door smile before Ray saw what happened.

"He was SF medic in 7th Group and finished top of his class in three of four phases of the Q course. Pretty sure he can take whatever we throw at him. We're gonna start with run-throughs in the shooting house today. We won't start with live hostages, though." Ray motioned to Grant to take the vacant seat next to Shuler.

"Moving on," Ray said.

MACK SIMPLY RAISED a brow at Ray when the team broke for lunch after a few hours in the shooting house. Since Ray handed him the ammunition magazine, he speculated the weapon malfunction on the latest hostage-rescue drill was intentional.

His team leader's cocky smirk confirmed it. "Knew you'd hate that. Grant hesitated, but he recovered and picked up your sector. Hits could be cleaner. We'll do a couple more run-throughs after lunch, see what happens when he gets fatigued. I want this team mission-ready within the month."

"No rest when you got Bad Karma to dish out." Tony sank onto the picnic table bench while Grant and Kyle Lin walked toward the compound to retrieve the food. "Hey,

Grant, bring extra ice and waters when you come back. And hustle up, newb. I'm starving."

"Yes, Sergeant."

Rozanski rolled his eyes. "Yes, Sergeant? What next 'My pleasure'? Or apologizing to the targets for shooting them?"

"He's not *that* polite. He flipped off Dominguez," Tony pointed out.

"I bet he flashes that GQ smile and offers to help old ladies cross the street," Dominguez put in.

Everyone went silent. Tony laughed first, and the other men joined in. Most Special Ops guys earned nicknames. It usually took a few weeks for the right one to click. Until then, they were *new guy* or *newb*.

"'Boy Scout.' All in favor?" Ray asked.

Everyone's hand went up. With the newbie's nickname decided, Grant was a step closer to sealing his spot on the team.

"Mack, you want to hit Jumpy's Place with us?" Juan asked while they ate.

"Can't. I have the girls this weekend."

"Vincenti, you want to come? Be my wingman," Juan asked.

Tony snorted. "Pass."

"You already have plans? Doesn't have to be Jumpy's. Where you going?" Juan persisted.

Without responding, Tony took another bite of his sub.

"All right. You don't have to stick around and be my wingman."

"If you need a wingman to meet women, then there's probably something wrong with your approach. Or your reputation."

"Oh, like you're so different." Juan rolled his eyes.

"Yes, I am. And because you don't see it is why I'll never be your wingman."

"Enough. We're a team. You don't have to like each other, but we need to work together to get the mission done." Ray put an end to their back-and-forth before it escalated.

Mack understood the chief's point. And *he* wasn't going to call attention to how much Tony and Juan had in common when it came to hitting bars and leaving with women they'd just met. Juan might go on a few dates with them afterward, but Tony seemed to take what was offered without making promises.

Mack wanted more for himself. Maybe he'd matured. Or having Amber and Darcy made him realize he wanted a woman he could eventually introduce to them. A woman looking to hook up with a Spec Ops guy wasn't the example he wanted for his girls. The last time he'd gone to Jumpy's, one of the women he'd talked to did everything but come right out and ask if he'd killed anyone—like that turned her on. Pass.

"Time to get back to work," Ray declared.

Tony crumpled the wrapper from his sub. "Tell the girls Uncle Tony says hi. Or maybe I'll come by."

"Darcy'd love that." Which was true. Rather than be intimidated by his tough exterior, she climbed on Tony like he was her personal jungle gym, and he ate it up.

The chief was right about them being a team. A band of brothers. Bad Karma Brothers. They all had extended family, but this team had a disproportionate number of single guys.

Lin and Porter were young, yet old enough to be married, especially by Army standards. Rozanski proposed a month ago, though he wasn't getting married until after their upcoming deployment. Grant didn't wear a wedding band, but that didn't mean he wasn't engaged or married.

Tony was Mack's best friend, but even he wasn't sure what Tony's deal was. He sure didn't act like he was looking for a mate, despite his love of kids. Juan had two divorces under his belt and wasn't going that route again anytime soon, or maybe ever. Shuler was on his third marriage—not unusual in their world—and expecting another kid.

Mack rounded out the bunch with his recent divorce. Only Ray had it all: his Spec Ops career; a devoted, understanding wife; and a daughter who had it together, too. The Lundgrens gave him hope that one day he could have it all again. He needed a woman like Stephanie, one who wouldn't give him an ultimatum—career or family. He wanted it all. For him and his girls.

ELEVEN

THE GENTLE HUM of her tires on the interstate calmed the nerves that flared back up when Kristie saw the road sign giving the mileage to Fort Bragg. This move would be a good thing. Here, she wouldn't be "the poor widow." It'd be a fresh start. A chance to make new friends. A step toward her dream job.

She'd only be infringing on the Lundgrens for a few hours in the evenings—and she'd probably be flying lots of nights. She'd find a permanent place near the airfield within a few weeks.

And it wasn't like she'd be smack-dab in the center of Ray and his Spec Ops buddies. Keeping her distance would be easy. She might encounter them in the commissary or other businesses, but those guys trained clear on the other side of post. She might fly over them, but that's it. She had this.

By the time she turned onto Ray and Stephanie's street, her confidence trumped her reservations again. Everything was as it should be. The sky was a vivid blue. Trees were in full leaf; flowers bloomed. American flags flapped in the breeze, and a man pushed a lawnmower across his lawn. A child wearing a purple helmet rode a pink bicycle in the street while a man ran behind her, holding the bike seat. The sunshine accented the red tones in his hair.

Mack?

When the child saw the car coming, she veered to the right, running up a driveway and onto the grass before toppling to the side.

Oh, no. Kristie braked. Before she could get out of the car, Mack waved, letting her know his daughter wasn't hurt.

Mack. On Ray's street. Really? What the …?

She waved back, then parked in the Lundgrens' driveway.

"Time to give your old man a two-minute break." Kristie overheard Mack say when she got out of her car.

"Sorry. Didn't mean to run you off the road," she said as the pair ambled her way.

"Not your fault. Somebody panicked a little." Mack gave his daughter a mock frown. In return, the girl's pink lips curved into the most precious smile. Brown eyes bordered by to-die-for lashes looked up at Kristie. Wisps of red hair a few shades lighter than her father's peeked out from the helmet. "This is my daughter, Darcy. Miss Kristie is going to be staying with Uncle Ray and Aunt Stephanie."

"Hi, Darcy. Looks like you're getting the hang of it."

"That's what I've been telling her." Mack wiped away beads of sweat, drawing Kristie's attention to the freckle touching his bottom lip.

"Daddy, can I get a drink?"

"Sure, monkey, but we aren't done yet, so make it fast and bring me a bottle of cold water, too, please."

"You, uh, live on the street?" Kristie asked the obvious.

"Right there." He pointed to the house where Darcy headed.

Right across the street. Talk about a damper on her plans to steer clear of Ray's Special Ops pals—particularly Mack. *Ohhh, brother.* Okay. It's not like this was some setup. She could deal with this for a few weeks.

"Looks like the only gear she still needs is a Kevlar vest." Kristie grinned at the way Darcy waddled due to the knee pads, elbow pads, and wrist guards. It fit with Mack being a protective father.

"Don't give her ideas." Mack's throaty chuckle made dragonflies flit in her stomach. "Our first attempt to ditch the training wheels ended with badly scraped knees and hands. She was afraid to get back in the saddle right away. Kinda surprising for a kid who got her nickname by climbing anything, or anyone, she could and swinging upside down. Anyway, I was deployed last summer, and now that the weather's nice, all her friends are riding, and she's feeling left out. She is learning to ride it *today.* Before she goes back to her mom's."

"Good luck."

"Thanks. We're gonna need it. I saw your hosts head out a while ago," he said before she could slip away—and stop obsessing over that freckle.

"They had to leave for a church-group dinner." She'd told them to go since she'd gotten a later start than planned. Late because packing up and saying goodbye to friends had been harder than she anticipated. "They left the door unlocked for me."

"Pretty safe neighborhood," he drawled with an easy grin. "You need help moving anything in?"

"I didn't bring much, but if you could grab the box in the back seat, I'd appreciate it."

She got the two suitcases from the trunk while he reached in and hefted the heavy box with ease, then followed her up the drive to the door. The quiet surreality of entering Ray and Stephanie's home hit hard.

With Mack on her heels, she headed to the guest room rather than hesitate and risk showing vulnerability. This was temporary. A transition to a new life. She didn't plan to forget her past with Eric, but the time had come to move forward.

"You can set that in the closet." She stationed the suitcases next to the dresser, suddenly anxious to get out of the bedroom. How long had it been since a man had been in *her* bedroom? Way too long. Better to not give Mack time to think about them being alone, even if neither had inappropriate intentions.

As Kristie returned to her car for another load, Darcy trotted across the street, holding water bottles to her chest. She handed one to Mack.

"I brought you one." The girl offered a bottle to Kristie.

"Thank you. I am thirsty after the drive up." The child's thoughtful gesture touched her. The familiar ache for a child clutched at her heart and robbed her limbs of energy. She managed to unscrew the top and take a swig of water without her eyes getting too misty.

"Once we've mastered the bike, I'm going to grill some burgers. You want to come over and have dinner with us? There'll be plenty."

I'd love to. She pictured Mack at the grill. Sitting around a table to enjoy a meal like a family sounded better than her norm of sitting on the couch with the TV on to feel less alone. But he wasn't a part of her future, so she better shut down that daydream. "I don't want to intrude. Besides, I should get unpacked and settled in since I have to hit the tarmac running tomorrow."

His lips puckered, and his gaze locked on her eyes as if he saw right through her excuses. "Okay. Maybe another time."

She nodded meekly. "I'm going to be peeking out to see how the bike riding is going." It was easier to address Darcy than quote fraternization regulations. He knew as well as she did that even casual relations between non-commissioned officers and enlisted personnel were prohibited. And with almost two years of required service left, she couldn't afford to mess around.

"Need help with anything else before we start up again?" he asked.

"I got it, thanks."

"Okay. Mount up, monkey." He set their water bottles on the grass and checked the chin strap on Darcy's helmet.

"Good luck!" Kristie went to the car and scooped up an armful of hanging clothes from the seat. After she carried in the last load of things, she unpacked the suitcases, then found room in the hall bath to stash her toiletries.

She was putting the smaller suitcase inside the larger one when Darcy's squeal and Mack's comforting encouragement drew her to the window. She looked out in time to see Darcy wobbling on the bike while Mack ran alongside, his arms spread out but at the ready as she took flight on her own. She made it past two houses before running up into a front yard.

You go, girl! Kristie cheered her on. Darcy set her fists on her hips in a scolding manner when Mack tried to high-five her.

Mack's rich laughter carried even from a distance. The proud smile on his face as he picked up the bike and set it upright nudged at Kristie's heart. Handsome, fit, and confident, with an enjoyable sense of humor. Throw in great fatherhood qualities, and it added up to a man most women would find desirable.

Could she fix the flaw in her plan to avoid Mack and the rest of Ray's team? She couldn't surrender already, but she was going to have to fight hard—against herself—to win the battle her heart waged. A chance to be part of a whole again. She could have it. But she should wait for the right guy, rather than set her sights on the first guy who appealed to her when the rank issue could endanger her career—and especially since his Spec Ops career could land her heart in double jeopardy.

TWELVE

Kristie stopped at the gas station on post to fill up before heading to the Lundgrens'. Overall, her first week had gone well enough. She'd met most of the men in her new company, and they were welcoming. Next week, she'd meet the two pilots who'd been on leave.

Her first two days had been easy flying with the head pilot, James Lee. As she got familiar with the area around Fayetteville and Fort Bragg, they caught up on life since they served together at Fort Lewis. She also liked the two other pilots she'd flown with.

Staying with the Lundgrens made the transition easier, but over the weekend, she'd get serious about looking for a permanent place to live. She couldn't stay with them forever. Things would settle into a new normal soon.

As the gas pumped, her gaze locked on a man fueling a gray truck at another row of pumps. He stared directly at her.

In that fraction of a second, she recognized Bryan Sheehan. Of all people to run into. She'd hoped never to see the misogynistic ass again after their last deployment. Could she not catch a break?

His icy look chilled her from a good twenty-five feet away. No surprise since he'd blamed her for the Article 15 disciplinary action resulting in his demotion. What were the chances he'd transferred to Bragg, like fifteen percent? Shit. If he was in one of the aviation units at Simmons, she wouldn't be able to avoid him, even if he was working on a different aircraft type now.

She stood straighter. If he'd done his job right or admitted to the screwup, and had not been an insubordinate asshole, he wouldn't have gotten written up.

As if by tacit agreement, they broke eye contact. After he replaced the nozzle, Sheehan climbed into his truck; only he didn't leave. She tried to ignore his existence as she cleaned her car's windshield and rear window. Still, he sat there. Maybe he was staring at her backside. Whatever. Just finish and go. Once her tank was full, she got in her car and cast a quick glance in her rearview mirror.

While she waited for an opening in the traffic, the rumble of a large truck engine came from behind. *Son of a bitch.* Sheehan's bumper nearly kissed hers. Surely, he wouldn't … She pressed harder on the brake.

As soon as she could, she pulled out. Sheehan had to wait for another SUV to pass, but thirty seconds later, he tooled along behind her. He turned the same way leaving post, and a mile down the road, he was still there. Not on her tail, but one car behind. When she turned, he followed. For her next turn, she didn't use her signal. Neither did he. Now there were no cars between them.

Surely, he wouldn't try anything. Not on a busy road with people around. Then again, acting now, before she could tell anyone about him, meant he wouldn't be a person of interest if something happened to her.

She fished her phone out of her backpack, turned on the

video, and put it on the dash mount. "In the gray truck behind me is Bryan Sheehan. He's been following me since I left the gas station on post."

Was she overreacting? Probably. She could always erase the recording. Better than calling the police, or Ray, when the jerk was merely following her at a safe distance.

There was no way in hell, though, she'd let him follow her to Ray and Stephanie's. She had to be smart. Since she didn't know the area well enough to outrun or ditch him, she looked for a place to duck in. Somewhere with people around but wouldn't make him think she was afraid of him. Someplace like that strip shopping center.

She flicked on her turn signal and turned in, eyeing the storefront signs as she cruised the parking lot. Dry cleaners, Chinese takeout, cell-phone repair, nail salon. Perfect! He wouldn't follow her in there, right? If he waited instead of driving off, she'd splurge for an overdue pedicure. And while he probably didn't have a clue how long a manicure or pedicure took, she couldn't see him waiting in the parking lot that long.

After taking the empty space in front of the salon, she craned her neck, picking out Sheehan's truck two rows over. He idled rather than park. Was he making sure she didn't get his plate number?

Trying her best to appear casual, she got out and didn't glance in his direction on her way in. Overhead, the bells chimed, and an overpowering chemical smell assaulted her nose. While waiting for one of the staff to greet her, Kristie caught a glimpse out the front window as Sheehan drove slowly past.

"Do you have an appointment?" A young woman asked in accented English while filing a brunette's nails.

"No."

"What would you like?"

"Uh, a pedicure." Which might mean waiting as two other women were in various stages of manicures, and three of the five pedicure chairs were occupied. Another customer sat in a seat by the front window, scrolling through her phone.

The nail technician's eyes roamed over Kristie's uniform and down to her boots. "Sign in." She gestured to the sheet on the counter. "It'll be about half an hour. Pick your polish." Her head dipped as she resumed working.

Kristie signed in, then kept an eye on the window as she browsed the rack filled with hundreds of polishes in every color of the rainbow. Regulations prohibited most of them on her fingernails when on duty, but her toes were usually the bright shade of Blue-My-Mind or I'm-Not-Really-A-Waitress red. She checked the label on the bottom of a sassy fuchsia. Her mind and attention were incapable of making a simple decision, though. A stop-sign red to signify danger?

Damn. Sheehan was getting to her. Getting a pedicure should be a relaxing event. She sighed and summoned up her courage. She'd flown dozens of combat missions, recently exchanged fire with cartel gunmen, and performed a risky-as-hell extraction. She'd stood up to Sheehan on her last tour, and he'd deserved it. He needed to man up and face the consequences rather than blame her. Hadn't he learned shit from getting reprimanded?

Well, maybe he had. The truck exited the shopping center and headed back in the direction they'd come. She watched until the pickup disappeared from sight. Time to bolt—in case he circled back.

She returned the polish to the rack. "I'll make an appointment for a better time," she said to the employee nearest the desk.

Kristie kept an eye out for gray trucks as she drove home.

She made it to the Lundgrens' certain she hadn't been followed. Hopefully, Sheehan had his fun jerking her chain and would be satisfied. She would avoid him going forward. But if the jerk followed her again, she wasn't running away. It'd be time for confrontation and involving the authorities.

THIRTEEN

FRIDAY EVENING, Kristie navigated around the cars lining the street as she neared Ray and Stephanie's house. She'd never seen so many cars on the road. Based on the black SUV, the sleek, red motorcycle, and faded-silver Honda with dents in the back bumper and side panel parked in Mack's driveway, he must've had buddies over.

In addition to those vehicles, a white minivan blocked in Ray's SUV. As Kristie parked behind Stephanie's car, the skin on her arms prickled. Her internal warning system telling her something was amiss rarely failed her.

She made her way to the side door and glimpsed a woman standing by the kitchen island talking to Stephanie. Kristie opened the door, and a multitude of voices greeted her. Nope, not Mack's place. Too late to duck out now.

Stepping into the kitchen, where food covered the table, she inhaled the tantalizing aroma of barbecue pork. Her stomach rumbled, reminding her how long ago she'd eaten an apple and protein bar. Memories returned of team get-togethers at the Lundgrens' when they'd been at Fort Lewis.

"Kristie!" Stephanie welcomed her. "Did the guys leave you a spot to park?"

"Yeah. I didn't realize you were having a party."

"I mentioned we were having a barbecue."

"You said we were having barbecue *for dinner*."

Stephanie smiled, the picture of innocence. "Can I get you something to drink?"

"Let me change first." She smiled back at Stephanie and the woman beside her.

Kristie didn't have a choice other than to pass through the living room filled with people. Luckily, most focused on the TV. Out of the corner of her eye, she spotted Ray seated at the dining room table with Mack, two women, and several men she remembered from the cantina in Colombia.

She hadn't laid eyes on Mack since Sunday. So much for thinking she could continue to avoid him. In the hallway, she nearly collided with a fresh-faced young man coming out of the bathroom. He did a double-take, scanning her uniform. "Sorry, ma'am."

Oh, great. Now I'm "ma'am." Another reminder of the rules and regs. With Eric's team and friends, she'd been Kristie, Eric's wife. A part of the group, despite being an officer.

What were the chances she could hide in her room? Knowing Stephanie, zero. She ran through several evasive maneuvers while she slipped out of her boots and uniform.

Move on. Keep living life, Eric's voice prodded in her head. She peered into the closet, settling on a pair of denim capris and a red V-neck. While she studied her reflection, she traded her small stud earrings for a pair of silver hoops.

Before joining the party, she ducked into the bathroom and applied a touch of eyeliner and lipstick. Then she took a long, deep breath while debating her options. Should she do this? Go back out there and mingle with Ray's team? Part of her wanted to. It was no big deal. Just hanging out, making new friends.

Passing back through the living room, she glanced around. Mack and several of the other men checked her out, making a flush heat her face. Ray had his mouth full, and though he motioned to her, she acknowledged him but didn't pause for introductions to the rest of the team.

Kristie found Stephanie still in the kitchen. "Where's Alexis tonight?"

"Babysitting at my house," the woman with Stephanie answered, killing Kristie's improvised escape plan of taking Alexis to a movie.

"Kristie, this is Tammy Shuler," Stephanie introduced them.

"You're a pilot. I saw the insignia patches on your uniform," Tammy explained.

"I fly Black Hawks. I just joined the 82nd Aviation."

"My first husband flew Kiowas in the 159th."

"Oh." Something in Tammy's voice made the hair on the back of Kristie's neck stand on end.

Tammy's eyes flicked to Stephanie. "He was killed when his helicopter went down in Mosul."

Kristie's head jerked involuntarily. "I'm sorry." Damn. Even though she hated that empty platitude, it still slipped out.

"It's been hard ... but you have to go on. I had kids to take care of. And then I met Walt." Tammy gestured toward the living room.

Kristie cut her gaze to Stephanie. Had she told Tammy about Eric? She grasped for something to change the subject. "How old are your kids?"

"Mine are seven and almost five." Tammy patted her

stomach, drawing attention to the slight mound. "This will be our first together."

"Congratulations."

"Thanks. Walt has three girls—fifteen, ten, and eight. It'll be a full, crazy house when they're with us. We don't get to see them much, especially his oldest since she lives with her mom in Kentucky. Now, let's get something to eat before the guys come back for seconds," Tammy said like they were old friends.

Kristie nodded. Okay, this widow had moved on. Remarried. Was having kids. Her story should inspire hope, not feel like a swift kick in Kristie's gut. However, between her new job, needing to find a place to live, and now Sheehan following her, she didn't have the energy to deal with one more thing.

Tammy seemed happy. Marrying a guy who had at least two exes, which wasn't all that uncommon in the Special Ops community, took a lot of courage, especially for a woman with kids.

Stephanie motioned Kristie to the table. Tammy loaded her plate with generous helpings of barbecue, slaw, potato salad, and beans. Mack walked in as Kristie finished filling her own plate. She didn't let her gaze linger on him long. The sensation of being watched was probably her imagination.

Why had Mack and his wife split? Infidelity? Deployments?

Why the hell did it even matter?

Maybe someday she'd remarry, but not to another man in Special Ops. Not with the risk of losing him in combat or the high divorce rate in units like this. She couldn't handle more loss or heartache. And she wouldn't settle or marry just to have *someone*. She didn't have kids, and she could take care of herself. Finding a compatible spouse was like winning the lottery. Better to invest those winnings to make them last for a lifetime.

When Kristie wandered into the living room, Ray nabbed her and introduced her to the team. Rather than take the chair at the table across from where Mack sat a minute ago, she headed to the couch. "There an empty seat here?"

"For you? Definitely." The guy edged over. "I'm Tony."

"Kristie." She eased down in the middle. "Who's playing?" She cringed as a hockey player in red slammed another player into the wall.

"'Canes versus some Yankee team." Mack rounded the end of the couch and sat in the vacant spot next to her.

Did he have to do that? Trapped between the two, she had no easy way to escape.

"Funny," Tony remarked to Mack, then turned to her with a conspiratorial grin. "Buffalo Sabres. I'll give you five bucks to cheer for them with me."

"You from Buffalo?" She pointed her thumb toward Tony's Buffalo Bills T-shirt, trying not to think about Mack's leg rubbing against hers when he leaned forward to set his cup on the coffee table, pushing another plastic cup aside.

"Small town just outside."

"Thanks a lot." A handsome Latino soldier with a short beard scowled down at Mack on the full couch.

Tony jerked his head toward the adjacent dining area. "There're seats at the table, Dominguez."

"I want to see the game." Dominguez picked up his cup from the edge of the table.

"You don't even like hockey," Tony said.

"I like the fights."

"Here. I can—" Kristie started to rise.

Tony moved a hand to block her. "Three guys on the couch? Not happening."

She glanced at Mack, who didn't budge, then gave Dominguez an apologetic shrug.

Grumbling under his breath, he stepped over and cleared a space on the coffee table. He set his plate down, then grabbed a chair from the dining area and sat near the end of the couch.

When the Hurricanes scored a few minutes later, everyone cheered, except for Tony.

He frowned at her. "Thought you were rooting for my team."

She would have been intimidated except for the amusement in his chocolate-colored eyes. "Gotta cheer for the home team," she answered.

Tony was attractive in a bad-boy way. However, it was Mack's smirky grin, those enthralling blue eyes and dusting of freckles she found immensely attractive.

"How you like that, Vincenti? Two to zip," Dominguez crowed.

"It's the first period, and we're up two games to one. Don't get ahead of yourself."

"How was your first week here?" Mack swung his beer bottle back and forth by the neck.

"Good. I flew some. Mostly, I reviewed flight logs to plan training and got to know the guys in the company."

"What do you fly?" Tony asked.

"Black Hawks."

"Really?" Tony's lips curled up, and his head bobbed.

"Yeah. You've flown with her, dumbass." Dominguez took a potshot.

Tony's brow furrowed. "When?"

"Last time you got shot. Remember that?" Dominguez sneered at Tony.

Tony studied her, though he appeared to bite the inside of

his cheek in an attempt to ignore Dominguez. "Colombia? That was you? Nice flying."

"All in a day's work. How's your arm?" she asked.

"Eh, arm's fine. Messed up the ink a bit, though." Tony pushed up his left sleeve, revealing a tattoo banding his arm. The skin puckered where the bullet had torn through his muscle, leaving a scar that distorted the intricate design of the woven, thorny branches.

She gave him a sympathetic nod and turned her attention back to the game, trying not to think about Mack's bicep grazing her arm. Why couldn't she be attracted to beta males? There was so much testosterone in the room, it made a girl lightheaded.

She was used to being outnumbered by males. This was different. Most of these operators were above-average look-ing, and it was more than their strong jaws and athletic builds. Not one of them slouched. Each had a swagger about them, but not in a cocky way. They had a quiet self-confidence that was downright, undeniably sexy. Here she felt safe. No worries about Sheehan while surrounded by these guys.

"You know, we need to give Grant a workout with the team on field ops." Ray's booming voice commanded every-one's attention. He rested a hand on the shoulder of the young man she'd encountered in the hallway, but Ray's sights were focused on her. "You've got newbies to break in, too, don't ya, Kristie?"

"I do. What did you have in mind?"

Ray's wicked smile told her everything. "I'm thinking spot jumps. Fast roping. Different insertion scenarios." His smile widened at the chorus of "Hooah!" around the room. "I'll make a request to set it up."

Ray's proclamation sent a buzz of anticipation through her, making her arms and hands tingle. In the past, flying similar training ops had been her favorite activity, but this didn't fit into her plan of avoiding Special Ops guys. Sandwiched between Tony and Mack, she couldn't help but let her mind wander to places it had no business going, especially since she had to keep her relationship with Mack professional.

At the end of the game's second period, she escaped into the kitchen. She spooned a serving of banana pudding into a bowl before she caught sight of Mack and Tony following her lead.

"Better have a cannoli, or you'll hurt Vincenti's feelings," Mack advised, eyeing her with a playful smile.

"Did you bring them?" she asked.

"Bring them?" Tony huffed and puffed out his chest. "I made them."

"I would love a cannoli, then."

Mack placed one in her bowl. Their eyes locked again, and her heart skipped a beat. Her gaze dropped to his lips, then shifted back to his eyes.

"Thanks," she said with an internal sigh.

Tony cleared his throat.

"Sorry for holding up the line." She didn't dare make eye contact with him—even when he gave a rough chuckle.

MACK WATCHED Kristie take a seat at the dining room table—instead of beside him on the couch. He'd noticed how quickly, yet subtly, she'd moved aside when his leg brushed hers earlier. The last thing he wanted was to give her more reasons to put distance between them, so he feigned interest in the game.

His jaw hurt from grinding his teeth while Tony had

chatted her up. He glanced over to where she sat next to Grant, but she was talking with the women. When the game ended, Kristie disappeared into the kitchen with Stephanie. He heard the clattering of dishes being stacked and loaded.

Walt and Tammy were the first to head out. The other guys made their way through the kitchen to say goodnight. As expected, Stephanie had set out containers of leftover barbeque. Dominguez, Rozanski, and Porter each snagged a container, thanking her and Ray before they ducked out.

"Thanks for bringing the cannoli, Tony. Hope you don't mind that I kept a few. Alexis requested one." Stephanie handed Tony a clean platter and tub of barbeque.

"No problem. Thanks for having us. Nice to meet ya, Kristie. See you soon. Night, Mack."

"I'm coming, too." He ignored Tony's surprised expression and targeted his eyes on Kristie. "Good night ladies." Stephanie pressed the last container of barbeque into Mack's hand. He took one last peek at Kristie and trailed Tony out the door.

Dominguez backed his beat-up car out of Mack's driveway as they walked across the street. Heavy-metal music blared from his open window. Grant lowered the face shield on his helmet and started his Ducati. Cruising down the driveway, he followed Dominguez's taillights.

"You want to come in for another beer?" Mack asked Tony.

"As consolation for my team losing, or so you can make sure I don't invite your girl out?"

"What are you talking about?"

"Kristie."

"Nothing's going on there."

"Why not? I saw how you kept looking at her. And being

around you made *her* nervous like a schoolgirl with a crush on the quarterback."

Shit. He thought he played it low-key. Apparently, not low enough. "She's a warrant officer."

"So? Breaking rules adds danger and excitement to the mix."

He shook his head, not that Tony's suggestion surprised him. "I don't think she's willing to risk it."

"You know this because ...?" Tony drew out the last word.

He shifted his weight and broke eye contact under Tony's stare. "I kinda tested the waters. Got shot down."

"Sure it wasn't a warning shot? 'Cuz it sure wasn't a kill shot based on what I witnessed. I was barely a blip on her radar. Don't worry about me trying anything, but keep an eye on Dominguez." Vincenti opened the door of his SUV.

Mack tried to laugh it off—though his buddy was an expert at reading people. The idea Tony picked up on something he missed played across his mind. After taking another glance at the Lundgren house, he headed inside, contemplating her reasons for brushing him off.

It made sense she wouldn't cozy up to him in front of others due to rank. The Army drilled rules about fraternization into you from boot camp on. However, with the amount of money invested in training and retaining operators, people tended to look the other way for minor things. Aviators had a lot invested in their training. Maybe that gave them leeway to skirt the official rules and regs, at least enough for them to discreetly explore if they wanted a permanent solution. He'd watch his step.

Land mines were only dangerous if you stepped on one.

FOURTEEN

IT HAD BEEN a good afternoon of flying, and Kristie hoped that was a good precursor for the apartments she was scheduled to tour. The potential roommate situation she'd checked into last night had been a non-starter.

Ray choked from laughing so hard when she told him and Stephanie about the woman having a stripper pole—in the living room. The pole had been the first warning sign. Lots of women did pole dancing for exercise. Maybe. But the number of liquor bottles in the kitchen and what she'd glimpsed in the woman's bedroom were also indicators they might not be compatible roommates.

As she left the airfield Wednesday afternoon, she turned right onto Honeycutt Road. When she passed Texas Pond, a dark vehicle pulled out behind her. She wouldn't have thought twice about it if Sheehan hadn't followed her last week and then learning he was indeed working in the maintenance company at the airfield.

It took several seconds of watching in her rearview mirror to be sure it was a large SUV—not Sheehan and his big truck.

A similar SUV parked near the entrance to the pond's parking lot had caught her attention yesterday.

A few miles later, she navigated onto 401 Business. What appeared to be the same SUV turned and stayed a few cars back. Was it her imagination? Probably coincidence since this was a thoroughfare lined with restaurants and shops. Still, the déjà vu of Sheehan following her made her check her rearview mirror again. Would he resort to driving his wife's car, hoping Kristie wouldn't know it was him?

What would be his endgame? A little payback? Intimidation? The glare of the sun on the SUV's windshield kept her from confirming it was Sheehan. If he pulled up next to her and it was him, she'd look him right in the eye. Bullies tended to back down when someone stood up to them. Or if she called the MPs—and she sure as hell would report him again if he kept up this stalking bullshit.

Instead of riding her tail, though, the vehicle hung back. Why? If he was trying to follow her home, she'd make it easy for him—kind of.

Instead of going to the complex where she had the appointment tonight, she continued to the one she'd seen last night. She had no intention of living there.

If he had followed her last night, she might have missed the SUV in her rush to get here after work, but tonight when she parked at the building next to the sales office, she watched the SUV cruise in and park two buildings away.

Here goes nothing.

Getting out of her car, she slung her backpack over her shoulder and strode to the stand of mailboxes like she did this every day. While pretending to check for mail, she kept an eye on the SUV. No one got out, and she still couldn't see the damn driver.

Did she dare walk by the building where he was parked?

Probably best to act as though she wasn't aware she'd been followed.

She crossed the blacktop to the building and climbed to the second-floor landing where she made the turn, so she'd be visible if he was watching. After a few moments, she hugged the banister and snuck down to the ground floor. She ducked out the back, using the courtyard walkway connecting the buildings, then eased toward the entrance. She peeked at the parking lot in time to see the SUV leaving.

Ah, ha! He *had* followed her. It had to be Sheehan. She fumbled for her phone to get a picture, but she was too late.

She blew out a deep breath, and just in case, waited another minute before returning to her car. She kept an eye out on the short trip to the other apartment complex. If her plan worked, now he would think she lived here. Good luck with that.

FIFTEEN

SATURDAY NIGHT, the headlights of a passing car shone through the Lundgrens' front door sidelights, catching Kristie's attention because of its snail's pace. Muffy, their gray tabby, slept stretched out on the floor. Too bad that Ray and Stephanie didn't have a dog. It was her second night alone with the Lundgrens away at the beach, and she didn't need to get paranoid already.

She hesitated, then laid her book on the couch and crossed to the foyer to peek out. It wasn't Sheehan's truck, but a dark SUV idled across the street. Was it the same one that had followed her three days ago? The headlights were off now, but in the faint glow from the dashboard lights, she could make out a person in the driver's seat. Seconds ticked by with no one getting out.

Staying far enough back so her silhouette wouldn't show, she edged closer to the window.

Could it be Sheehan? Mack's truck was in his driveway. If she had his number, she'd recruit him to check it out. Calling the police would be overkill. It might be someone who pulled over to text. Right, safety first.

She waited. The car didn't move. Finally, she grabbed her phone and her pistol. After she tucked the weapon into the waistband of her shorts, she slipped out the kitchen door on the side of the house. As a precaution, she snuck through the neighbor's backyard.

The SUV hadn't left when she edged around the side of the house. Confronting whoever was in the car on her own, especially at night, wouldn't be smart, but if she could get closer, she'd snap a picture of the license plate. Ray would have access to someone who could find out who the vehicle belonged to. If she had evidence, she could do something. And in case they saw her and tried something, she was armed.

She activated the camera on her phone and turned off the flash before making her way to the front of the neighbor's house. If the neighbors saw her and came out, she'd be okay with that.

Even at maximum zoom, she couldn't capture the numbers on the plate in the dark. She had to get closer. If she had a dog to walk, that would make pulling this off a lot easier.

Kristie stood on the sidewalk about to take a picture when the SUV's passenger door opened. She snapped the picture as quickly as possible, then reached for her weapon, keeping it at her side. Her breath rushed out when Mack climbed out. She froze, hoping he wouldn't look her way.

He said something to the driver, then closed the door. He started to turn, caught sight of her, and did a doubletake.

"You looking for me?" His voice had a teasing lilt.

"No, I'm just, uh …"

Mack kept approaching, giving her some time to come up with a story. Why couldn't Muffy be a Labrador or a mutt? She slid her hand behind her and tucked the pistol back into her waistband.

"Just, uh, what?" he pressed, stopping short of invading her personal space. His eyes crinkled in suspicion, then cut to her hand as she brought it to her side.

"I saw a suspicious vehicle idling outside. I thought I'd get the tag number in case …"

"That was Tony. We went to dinner. You got a case of PDTS?"

"No, I don't have *P-T-S-D!*" she corrected him.

"Not PTSD. PDTS—post-*deployment traffic* syndrome— where you evaluate every vehicle to determine if it's a potential threat."

"I can do my job without it causing problems."

"Then what's got you so spooked that you came out packing?"

Shit. He'd seen her weapon. She huffed. "Someone followed me last week."

"What do you mean, 'followed you?'"

"The first time—"

"Wait, wait. First time?" Mack stood straighter, his eyes wide and wary. "Let's go inside to discuss this."

"There's nothing to discuss. I'm handling it."

"Handling it by checking out cars with a weapon in hand? Inside," he ordered.

"But—"

"My place or yours? Never mind." He angled his body to corral her in the direction of Ray's house.

"Front door's locked." She veered off toward the side of the house.

He stayed right on her heels, already doing surveillance like a bodyguard.

"Coffee?" she offered once they were inside, hoping to gain a few seconds to plan her explanation so he wouldn't overreact.

"Sure. Give me details," he ordered while she spooned coffee into the machine's basket.

"I ran into a guy who has an old beef with me at one of the gas stations on post. He rode my tail then followed me for a few miles. I ditched him in a shopping center, and he left."

"Good that you know who the guy is, but he did it again?" The concern in Mack's voice was undeniable.

"The other night, an SUV followed me from the airfield when I went to look at apartments." She swore silently when water sloshed onto the counter instead of making it into the coffee maker.

"Same guy?"

"I can't say for sure. It wasn't Sheehan's truck, and he didn't tailgate me like before. He hung back, and I couldn't see who was driving. I parked and pretended to go inside an apartment building, and the SUV left a minute later. Maybe I'm being paranoid."

"I don't like it. I can see him being a dick the first time, but if he made a plan, waited, and stalked you, he could be escalating. What's this Sheehan's first name?"

"Bryan. With a *y*."

Mack typed the name into his phone. "Is he assigned to an aviation unit?"

"He's in the maintenance company."

"What's your history with him? Ex-boyfriend? Promoted over him? Gave him a bad review?"

"More complicated than that." *Come on, coffee.* Based on Mack's raised eyebrows, she had a feeling they were going to need it.

"My last tour, I asked Sheehan, the senior crew chief in our maintenance shop, to check my aircraft after I detected a vibration. When we took the bird up the next day, I still felt it. We returned to base, and I went to the Maintenance Test

Pilot. Horton called Sheehan over and asked him what he found. Sheehan said everything checked out and insinuated that I was being paranoid. The week before, a craft experienced mechanical failure and made a hard landing. Everyone survived, though both pilots suffered spinal injuries, and the crew chiefs were banged up, so I was being cautious."

"Understandable," Mack agreed.

"My co-pilot, Kerns, told Horton he felt it, too, so he ordered Sheehan to take another look, then assigned us a new bird. We wrapped up missions that afternoon, and Sheehan came back, said he didn't find anything, but he tightened some bolts. Horton took it for a test flight, and it was good to go. Sure enough, no vibration."

"You think he didn't want to admit missing something?"

"It sure felt that way. He's also an ass who doesn't like taking orders from a woman. If Kerns asked the first time, he probably would have been taken seriously. I didn't raise a stink, but then one of the maintenance guys, this kid Pawley who I like, told Horton he'd seen Sheehan replace a part in my tail rotor."

"What a prick. They bust him?"

"He said it wasn't related, just doing preventative maintenance while the bird was there. The part was gone, so no solid evidence, but Horton didn't buy it. Wasn't the first, nor second complaint about Sheehan's work—or lack of—and Horton did reprimand him. Somehow Sheehan blamed me. Started talking smack about me to the men reporting to him that there was nothing wrong and that I'm making up shit about him not doing his job because I'm afraid to fly after Mears and Boushey's crash."

"Even though you'd gotten another craft and gone out?"

"Exactly. And flew every mission assigned to me after their crash. I have to look after the safety of my entire crew, and when Sheehan wouldn't knock it off, I had to bring him up for insubordination. Coupled with the other complaints already on his record, he got an Article 15, which kind of sent him over the edge. I went directly to Horton for any maintenance needs and steered clear of Sheehan."

Sheehan kept his mouth shut, but either treated her as invisible or shot her death glares if he could get away with it. Hardly a fun working relationship. "He was such an ass that he had no friends in the unit. Apparently, he read the writing on the wall because he requested a transfer before Colonel Muñoz found a way to force him out."

"And ended up here. Lucky you."

"I was hoping to never deal with him again, but aviation is a small community." Very small, and despite the fifteen-percent chance of being at the same base, the chance of crossing paths was way too high.

Mack sipped his coffee and stared at her over the rim. "Have you told Ray about being followed?"

"Not yet." She'd put that off, thinking she'd handled Sheehan after he followed her to the apartment complex. "I'll tell them, and if I can't find and get in an apartment before they get back from the beach, I'll get a hotel."

"That's not why I asked. Here, you've got Ray, there's a security system, and I'm right across the street. You're safer here than in an apartment or hotel."

"But I can't take the chance of putting Stephanie or Alexis in danger if Sheehan becomes unhinged."

"It's not like this is some Colombian drug lord after you. You can tell them when they get back, and let them make the call. You know we're the Bad Karma team. Dishing out karma to evil-doers everywhere."

"You can't go vigilante on him." That sounded exactly

like what Eric would suggest if he were here. "A strong warning would be okay, though," she relented.

Mack's sexy, throaty chuckle melted the tension that had made her arms rigid.

"I can't let you get in trouble because of me," she warned.

"No worries. We know where to draw the line. And how to cover up things." He didn't quite hide his grin behind his coffee mug. "Do you change up your route regularly?"

"Yes. And after he followed me the first time, I haven't come straight here. I've been changing routes, stops, and times."

"Good. It's not likely he followed you then, but I'll check your car for tracking devices in the daylight. Tonight, either you stay at my place, or I'll stay here with you."

"You don't need to do that. I can set the alarm, and I have my weapon," she protested.

"I don't *have to*, but otherwise, I'm going to make perimeter checks every half hour and sit across the street watching the house all night. I'll get a better night's sleep if we're under the same roof where I can react quickly to any threats. So, which is it? You can take one of my girls' bedrooms, or I can sleep here on the couch."

Her fingertips drummed on the tabletop. "You shouldn't have to sleep on the couch. I can change the sheets—"

"I'm not sleeping in the chief's bed. Or his daughter's. The couch is fine. Trust me, beats a lot of places I've slept. All I need is a pillow."

He maintained eye contact as if hoping she'd offer another alternative. The refrigerator hummed and hummed.

"I'll get you a pillow," Kristie caved, pushing up from the chair.

"I'll get one. I'm gonna grab a few things from my house. Be right back."

While Mack was across the street, she put her weapon away. Was this a good idea? The two of them spending the night under the same roof? It was early. If she begged off to go to bed now, he'd know she was avoiding him. It'd be rude.

Being together like this wasn't fraternization —technically.

They should make the most of it. As friends. Nothing more than Mack making sure she was safe from the likes of Sheehan.

She turned on the living room TV and searched the channel guide. Good old TV Land came through.

When she let Mack in a few minutes later, he broke into a smile when he saw *M*A*S*H* on the screen. He set his bag on the floor and his pillow on the couch. "You going to watch with me?"

"If you promise not to call me Hot Lips."

"Yeah. You're not her biggest fan, are ya?"

He remembered. That little fact sent a buzz through her body. A hot, sensual buzz that made her tingle in all the right places. *No.* Wrong places. The *wrong* places. She swallowed down the desire welling up. "You want a beer?"

"Sure. Got any peanuts or pretzels?"

"I'll check." And take a minute to get it together. At least the upside was she wasn't worried about Sheehan anymore.

It was hard to think about Sheehan with Mack sitting beside her, though he wasn't making it easy to keep her thoughts on the show and off him—by being Mack. Funny, charming, easy to be with.

"*Eck*," he grumbled and picked up the remote, muting the volume when a different show started after the second episode of *M*A*S*H*. "Sorry. Can't stand that show."

"Me, either. You can turn it off. I should let you sleep."

She got to her feet and carried the dirty dishes to the kitchen. He followed with his empty beer bottle.

Mack checked the doors before he turned off the lights throughout the house. She thought he was being overprotective, but he had a point. Pawley and Horton told her how pissed Sheehan had been that she went to the colonel about his insubordination. She'd first envisioned Sheehan doing some property damage, but would he do something stupid? Try to hurt her?

She didn't lock the bedroom door. Mack was here to protect her. A simple lock wouldn't keep him out if he wanted in. She had to keep trusting him.

And try to keep things professional. Even though it'd been so damned hard sitting next to him watching TV. It felt good. Comfortable. The way she hadn't been comfortable with a man since Eric. She hadn't wanted to tell Mack, or anyone, about being followed and risk looking weak, but he hadn't belittled her at all.

She settled into bed, hyperaware Mack was right down the hall. Sleeping on the couch. A *couch*. Good thing he couldn't read her mind. Were the same thoughts running through his head?

Stupid Army regulations. They weren't in the same unit, and never would be. She'd never have to give him orders. Though she could think of a few she wouldn't *mind* giving him.

SIXTEEN

KRISTIE APPEARED while Mack knocked out his push-ups in the living room. "Morning," he said, pumping out another. He stopped and got to his feet. "I made coffee."

"Thanks."

"You're up earlier than I thought, with you being an aviator."

"Really? You're going to rag on aviators even after I pulled you out of the jungle?" Kristie grinned but shifted to neutral when her gaze briefly dropped to his bare torso.

"All right. I take it back." He picked up his shirt and pulled it on. "Didn't want to leave for a run and make you think I'd abandoned my post."

"I don't see that happening. Have you eaten?"

"Not yet." He hadn't wanted to make noise and wake her.

"Want some eggs?"

"That'd be great." Was she checking out his arms now, or was that his hopeful imagination?

"How do you like them?"

"Over easy, if it's not too much trouble. I'm going to give your car a once-over. I need your keys." He followed her into the kitchen, waiting while she dug them out of her purse. "Do you keep it locked?"

"Always."

"Keep that up."

Outside, he checked the wheel wells first. Finding nothing, he dropped to the ground and lay on his back, wiggling his way underneath. Starting at the back bumper, he used his tactical flashlight to examine the undercarriage for signs of a GPS tracker, then checked the interior and under the hood. Once he was satisfied, he closed the hood and locked the car before stepping back into the kitchen to the sound of meat sizzling.

"Car's clean." He moved to the sink to wash the dirt and grease from his hands.

"That's a relief."

"You still need to be careful. Check your car, change up routes, park in well-lit areas."

"I—"

"I know you know this." He guessed her response based on the defensive angle of her head. "But I feel better saying it."

She dropped the death glare and turned the sausages in the pan. "How runny do you like your eggs?"

"Anything between raw and rubbery, and I won't complain." He watched her separate the eggs in the skillet, then carefully flip them.

"Would you get the jelly out and pour some juice?"

He did as instructed and grabbed napkins and silverware while Kristie served up the plates. Sitting next to each other at the round table in the sunny kitchen brought back memories of the early days of his marriage. It'd been years since Rochelle asked how he wanted his eggs. He always got scrambled because that's what the girls liked. Making them the same way meant less work for her. Kristie fixed herself an omelet but hadn't even suggested he have one, too.

Rather than expecting him to read her mind or telling him to stay out of her way, Kristie asked for help. He'd nearly forgotten that putting a meal together could be enjoyable when done as a team.

"This is great. Thanks. I may have to try an omelet next time."

"You're not planning on being my personal bodyguard twenty-four seven, I hope."

"Not twenty-four seven. I'm gonna go home to give you some space. Mow my grass. Get a shower. You're free to run errands—preferably in daylight. I'll check in, so hope you're quick to answer texts. What's your phone number?"

She didn't hesitate to supply it. He might as well try pushing a step further. "Tonight, I can grill out, or we can order in pizza. Watch more *M*A*S*H* or a movie." A smidgen of guilt poked him about using this situation to his advantage as he saved her number in his phone.

Now she did hesitate, eyeing him.

"Unless you'd rather be here all alone, knowing that I'm across the street, watching. Not in a creepy, stalker way, just, you know, protecting you from afar. If you had a dog, I wouldn't have to do that, but—"

Kristie laughed, a delightful, musical sound, and graced him with a smile that made him long to reach out and touch her.

"Maybe I'll stop by the animal shelter or see if I can foster a pit bull for a while." She played along.

"Now, you're talking. Though, a yappy little dog can be even more effective. More warning time for you to grab your weapon." He raised his eyebrows and grinned at her. "I could call Hightower and see about borrowing Dita for the night."

"I better not bring a dog into Ray's house without permission, and I'm not explaining why I'm asking over the phone. You know Ray, he might use that as an excuse to ditch the vacation and come home. But I can't let you keep sleeping on the couch."

His expression must have given away where his mind went because she shook her head faster than a SASS sniper round.

"I'm going to change the sheets, and I'll sleep in Alexis's bed, and you can have the guest room until they get back from the beach."

"I hate for you to go to the trouble of changing beds and moving your stuff."

Kristie's gaze lingered on him long enough to give him hope. "You can change the sheets on one of the beds then. Unless you've decided you're comfortable sleeping in your boss's daughter's bed."

"*Ye-aah*, no. I—No. I'll help change sheets." He took a bite of sausage, doing his best to remain low-key and not get ahead of himself.

"How about pizza for dinner? My treat. I like pepperoni with pineapple."

"Seriously? Not Hawaiian with ham and pineapple?"

"You can get whatever you want on yours," she said, not backing down.

Good thing he liked a challenge.

SEVENTEEN

AT THE END of the day Monday, Mack waited for the guys to head out of the team room. Tony Vincenti lagged behind, as if on purpose.

"Was that Kristie you went to talk to when I dropped you off the other night?" Tony grinned in a hopeful way.

"It's not what you think. She was worried about the suspicious car sitting out front. Came to check it out. Not to see me."

"We were only out there a couple minutes." Tony looked perplexed.

"She ran into some jerk she used to work with, and the dude followed her in a harassing way. Then she thinks he followed her again in a different vehicle last week."

Tony moved closer. "Seriously? Why?"

Mack leaned back in the wooden chair and rapped a fist on the tabletop. "He's a douche guy, who was in her old maintenance shop. He didn't do a repair, then gave her crap, so she reported him for insubordination. He got written up with an Article 15 and transferred after the deployment. He's here now."

"You aren't planning something stupid, are you?"

"Maybe. We got a couple of spare GPS trackers?"

"I'm sure we do." Tony moved to the equipment cage and pulled down a box, sorting through the electronics before pulling out two trackers. "What are you thinking?"

"Thought we could go to the airfield, let her point out his truck. I'd put one on his vehicle. Put one on hers, too. Then, if he goes near Kristie, we've got proof he's harassing her."

"Straightforward enough. I'm in."

"You sure?"

"You might need a lookout. And if we have to track him, it's harder for him to pick up a tail with two of us following him."

"I'll text her to see when works."

Tony sang *Bad, Bad Leroy Brown* as Mack texted and waited to hear back.

THURSDAY AFTERNOON, Kristie climbed into the back seat of Tony's SUV. Mack had installed a dashcam in her car on Tuesday, and she'd reluctantly gotten on board with their plan to put a tracker on her car and Sheehan's.

She hadn't seen his truck in the lot on Tuesday. Though there had been several SUVs, she couldn't swear one was a solid match to the one that followed her to the apartment complex. Last night was Mack's night for dinner with his girls, so she agreed to give it another try after she cruised through the lot near the maintenance hangar and picked out his truck with its distinctive grille guard.

"Are you sure about this? If the maintenance guys finish their work, they could knock off for the day soon." It wasn't like there'd be an end-of-day bugle to warn them.

"It'll only take a few seconds to plant it under the truck."

"Still, it's broad daylight. What about following him home and doing it there at night?"

"Home could be a problem. We could lose him. He might park in a garage. Or have a dog, or motion-sensor lights. Nosy insomniac neighbors." Tony made valid points.

"Tony's the lookout. Trust me. We've got this," Mack assured her.

They cruised the lot, and she pointed out the big, dark-gray GMC truck. Once they mapped out their tactics, Kristie hunched down in the back, peering out between the seats.

Mack and Tony made it past the door to the maintenance hangar without anyone coming out. She lost sight of Mack when he ducked between two vehicles. The covert mission had her heart pounding, but when a pair of soldiers exited the hangar, it beat harder and faster. She couldn't read Tony's lips, but he saw the men headed his way. *Come on. Come on.* No sign of Mack yet.

Why was Tony standing in plain sight? What if one of the men looked his way and caught Mack? She hated being outside the loop.

The hangar door swung open again, and none other than Bryan Sheehan strolled out. *Shit!* Of course, he headed right toward Tony, who wouldn't recognize Sheehan. This was going to look so bad if he discovered them planting the tracker.

In a flash, she slipped out of the SUV. She left the door cracked, then jogged after Sheehan.

"Hey, Sheehan!" she called loud enough to get not only his attention but the other two soldiers, as well. Crap, one of them she'd met, and he recognized her.

Sheehan shook his head as she approached. "What?"

"Following me the other night was not cool."

"Maybe I was going to the same place."

"Why didn't you go into one of the stores then?" She held his attention. "And what were you doing at the apartment complex?"

"Apartment complex? What the hell are you talking about, Donovan? You got a lot of nerve showing up here and making shit up again. Quit trying to fuck up my life."

She needed to buy time for Mack and Tony. "I think you did that on your own." If he had switched vehicles to follow her, he wasn't going to come out and confess.

He stalked a few steps in her direction.

"Let's agree to do our jobs and steer clear of one another." Her offer defused him enough to hold up. Or maybe it was the other pair of soldiers within earshot.

Tony and Mack strolled into sight. Mission accomplished —on their end.

"Happy to keep my distance. Don't want to get associated with the pilot who's paranoid about every vibration in her aircraft. Hate for you to get labeled as *that* pilot by the guys in the maintenance shop." He smirked.

Was that a threat? Or an attempt to mess with her head? One word from her, and Mack and Tony would be happy to show Sheehan the true meaning of intimidation, based on the scowl on Mack's face.

"Never have before, and there's nothing in my file about me not doing *my* job," she said as her warning shot before turning on her heel. The last thing she needed was a rumor swirling that she was unstable, blowing her shot at MEDEVAC.

She didn't look back as she strode toward the Charlie Company hangar, but she listened. No deep voices. No scuffle. And seconds later, the slam of car doors.

Once she crossed the airfield and got into her car, Kristie

turned the air-conditioning on high. A lengthy exhale and distance from Sheehan slowed her heartbeat to normal. Though confrontation was not her thing, calling him out bought the guys more time, and it empowered her. She hoped it was enough. If Sheehan didn't live up to his promise to keep his distance, they'd get proof of him harassing or stalking her.

Her phone dinged. Had to be Mack. Yup. His text said to meet him back at the house. The wording poked at her heart. The house. Lundgrens', not her home.

The last bit of adrenaline drained away. There was no need for Mack to continue to protect her. No reason for him to stay or them to spend time together. No more living in her little fantasy world.

She should offer to cook dinner for him as a thank-you. Maybe she should invite Tony, too. She was stalling. Best to go cold turkey.

See you there, she texted back.

She'd only been at the Lundgrens' a few minutes before Mack knocked at the kitchen door.

"Did you get the tracker on the truck?"

"Yes. He won't find it unless he crawls underneath." Mack grinned. A smudge of dirt or grease ran along his cheek. "Once we determine where he lives, I'll go by and see what other vehicles are there that he'd have access to. I'm going to make sure he doesn't happen to drive down this street. What exactly did you say to him?" He nodded as she summed it up. "Quick thinking. Thanks for buying us extra time."

At least he didn't scold her for getting out of Tony's SUV. "Thanks. I appreciate you guys helping me handle this. Don't worry about stripping the bed. I'll take care of it."

His grin disappeared. "Kicking me out already?"

"More like not infringing on you any longer." It took effort to sound lighthearted. "I'm sure you'd like to sleep in your own bed. And you have your girls coming tomorrow for the weekend. You can't keep sleeping here."

He kept staring at her rather than move to get his stuff. "Look, I'll go home—because I feel like you're safe. But being here with you hasn't exactly been a hardship. And before I go, we need to address this." He waved a hand between them.

"Mack—"

"No. Let me finish. There's something here. Between *us*. We've been tiptoeing around it the past few days, and it's not going away just because we're not under the same roof."

"I admit," she struggled for the right words, "you made me feel safe. And being with you was easy and fun."

"We could have something good together if—"

"If what, Mack? If it weren't for Army regulations that prohibit it?"

"There are workarounds."

"I have two years left on my service commitment, but I plan to do twenty for full retirement. Do you think we could sneak around, hoping we don't get caught? That's not going to happen. I can't afford to risk everything by violating regulations."

"You and I aren't in the same unit, and it's not a big deal in my unit."

"Well, *hooyah* for you, but it is in mine. I just got here, and I'm in line for my dream job. I'm not willing to risk getting busted in rank or court-martialed." It was the superior-ranking officer that would face charges.

"You can't let flying be your whole life. Because it's not enough. I know. I love my job, and I do it to protect the people I love, and it totally sucks that my ex thought I was selfish for risking myself to protect her and the girls from the bad shit they don't see. I need a reason to do what I do. Someone to come home to. Especially since there will come a day I—you—can't do it anymore. When were you happiest?"

"What?"

"In your life. When were you happiest?"

She stared at him. If she told him, he'd use it to his advantage. Yet she couldn't lie. Not about this. "When I was married to Eric. When we were both doing what we loved." She hesitated. "When we were planning a family."

"Exactly. You may think you can't have it all again. But you can. Wasn't your husband an NCO?"

How did he know? "Yes, and so was I when we got married. We moved up the wedding to avoid problems after I got accepted to Warrant Officer Candidate School."

"Ray's suggested I apply to WOCS. Dealing with the politics kept me from pursuing it. With some more motivation I might reconsider." His soulful eyes bored into hers, and he took a step closer. "I want a second chance. With a woman who'll support my career."

He'd pushed her into a corner. She needed to come clean rather than give him false hope. "Then I'm not the right woman for you."

"Why?"

"After losing Eric, I swore I'd never get involved with someone in Special Ops again." She would not, could not, put herself in that position again.

"What happened to your husband sucks, but it's not going to happen again."

"You can't promise that. No one can. I can't live worrying whether a man I care about will come back alive every time he leaves on a mission. That's not fair—to you or to me."

"With our training, and working with the best of the best, our casualty rate is lower than regular Army."

"You can quote percentages, but that doesn't change things."

"Are you saying you won't date anyone in the military then, or just no one in Special Ops?"

She refused to answer or fight with him on this. He wouldn't leave Special Ops. He might get out and work for a private contractor—doing the same dangerous stuff—but there was *no* going back to regular Army for these guys.

"Have you realized it's a little hypocritical when you're flying and risking *your* life? That you'd potentially be putting some banker or accountant in your boots if something happened to you? You'd be better off with someone who knows and accepts the risks. Honestly, do you think settling for safe is gonna do it for you? Or is what your husband would want for you?"

He brought up rational arguments, but her brain couldn't override her fears. "It's better if we acknowledge that this wasn't meant to be and stay friends." Before he got her to let her guard down any further.

"Friends?" He sighed out the word with more than a hint of frustration. "Sure, if that's what you want."

"Mack, I don't want things to get awkward between us."

"Sometimes it doesn't matter what we want. Things are what they are." With that, he retreated to the Lundgrens' guest room.

Dammit. Way to shoot a guy down after he put himself out there.

She should have seen it coming and tried harder to keep things in the friend zone rather than send him mixed signals with the teasing banter the past few nights. But he knew the rules as well as she did—even if operators got special treatment due to their elite status. He knew how Eric died. He may not think it could happen to him, but she'd seen firsthand how close he'd come a few weeks ago.

Mack came out a minute later with his bag. "Guess I'll see you around." He headed to the kitchen door, then stopped and looked over his shoulder at her. "Call me if you see Sheehan or if anything, and I mean *anything*, feels off."

"I will," she promised. But it'd be wrong to hope for something that would bring them back together.

EIGHTEEN

"I'LL GET straws and napkins, Daddy." Darcy spun on her heel and wove through the customers behind them while Mack handed cash to the teenager manning the register.

"How'd the social studies project turn out?" he asked Amber while they waited for their food.

Her head tilted up. "I got a ninety-eight."

"A ninety-eight? Wow! Where'd you get all those brains?" he said loud enough for others to hear and ruffled her hair. "I'm proud of you, girl. Keep it up."

"I have a science test tomorrow on landforms."

"You already study?"

"Yeah, but I have a math worksheet to do."

"Did your mother know that?"

"No. I brought it." Amber patted her pocket. "I'll get it done."

"Deal." He didn't want her getting behind in school, but he also didn't want Rochelle carping about the few hours he got with the girls during the week were interfering with their homework.

He turned around with the tray; only Darcy wasn't at the condiment counter. His head jerked around, surveying the dining room. When he spotted her standing next to a table talking to a man he didn't recognize, his grasp on the tray tightened.

Before he charged over, he checked out the man's dinner companion. Even from behind, he recognized the French braid of the uniformed woman talking to his daughter. Setting the tray on the condiment counter, he choked down the lump in his throat as he grabbed several packets of ketchup.

Kristie shot him down when he said he wanted them to move things forward. And now, less than a week later, here she was in a restaurant having dinner with another guy.

Damn, that didn't take long.

The guy she was with was also in uniform. Mack strained to make out the rank insignia on his chest. A warrant officer. Probably another pilot. Figures. Seeing her with another guy felt like a kick in the 'nads. It didn't really surprise him. She was the total package.

He clenched his teeth as Amber headed toward Darcy. A low growl formed in his throat. He'd prefer to sit across the room and call to Darcy.

Ignoring Kristie would be rude though. Especially since, on Sunday afternoon, he'd found her in his driveway—she and Alexis each holding the ends of the long rope as both of his girls jumped together.

There was no need to be an ass, even if she was on a date —with a loser who took her out for fast food. Classy. Maybe officers didn't need to impress other officers.

"Hey. Sorry for the intrusion. Girls, come on." He motioned for them.

"They're fine," Kristie said.

A notepad sat on the table near Kristie's elbow. At the far

end of their table, a tray held empty food wrappers. Her date's gaze shifted between Kristie and Darcy.

This was killing Mack. Time to escape before introductions were made. "Have a good night." He turned to find Amber sitting at the table catty-corner to Kristie's booth. *Great.* He handed his girls their sandwiches as Kristie's date carried their tray to the trash.

"Be right back," the guy told Kristie.

Seated four feet away from them, Mack couldn't help but overhear. Her date opened the door to the playground area, called out, then tapped his watch. A boy close to Amber's age, wearing a white karate uniform, joined the man, and the two returned to the table.

"Anything else before I head out?" the pilot asked Kristie.

"The colonel approved a training op with the Special Operations guys." Her head turned in his direction, but Mack didn't meet her eyes. He had been looking forward to that op —until now.

"Sounds good. Thanks again for meeting me here."

"It wasn't a problem. Good thing I saw you before Friday, Dalton. I wouldn't have recognized you. What has your mother been feeding you? You've grown a foot!"

"She says it's the Captain Crunch," the boy said, making Kristie laugh.

Even though she'd deflected Mack's interest with the rank argument, he wasn't willing to wave the white flag. This week, he'd pulled up the site and looked over the sample application for WOCS. If accepted as a candidate, it'd only take a couple of months to complete the course to become a Warrant Officer. A couple of months away from the girls. Away from his team. But it might be too late if Kristie got involved with someone else.

Mack caved to the urge to check out the guy's left hand

and saw the wedding band. *Alleluia.* His appetite returned. Darcy stared at him with a puzzled expression, so he made a silly face. Still, she regarded him with open curiosity.

"I appreciate y'all organizing the dinner," he heard Kristie say.

"Happy to do it. Once the women meet you, that'll put an end to any crazy talk. It'll be fine."

"Can I bring anything?"

"Call and check with Mary Kate. Okay, dude, let's go test for that blue belt."

"You'll do great." Kristie raised a fist, and the boy bumped it with his.

"You heading out?" the pilot asked her.

"I'm going to grab something to eat first." She slid out of the booth and moved out of Mack's line of sight and earshot.

As Amber talked about school and her friend's upcoming birthday party, he tried to focus on what she was saying.

"Miss Kristie, you can sit with us," Darcy's sweet voice piped up unprompted.

Kristie hesitated, a wistful expression flitting across her features as she returned Darcy's gaze. "I don't want to intrude on your family dinner."

"What's 'intrude' mean?"

"Um, go someplace you aren't invited," Kristie answered.

"I invited you." Darcy's lips turned down in a pout that usually worked magic.

Mack kept his mouth shut, watching Kristie's face as she wavered. When Kristie looked to him, he shrugged helplessly. "She's kind of hard to say no to." He edged over, giving her room to sit down.

"I can see that." Kristie transferred her food to their table, then stepped back to retrieve her notepad.

"Next time we're at Daddy's, you can come over and get your turn jumping rope," Darcy said as soon as Kristie joined them.

"I won't be around next weekend. I'm having dinner with friends, then I'm going to Charlotte to see my family. Maybe another time. Though I doubt I can jump nearly as well as you girls."

Kristie's tactful handling of his daughter's invitation sounded authentic, and it stirred something inside him. He couldn't quite identify it, but he liked it, and even Amber beamed at the praise.

"Do you work with Daddy and Uncle Ray?" Darcy took a gulp of milk.

"Not usually, but I will one day next week. I fly helicopters."

"Helicopters! That's so cool." Amber sounded impressed.

"Can we go for a ride?" Darcy's eyes opened wide. She bounced so hard on the seat the table rocked.

"I'm afraid I can't take you up." Kristie looked genuinely disappointed as she addressed Darcy. "But your dad can bring you out to the airfield sometime. You can check out my Black Hawk, then you can watch me fly."

"Really? Can we go, Daddy?" Darcy batted her long lashes.

Mack half-expected Darcy to come clear across the table. "I'm sure we can manage that." He liked the idea and the smiles on his girls' faces. The invitation to the airfield for a tour might be for the girls, but he'd make the most of the invite.

Kristie answered more questions for Darcy, and then she made a point to turn the focus back to Amber, engaging both girls in the conversation. He couldn't believe how well this was going—sitting here sharing a meal with his daughters, talking so easily with Kristie. It was a delicious kind of torture.

Darcy slurped the last of her milk. She glanced over her shoulder toward the play area, then swiveled back to face him. "Can I go play now?"

He nodded; normally, she wouldn't have stayed at the table this long.

"You wanna come watch me, Miss Kristie?" Darcy's eyes lit up as she scooted off the bench.

Kristie gave a light chuckle, and Mack guessed her answer before she even opened her mouth. His youngest was pretty irresistible, but this also allowed Kristie to escape.

Darcy paused as Kristie rose. "You comin', Amber?"

"I have to finish my homework." Amber's voice was flat, and her words drawn out as she looked at him, probably hoping for a reprieve.

"Duty first." He winked at her.

Amber sighed, reached around, and pulled the sheet and a pencil from her pocket. "You don't have to help me do my homework, Dad."

"All right. But math is my specialty. Just don't ask me to spell those words they give you brainiacs."

Amber rolled her eyes in that preteen way that was still endearing instead of annoying.

"I guess I'll be in the play area with the screaming kids, then." Usually, he avoided the play area, but tonight he had an incentive to sit out there—and he got to shoot down Kristie's evade-and-escape maneuver. He pushed open the door and saw Kristie sitting at a table, facing the playset.

"May I?"

Kristie tilted her head. "Of course."

Seated beside her, he scanned the interconnecting tubes until he saw Darcy crawling through. Pausing at the window, she waved to them and blew him a kiss.

"She is precious."

He angled his head to see Kristie's face better. "She got the red hair and freckles from me."

She gave a low chuckle but didn't tear her gaze from the children playing around them.

"So, you're having dinner with friends next weekend."

"Unit dinner party on Friday."

"There a problem?"

Her head rocked side-to-side before she scrunched her eyebrows at him. *Oops.* Not like he could help overhearing her conversation.

"A couple of wives and girlfriends weren't thrilled when they heard a female pilot was joining the unit since it means I'll deploy with the guys. James and Mary Kate thought if the women met me, it might eliminate their concerns, so they offered to host a get-together."

Flaunting a beautiful, single woman in front of them was supposed to make them feel better? He tried not to laugh. "You might need to take a date." She met his gaze head-on, not that he expected her to ask him. "Sorry. And sorry about stalking out the other night."

"It's okay."

"No, it's not okay. Or fair. This sucks."

Though barely perceptible, her head nodded in agreement. A muscle in her cheek shifted, and the corner of her mouth curved down.

Should he give up and end this emotional torture for both of them?

He caught sight of Darcy, who smiled and waved at them

again. He waggled his index finger to summon her. She disappeared from view in the maze of tubes, then slid out to his left. She bounded over, tiny beads of sweat dotting her flushed face.

"Do we have to go already?" She gave an exaggerated pout.

"Not yet. I just need a hug."

Darcy's face lit up. She threw her arms around his neck, and her slight frame snuggled against his chest. He wrapped his arm around her, stroking her back. Soft lips pressed against his cheek.

She eased back. "I love you, Daddy."

"I love you, too, monkey. Thanks for the hug."

Impulsively, she lunged forward and squeezed him again, giggling. Love for her radiated through him. He wished it were enough as he glimpsed Kristie out of the corner of his eye.

"You have an extra one of those?" Kristie asked before Darcy darted away.

"Uh, huh." His daughter beamed.

He watched as she threw her arms around Kristie's neck.

With eyes closed and a serene smile, Kristie returned Darcy's embrace. "I need to go, but thanks for the hug and dinner company." Her voice broke with emotion, not that Darcy noticed as she jogged back to the playset.

Kristie sniffed, drew in a deep breath, and exhaled slowly.

It took every bit of restraint to keep from slipping an arm around her and drawing her to him. He nudged her with his knee. *Look at me. Give me a nudge. Some hope.*

Kristie got to her feet and picked up her purse and notepad. She stood inches from him. His muscles flexed, but he kept his hands planted on his thighs. They stared at one another, her eyes filled with emotion.

"I'll see you later." Her tone was resigned.

His hand lifted in a half wave, and she reached out, her fingers grazing his before she walked away. Just enough of a touch—like a flame to kindling—to spark a blaze of hope.

Oh, yeah. You'll be seeing me. This was not over. Not by a long shot.

NINETEEN

KRISTIE TRAILED BEHIND HER CO-PILOT, Powell, while he completed the preflight inspection. A transport truck rumbled up and parked alongside the tarmac when they were nearly finished.

She cast a peek over her shoulder as men poured out of the truck. Her stomach constricted, churning the coffee she'd had.

You got this. It might be her first big joint op here with the Special Ops guys, but she'd worked with the Ranger battalion back in Savannah plenty of times. She loved this kind of flying. Mack's presence served as another reminder why anything beyond casual friends was not an option, but she was not going to let it rattle her.

The wolf whistle seconds later made her freeze in her tracks. *No way.* Surely Mack wouldn't …Tony? No. She overrode her initial impulse to turn, though Powell studied her with a dubious expression.

"That could be considered sexual harassment, Milledge," an unfamiliar voice chastised.

Jeremy! Relief flooded through her, squelching her rising

indignation. She turned and laid eyes on Jeremy Milledge and his ornery grin.

"It isn't harassment if she likes it. Right, darlin'?"

Jeremy using Eric's nickname for her gave Kristie a jolt. He spread his arms wide as he neared. His cocky attitude sparked guffaws from several of his team members. Mack and Tony exchanged glances.

"You're such a jerk." She hugged him anyway. "Who's your cute friend?" She extended a hand to the Belgian Malinois between Jeremy and the soldier holding the leash.

"This is Dita," the soldier introduced them.

She let the dog sniff her before she rubbed his tan fur and black ears. "So, you're going to fly with me today, huh, Dita?" The dog's rough tongue licked her hand.

"That means I get to fly with you, too," Jeremy smirked suggestively.

"Fine. But I am going to make you jump out of my aircraft," she retorted.

"*Oh,* you know I love it when you talk dirty," he purred.

She shook her head, leaving Jeremy and the members of his team to put on their chutes.

"You might want to be careful," her crew chief, Tinsley, said.

"About?" she asked.

"Flirting and hugging enlisted guys. Colonel Ball is a total hard-ass when it comes to relationships between the ranks."

"Jeremy and I are old friends—and he's married."

"Just saying. Ball's old school. Zero fraternization. Zimmerman, in B Company, was messing around with an enlisted chick, who got pregnant. Zimmerman went to the colonel, and she got kicked out of the unit."

"Warning duly noted," she conceded so Tinsley'd ease up.

It wasn't Jeremy Milledge she needed the warning about. But neither Tinsley nor Colonel Ball could read her mind when it came to Mack.

Nearby Mack, Ray, and another man stood talking with her unit's captain.

"We don't get to ride with you?" Tony walked past, a teasing smile on his rugged face.

"I guess not on this run." Though this way, she might get to watch Mack fast rope.

Don't go there.

The idea of him sliding down the rope from the craft to the ground taunted her as she boarded and buckled her straps, shifting in the seat to get comfortable. She started the engine, checked the gauges, then radioed the air traffic controller. "Tower, this is Renegade One-Three, holding short of the active for takeoff."

Having her feet on the control pedals and her hand on the cyclic control, with the whine of the engine vibrating through her, her earlier unease dissipated. Handling this aircraft was second nature. It gave her purpose. It enabled her to survive all she'd been through the past two years.

"Renegade One-Three, winds are zero-six-zero at six, altimeter three-zero-zero-one. Runway two cleared for take-off," the controller responded.

"Roger that, Tower."

She peered into the body of the aircraft and got a thumbs-up and wink from Jeremy before she throttled up the aircraft's engines. The sight of Dita in his custom goggles and harness made her smile. *Let's give these guys a ride and have fun.*

Her Black Hawk gained altitude. James Lee took the lead position in his aircraft heading to the jump point. The men jumped, and the aircraft circled until they landed. She set down in the cleared landing zone to pick up the men for the next part of their exercise. The men resituated their loaded packs to their backs, then scrambled aboard.

With Powell manning the controls, they skirted the forested area surrounding the clearing, flying in fast and low. The late-morning sun glinted off the plexiglass windshield while the men kicked out heavy, three-inch-thick nylon ropes. Kristie watched them step from the edge of the open doorway of James's aircraft and slide down the rope to the ground.

With helmets and goggles on, she couldn't make out who was who—though she tried to identify the men based on body type and size. It only took five seconds for each to reach the ground. Watching sent ripples of desire through her.

Whoa. Focus! She blinked and scolded her wandering imagination.

The men hit the ground and moved out to establish a tactical perimeter. Once they were all down, her crew released the ropes.

While Powell maintained a steady hover, Kristie watched the men run their plan, alternately advancing to cover each other. The aircrews scanned the area, providing cover in the event the "enemy" attacked—which they did. She observed Powell and his reaction when he saw the "insurgents" emerging from the woods to the left of the advancing teams.

Next, they ran several urban-insertion scenarios at a fake community. Though on a smaller scale, it truly resembled an Afghan village.

When they picked the men up after each practice run, there were no grim faces. It was evident in watching the men of the Combat Applications Group, they were a unique breed and thrived in their element. Mack couldn't give up being in the CAG any more than she could give up flying. They shared more than a sense of duty; they loved their jobs. They needed the purpose. And they used the adrenaline rush that came from doing what they did to compensate for what they lacked in other parts of their lives.

But Mack had come out and admitted he wanted more than his career. Guys in his line of work needed a reason to make it home. He had his girls, but he had physical needs, too. She got that. Hell, it'd been almost two years since Eric died. Because he'd deployed three months before his death, even longer since she'd been with a man. She deserved a freaking medal for not jumping Mack when he'd put out the signals and then spent the night in the next bedroom.

Watching him and his team today, she wanted to chuck the rules out the window. Good thing the Lundgrens were home, and she and Mack weren't alone together anymore.

TWENTY

BACK AT THE AIRFIELD, the men debarked and gathered to discuss their run-throughs. From his position, Mack watched the aviation crew tie down the blades of the Black Hawks, then meander past the operators before they disappeared into the office where the flight crew debriefed.

The pilots and crew filed out of the office minutes later. "Any thoughts, Sergeant Hanlon?" Ray drew Mack's attention back to their wrap-up.

"You guys sucked. We need to run these exercises again tomorrow. Maybe a few days next week, too." His gaze followed the pilots, well, Kristie mostly, coming in their direction while the men groaned and disputed him.

Mack watched her scan the faces of the men, lingering when meeting his eyes before she glanced away and focused on Ray.

"Lunch?" The pilot Mack had mistaken as Kristie's date last week issued the invite.

"Sounds good. You guys buying?" Ray attempted to keep a straight face.

"Shouldn't it be the other way around?" the pilot countered.

"We're doing the dangerous stuff," Dominguez protested with several of the team chiming their agreement.

"Oh, poor babies," Kristie lamented. "Next time we won't make you jump out of our perfectly good aircraft. You can just sit back and enjoy the ride."

"You wouldn't do that to us, would you?" Jeremy Milledge feigned horror.

"It'd be torture, wouldn't it?" she teased.

"Hell, yeah!" Milledge voiced for the group.

"Tung Sing Buffet over on Bragg Boulevard?" one of the pilots suggested.

"We'll meet you there," Ray agreed.

"I get to ride with you, sweet cheeks?" Milledge tried to slip an arm around Kristie's shoulders.

"*Sweet cheeks*? Seriously? Go ride in the truck." She elbowed Milledge in the ribs hard enough for him to wince and rub his side.

Clearly, they knew each other. But how? At least she wasn't taking his flirting seriously. Mack loved how she didn't take guff from him or the guys. Though Rochelle interacted with the guys at numerous get-togethers over the years, she never acted this comfortable around the men on his team. The pull in his gut returned as he envisioned Kristie hanging out with him and his friends.

If he could knock down the brick wall—or get her to unlock the door …

INSIDE THE RESTAURANT, the aroma of spices made Mack's mouth water, and his stomach rumble. The diminutive

Chinese hostess eyed the group of uniformed men filing in. She muttered something under her breath, pointed to several empty tables, then scurried to the kitchen.

The group pulled tables together. Mack hung back, hoping to sit next to Kristie, but Milledge edged in and took the vacant seat on her right. Pick your battles. Making a scene over a seat could draw unwanted attention. He stepped around to the other side of the table, where he could sit and enjoy the view.

After giving their drink orders, the group headed to the buffet. At the back of the pack, he encountered several all but empty pans as he moved down the line. He scooped out the last spoonful of Hunan beef and added it to his lo mein when Kristie walked past. Her steps slowed enough for him to notice. She met his gaze. Though he couldn't read her expression, his mind went into overdrive.

At the table, several conversations went on around them, but he primarily listened to Kristie. Hearing her views and observing her interact with their peers had the longing for more clawing its way out of his stomach.

"We need to do this kinda thing more often," Kristie's young co-pilot, Powell, stated.

"We were saying the same thing," Ray agreed.

Mack didn't fess up to the real reason he wanted more joint missions.

"I wasn't expecting your guys to come out of the woods." Powell shoveled a forkful of food in his mouth.

"Grant wasn't supposed to expect them, either," Mack said. "Anybody warn him?"

"Not me," Dominguez answered.

The rest of the men shook their heads.

"Prepare for all contingencies," Grant said.

"Be prepared? Told you he's a Boy Scout." Vincenti

leaned forward, peering past Mack at Grant. "Did you get your Eagle badge?"

"It's not a badge. You have to earn Eagle Scout."

Vincenti laughed harder at Grant's correction.

"Give him a break. The kid did good today." Mack gave a nod of approval to Grant, then eyed the other Bad Karma members. "Better than most of you on your first air assault training with the team."

"Boy Scout," someone coughed out.

"Naw. He's just *smarter than the average bear, Boo-Boo*," Dominguez mimicked, punching Grant in the arm.

Grant sneered at Dominguez, though Mack could swear the kid was blushing, too.

"You liked today, Grant?" Mack already knew the answer. Something about the newbie's enthusiasm took him back to his own early days in Special Operations.

"Oh, yeah. Especially the jump." Grant's face lit up like a kid on Christmas morning.

"It was cool, but coming in fast and low over the treetops was *sweet!*" Powell speared a piece of chicken and brought it to his mouth.

"Donovan here's a Special Ops groupie. What was your favorite part today?" Milledge bumped his shoulder to hers, jarring her enough to spill the food from her fork. "It was the fast-roping. Don't try to deny it. I remember how you and Eric would—"

"Shut up! TMI."

Based on the way Milledge jerked, Kristie must have kicked him under the table.

"Okay, okay. Geez. I was just gonna … Never mind."

The glare she fixed on Milledge made Mack want to strangle him. Shit. Milledge couldn't keep his big mouth shut.

After several tense, silent moments, Milledge leaned over

and whispered to her. She nodded and gave Milledge a sad smile. Whatever he said next made her rear back, eyes wide before they narrowed, and she elbowed his arm, unable to suppress an exasperated laugh.

She discreetly contemplated Mack for several seconds, then took a few bites, but mainly pushed food around her plate for the remainder of lunch. She didn't say much else, either, appearing to listen to others, wearing a distant look as if she was off in her own wounded world.

TWENTY-ONE

"You want to run over and ask? Kristie?"

Stephanie calling her name jerked Kristie's thoughts out of the clouds and back to the present. "Sorry, what were you saying?" She paused in the act of slicing the cucumber and willed her brain to process what Stephanie had asked but came up empty.

"The first time or second?" Stephanie teased.

"Um, both. Guess I was, uh …"

"Distracted?" She laughed. "I noticed. That's why I asked if you wanted to go over and invite Mack to dinner."

"Why? What did I …?" *Shut up.* As it was, Stephanie read Kristie like a roadside billboard.

"You can drop the act. I've seen you look across the street seventeen times in the past ten minutes."

"I have not."

"Oh, did I miss one? Eighteen?"

"Why would I be watching for Mack?" She resumed cutting to hide her face.

"You tell me," Stephanie persisted.

"There's nothing to tell." Kristie had told Ray and

Stephanie about Sheehan following her, Mack and Tony planting the tracker, and even that Mack had stayed overnight —on guard duty.

"A blind woman could see you two are attracted to each other."

"He had my back with Sheehan, but nothing is going to happen with Mack and me." She dumped the cucumber into the salad bowl and began peeling carrots.

"Why not? You two would be great together. He's a lot like Eric."

"Exactly. He's Special Ops."

"Just your type."

"Not anymore."

"*Right.*" Stephanie didn't even try to hold back her smile while she sprinkled seasoning onto the burgers. "You're into what, teachers and lawyers now, because they have safe jobs?"

"I'm not looking for another man. Why can't I be happy alone instead of disappointed when a relationship doesn't live up to what I had with Eric?"

"Who says it won't? I mean, it will be different, but it might be better."

"Are you forgetting Mack's an NCO, and I'm a warrant officer?" Tinsley's warning about Colonel Ball echoed in her head.

"You could transfer to the Reserve or the Guard."

Her friend meant well, but this wasn't helping. "Why should I give up my career? What if things didn't work out? It's not worth giving up my shot at flying MEDEVAC."

Stephanie's skeptical look made Kristie want to shrink away. "You're afraid of losing another man, I get that, but don't give up on the things you *really* want. After Sam died, I was suddenly a young, single mom scared shitless about how

I was going to take care of myself and a child. Then Ray came back into my life. I knew what his job meant. I read the names of the military casualties they would list in the newspaper back then. I could have shied away and let fear keep me from taking another chance. But I would have missed out on a man who loves me more than I deserve and loves my daughter as his own."

The first time Stephanie had ever mentioned her first husband to Kristie was after Eric died. She'd told her then to help her through things, but Kristie's situation was different. She didn't have a child. She had a job—for now—and could provide for and take care of herself.

"Yes, something could happen to Ray on a mission. Or driving to the store." Stephanie threw up her hands. "He could get cancer. Or have a heart attack. He's more likely to live another sixty years. Ray and I've had thirteen great years so far and some not-so-fabulous times—but that's life," she stated in her pragmatic way. "If you could go back in time, would you still marry Eric if you knew he'd be killed in action?"

"Of course." Kristie didn't hesitate. "I might ask him to get out of Special Ops, though."

"And change him from the man you fell in love with?"

Ouch. She hung her head as Stephanie's point pierced her heart. She loved Eric for who he was. As he was. Giving up serving in the Rangers—a step toward his dream of Delta—would have changed him. She couldn't ask Mack to give it up, either.

"How'd you get over loving and losing Sam?"

"Realized I never would completely and that loving another man didn't diminish what we had. As much as I loved Sam, I love Ray even more. Just because your 'until death do us part' came way too early doesn't mean you can't have a second chance at marriage and a family. Unless you make flying that damn helicopter your life. It won't make you laugh or return your love. And it isn't always going to be there to help you escape. What then?"

Unable to answer, Kristie dropped her gaze to avoid Stephanie's challenging stare.

"My husband is as dedicated as any operator in the CAG, but they have more than their job. They have friends and families. Their service sometimes costs them their lives or their marriages, but life goes on. And when you find another shot at happiness, you grab on and hold tight. *'Tis better to have loved and lost than never to have loved at all.*" Stephanie picked up the plate of burgers. "I'm going to put these on the grill."

Kristie finished peeling the carrot with shaky hands.

If anyone knew both her and Mack, it was Ray and Stephanie. Stephanie wouldn't give her a shove in Mack's direction if she didn't think he was a great guy. She couldn't shoot him down solely because he was divorced. Divorce was all too common in the military, especially in Special Ops units.

The time she'd spent with Mack had been easy and enjoyable. He'd been appreciative of the things she did—like cooking, and he even helped with the cleanup. No red flags there. His sense of humor was easy-going and fun without cutting people down. She shouldn't base her opinion of him on physical attributes, but it didn't hurt that he had an appealing face, great smile, and solid muscles.

What were his flaws? Thinking he knew best. Yeah, she'd seen that. She hadn't minded his take-charge attitude too much. He'd actually listened. Okay, *not* a flaw. Based on what she'd seen of him with his girls and overhearing his conversations with them when he called each night, the man was doing all he could to stay connected to his daughters despite the divorce and work taking him away from them.

"Why did Mack and his wife get divorced?" she asked after Stephanie came back in and began washing the meat platter.

"That's not my story to tell. If you want to know, you can ask him. I'll just say he deserved better. Rochelle was no Kristie Donovan."

What the heck did that mean? Instead of backing up her reasons to steer clear of Mack, Stephanie had given her a lot to think about. For so long, she'd clung to the idea that Eric had been the one for her. What if there wasn't only one "right one" and she could have that kind of love again? What if she didn't have to give up her dreams of a husband and kids?

TWENTY-TWO

WAITING AT THE STOPLIGHT, Kristie picked out a quarter from the car's change holder. Heads with an eagle on the flip side. She twirled the quarter between her thumb and fingers. Heads or tails? *Heads, I use my head and play it smart, or tails, I put my ass on the line.*

The car behind her tapped on their horn after the light changed. She turned left, still holding onto the quarter. Letting a coin toss determine her future would be stupid. Why did it have to be an either-or decision?

She felt like a contestant on "Let's Make a Deal," where she could keep the current prize—her career—or give that up and *maybe* trade for something better. She didn't know what was behind door number three. She might end up with a booby prize. If only she could peek behind the curtain and see where things might go with Mack.

She couldn't give up her commission to date him. That defied common sense. But what about one date? Or two? They could fly under the radar. After all, who knew more about covert operations than Mack? Real life rarely lived up to fantasy and imagination anyway. They might not click. Or he might be a bad kisser. Then she could get him out of her mind.

On the other hand, it'd be nice to get attention from an appealing guy to ease the loneliness since losing Eric. *If* anyone questioned things, they could back off. She might get a verbal warning. A note in her file. Busted in rank. An Article—*Stop it! Don't think worst-case.*

What Stephanie said last night—about not being able to fly forever—hit her with a dose of reality. Yes, she had a career she loved, but was it enough? Maybe now. But would it be in five years? In ten?

Even Jeremy inadvertently brought it up when he went from saying he missed his buddy, to joking in true, inappropriate Milledge form about taking care of her "needs." It wasn't Jeremy she wanted taking care of the needs Mack had resuscitated.

Dammit, she deserved the chance at the future she wanted —and would have if Eric hadn't been killed in action. Who was the Army to say that more than eighty percent of its personnel were off-limits because they were enlisted? Being in different units, it wasn't like she'd be giving Mack orders, or he'd compromise her authority. Hell, she could always play the poor-widow card.

If his truck wasn't there, it'd be a sign. Divine intervention that would keep her from making a huge mistake. She cruised down the street, scarcely able to breathe, waiting for a sign to take control of her future.

IN HIS DRIVEWAY, Mack's truck was backed in, ready should

he need to make a fast getaway. *She* needed a fast getaway. No, she was going to do this. Before she lost her nerve.

She parked in the Lundgrens' drive, then crossed the street and rang Mack's bell. *One. Two. Three.* Maybe he wasn't home after all. *Four. Five. Six.* He could have gone to dinner with a friend. Or out on a date. No. Then he would have driven. Right?

She flinched when the door swung open.

"Hey." He looked stunned to see her.

"Hi. Can I, uh, come in?" Her tongue seemed swollen and thick in her mouth. Her heart pounded in her chest. This wasn't a conversation for the front porch where a neighbor might see or overhear.

"Yeah." He stepped aside, keeping some distance between them, his expression wary yet curious.

"You were right."

"Right? O-kay. A guy always likes to hear that, but about what? I'd hate for us not to be on the same page here."

The pressure in her chest didn't let up. "Us—being friends. It's, uh …" She shifted her weight as she scanned the room, her gaze finally returning to his.

He took a step closer, a smile spreading.

"I'd like to see if we could be more—than friends. If you still want …?"

"Are you saying if I asked you out, you'd say yes?"

"Uh …" Her heart sank from the invitation she couldn't accept.

"Right," he drawled. "You can't be caught in a compromising position." His lips disappeared as he studied her. "So, we can't go *out*."

Was he going to shoot her down? She probably deserved it. While she wanted to give this a shot, she couldn't afford to be reckless. Her unit followed the rules more than his, and if Colonel Ball found out, she could kiss her shot at MEDEVAC goodbye.

"Would we be dating, or are you just planning to use me for sex?"

Really? "No, I'm not planning ..." She hadn't thought that far ahead.

Yes, she wanted to strip off every piece of clothing they both wore and indulge in her lustful fantasies. Then what? Using him for her own needs wouldn't be fair, would it? Okay, he probably wouldn't mind.

What was she thinking coming over here? It was too late to take back what she'd said, and he wasn't going to let it drop based on the evocative grin that ramped up the heat radiating through her, making her damn near lose any last shred of common sense.

"I suspected you're an old-fashioned girl. Probably have rules about knowing a guy for"—his eyes narrowed, and his mouth shifted as if mentally calculating—"over a month. Or going on three dates before spending the night with him."

That he read her so well was comforting, and his teasing lessened her inner turmoil. She breathed easier. "That sounds about right," she admitted. "I never went on less than five dates before sleeping with a guy."

His eyes widened. "Five?"

"I might make an exception. Depending on how those first 'dates' go." She took a step closer. To three dates? Two? One?

"Well, all those nights at Ray and Steph's, having dinner and watching television, should count for at least two." He unhooked one thumb from his belt loop to count with his fingers.

"Because *you* insisted on acting as my bodyguard."

"You're right. I should get bonus points for that."

She couldn't help but laugh. "Really? You're pushing it, Hanlon."

With his warm hands now drawing her closer and his thumbs rubbing tantalizing circles over her hips, she melted faster than a snowman in the Sahara.

"I guess some things are worth waiting for, but we aren't waiting forever. *Tonight* is date night. We can't go out to dinner, and I've got nothing here worthy of this occasion. Either I go to the grocery store, pick up something, or we order delivery."

"What are you in the mood for?"

A laughing growl like a Humvee engine rumbled up his throat. "I can't believe you asked that."

"I was referring to food." Her skin heated as her body temp rose at his interpretation. Time to deflect. "If you don't mind getting us something to eat, I'll go change out of my uniform."

His eyebrows rose in interest.

Man, she really needed to pick her words better. "I kinda stink like jet fuel."

"I hadn't noticed." He bit back a grin. "I'll get the food. We can find a movie online to watch afterward. But first ..." He gave her hips a tug, his eyes dropping to her mouth.

She turned her face up and closed her eyes as his lips met hers with a kiss that drowned out the voices telling her she was playing with Hellfire missiles—because Mack was not a bad kisser. Not at all.

MACK TAPPED the horn before he got out of the truck. He

carried the pizza to the front door, glancing over his shoulder before going inside. No sign of her yet.

He set the pizza on the counter, feeling like he got his birthday, Christmas, and Valentine's Day all rolled into one. She'd opened the door to give him a chance. Unless … What if …?

He shouldn't have let her go across the street after kissing her. No. She wouldn't play him like that, would she? Why did Kristie make him doubt himself like some high schooler? He laughed out loud because he did feel like a love-struck teen.

"What's so funny?"

He jumped at her voice coming from behind him, then cleared his throat.

"Sorry. I didn't mean to surprise you. The door was open, so I came on in." Her lips curled in amusement.

At least I wasn't talking aloud. "I was, uh, thinking of how you handled Milledge yesterday."

"He has no filter, but he's usually harmless."

Mack pulled out two dinner plates, glad she bought his cover. "Sorry this isn't fancier." He'd been so shocked at her about-face he hadn't put any thought into doing something beyond how they'd spent the week at the Lundgrens'. Damn, he needed to up his game. "Table's kinda beat up. We can eat on the patio if you want."

"It's fine. I like the ambiance."

He fell harder when she smiled and traced a fingertip over the crayon marks from Darcy's various art projects. "Rochelle took most of the furniture when she moved out. I didn't fight her on it because of the girls. I've picked up things secondhand." He set the plates and paper napkins on the table.

"She let you stay in the house, though?"

"A third of the families on the street are military. She wanted to get away from all things Army, especially after word got out that she filed for legal separation while I was deployed."

Kristie winced and nodded, getting his drift.

"She got an apartment right before I got back. I thought about getting something smaller with less maintenance, but keeping the house lets the girls feel like they're coming home and still have a yard to play in."

"I'm sure the stability is good for them."

"Figured they'd need that. Sorry, I should not have brought up my ex." Wasn't avoiding talking about your ex one of the cardinal rules of dating? "I'm kinda out of practice at this."

"Me, too," she admitted.

He opened the pizza box and tried not to grimace.

"What?" She peeked at the pizza and smiled.

Oh, yeah, I remembered. "Who puts pepperoni *and* pineapple on their pizza? Pineapple with ham is one thing, but … I think it's so you don't have to share your half," he teased.

"You haven't even tried it."

"That's okay."

"Nope. Now you have to take a bite."

He kept his mouth shut, pulling his head back when she offered a piece. The staring showdown only lasted a few seconds before he gave in to her determined smile. He took a hearty bite. The sweetness of the pineapple complemented the spiciness of the pepperoni in a way that wasn't half bad. Sweet and spicy—like her.

"Well? What do you think?"

With her standing in his kitchen, teasing and flirting, it would be so easy to forget about the pizza. *Rein it in. Be a gentleman.* "I don't hate it."

"Then no more ragging on my choice of toppings, and I will share if you want a piece or two." She slid into a chair.

"Thanks." He was going to be a gentleman if it killed him.

HE CLICKED the volume button as the credits rolled to a Jackson 5 song. Though not a movie he might have picked on his own, the combination of action, comedy, timeless music, intergalactic adventure, and battles with quasi-superheroes saving the galaxy ended up being a great choice.

And, while tonight's date was much the same as the week they'd spent together, tonight was also different. The conversation over dinner was different. Holding hands while watching the movie was new and different. Missing bits of the movie because they were kissing was way different. Different in a very good way. But not so different that he wanted to push the physical aspects too far too fast.

"Are we going to make out more here, or am I walking you home to make out on Ray's front porch?"

"Let's not encourage Stephanie," Kristie said with a chuckle.

"Encourage her?"

"She knows I'm here, and she's been trying to set us up. Probably dropped a few hints to you."

"She didn't have to. I was interested from the first time I saw you. Well, after you took your helmet off, and I knew you were a woman."

"Good answer." She leaned over and kissed him, but he swore she looked disappointed that he mentioned her going home tonight.

He didn't trust himself to just snuggle if she stayed,

though. It'd been a while for him, but she'd made it sound like she hadn't dated since her husband died. Hadn't that been around two years ago? Two freaking long years. It wouldn't take much temptation for either one of them. This needed to feel like a relationship, not a hook-up. It'd be worth waiting for. He'd make sure she wasn't disappointed—in any way.

TWENTY-THREE

KRISTIE STRETCHED, then reached for her phone when she woke up. Mack had already texted. It'd been tempting to offer, or ask, to stay with him last night, but he'd worked so hard at respecting her instead of assuming by now that she was desperate to jump his bones. She wanted it to be special. What were another few days or a week?

Coffee or call him first? She propped the pillow up. Mack answered on the second ring.

"Good morning," she answered back. "Got your message."

"Thought I'd text since I didn't want to call too early."

"It's almost eight." The sound of his voice amplified the lustful electricity flowing through her.

"Rumors are you aviators have to get so many hours of sleep."

"Like I haven't heard that before." They fell into the easy pattern of keeping things light.

"How'd you like to go to a park? Hike a bit and have lunch?"

Though it sounded like an ideal way to spend the day

together, reality doused her with ice water. What if they ran into someone who knew either of them? "Um," she stammered.

"The park is about forty-five minutes away, so should be a safe distance," he set her mind at ease. "There are a bunch of walking trails. Mostly easy ones so we can talk and enjoy the scenery. I'm gonna run out to pick up some things for tonight, but I'll be ready by oh nine thirty. See you in a bit." He hung up before she could ask about tonight.

Okay, then. He wasn't issuing orders, but his take-charge approach appealed to her. Even better, he knew her concerns, took them seriously, and had done research on places for them to go. No excuses for her to back out as she took another step over the line.

Stephanie nodded knowingly when Kristie said she had plans. She headed out to Mack's truck after he texted her, and the grin on his face when she hopped into the passenger seat did things to her insides.

He didn't speak; just kept grinning as he headed out of the neighborhood. Coming to a stop sign, he checked the surrounding area before he leaned over—and waited. She caved to his implied request for a kiss. A tender, intoxicating kiss that made her toes curl inside her hiking shoes.

Once he started driving again, he handed her a map he'd printed off of the park. On the back were notes about sights along the different trails.

"Can't do the whole park today, but based on the pictures I saw, we'll want to go back."

She read over his scrawl. "Wow. Impressive research."

"I aim to please."

She could take that comment several ways. "You starred the Raven Rock Loop Trail. We'll start with that one."

He nodded agreeably, though one upturned corner of his

mouth confirmed the innuendo. Today might turn out to be very interesting.

They arrived at the park after a brief stop to pick up lunch. Kristie got out and turned her face up to the warm, late-spring sunshine. She breathed in the woodsy scent. The chirping of a variety of birds lent to the uplifting feel of a fresh start.

Mack pulled iced water bottles from a cooler behind his seat and loaded those and the food inside his backpack. "Before we go…" He raised his eyebrows suggestively, despite the presence of a couple by a car parked a few spaces away.

This time, she angled her head and waited, making him close the distance. His lips molded to hers, caressing them. His parted slightly, which enticed her to do the same. The feel of their tongues meeting ignited a heat that engulfed her body.

He pressed closer against her and slid his fingers into her hair, deepening the kiss. She'd almost forgotten how a kiss could make her weak in the knees. The kiss elicited more than desire. It inspired a potent wave of hope for a future where she could move beyond her past with Eric.

After the kiss, he stared in her eyes as if divining her deepest desires. The heat inside her crept up her neck to her cheeks. If his smile was an indicator, he liked what he saw. He issued a satisfied growl and shook his head as if to clear it before he clasped her hand in his and led the way across the parking lot toward the hiking trails.

Towering longleaf pines, hardwoods, and mountain laurel bordered the trodden dirt pathway, providing ample shade. The rhododendrons blossomed in shades of pink and purple. Birds chattered and flitted overhead. With the afternoon stretching ahead of them, they strolled along in no hurry.

"Aside from Sheehan stalking you, how are you feeling about Fort Bragg?" he asked.

"That's definitely been the downside." She hadn't seen Sheehan since their encounter, but she'd been watching. He certainly had proved he wasn't the type to let things go. "Did you find out if he has a black SUV?"

"Um, not yet. I didn't get by with having the girls last weekend. I'll get by there. Sorry." He gave her hand a squeeze.

"No problem. The guys in the company have been pretty welcoming."

That comment drew a sideways glance from him. "And the wives?"

"I think James and Mary Kate's get-together reassured the wives I'm not the man-hunter type sometimes associated with military widows. I got invited to Cindy Yang's baby shower, which is a good sign of acceptance." It wasn't like she could tell them any romantic thoughts involved Mack. "

"Milledge seemed pretty welcoming."

"You're not jealous, are you?"

"Should I be?" He sounded serious.

"No!" She replied so emphatically they both chuckled. "I love the goofball, but not that way. Jeremy and Eric shared an apartment at Fort Lewis when Eric and I were dating," she explained. "I know too much about Jeremy. By the way, he does not like spiders. In case that information comes in handy."

"Sounds like a story there."

"Let's just say he went too far with one of his pranks and payback was a bitch named Kristie. The payback involved a very real-looking, big, fuzzy spider in the shower."

Mack's throaty chuckle amped up her own giggles,

remembering the normally tough soldier's reaction to the encounter.

"Remind me not to get on your bad side."

"It was years ago. I've matured a bit since then—even if Jeremy hasn't."

They laughed together again. Mack was easy to be with. Things felt comfortable. Even familiar.

"Can I ask you a personal question?"

"You can ask." She braced for anything, her breath catching in her throat.

"It's not bad." He gave a reassuring smile and her hand a squeeze. "I'm not familiar with how aviation units work. Since you joined up wanting to fly MEDEVAC, how come you're still waiting for a slot?"

"When I went to Fort Rucker for WOCS and flight school, Eric transferred to Benning. We commuted the first two years of our marriage."

"That sucks."

"Yeah. When I graduated, the plan was for us to go back to Fort Lewis or Fort Stewart. Except there weren't any MEDEVAC slots available at either location, but I didn't want to wait longer to be with my husband. I planned on doing a deployment, build up my flight hours, and then transfer. Things got sidetracked. Until now." Hopefully.

"What made you want to fly—other than M*A*S*H?"

She chuckled and tucked the strand of hair the breeze kept blowing in her face behind her ear. She'd probably be explaining her career choice to people when she was in a nursing home. "My dad was in the Navy. Growing up, I never pictured myself in the service, though. Then we were at an air show where I met a female Army pilot. She let me wear her flight helmet and sit in a Black Hawk and told me I could fly, maybe even in combat one day."

"And the dream was born." He said it with an understanding most people didn't get.

"I used my birthday money to ride in this tiny sightseeing helicopter at the beach. My parents hoped I would get over my obsession."

"I see that didn't work."

"One flight and I knew it was what I wanted to do. Being up there—seeing things from a whole other perspective." She moved her hand through the air. "There's no speed limit or lanes to stay in. It's freedom." She met his gaze. "Sorry, I get a little carried away when I talk about flying."

"It's obvious you love it."

"Best job in the world."

"Right. Defying gravity with a million moving parts? I prefer boots on the ground, thank you."

"Flying is a heckuva lot safer than riding over the roads in Iraq or Afghanistan. And as I recall, you looked pretty happy about getting a ride not too long ago." She grinned at him.

"It was the best option at the time," he teased back. "I owe you one. You ever need rescuing, give me a call."

"I prefer not to have to take you up on that offer."

"I'd rather you not, either," he agreed.

Walking down the trail, Kristie inhaled the sweet scent of the blooming mountain laurel. Here in the sandhills, she hadn't expected the steep rock bluffs leading down to the river. Leaves rustled overhead, and Mack's warm hand gripped hers. He maintained an easy pace, allowing them to keep chatting. Even though they'd spent a few evenings together already, she picked up on the get-to-know-you shift now that their relationship had changed course. She wanted to know more, too.

"So, Mr. Boots-on-the-Ground, when did you realize you wanted to be in the Army—and Special Forces?"

"I kind of fell into it."

She laughed out loud. "You might fall into the military, but not Special Forces." Not with the amount of effort it requires. How few make it through the Qualification or Q course, as Eric had referred to it.

"Growing up, there was this older kid on our street who scared us."

"A bully?"

"Beyond that." He paused. "To give you an example, one night, Jordy's dad—he was a piece of work himself—called the police because the neighbor's dog wouldn't stop barking. The police showed up to talk to the neighbor, who said his dog was barking at the kids on the other side of their joint fence. The cops went in Jordy's backyard and found him and another kid in the trees at the back of the property smoking pot and drinking beers they've stolen from somewhere. They ended up getting busted and, man, was Jordy pissed. Not long after, the neighbor's dog went missing."

"No!"

"Yeah."

"What did he do?"

"Don't know. They never found the dog. There wasn't any evidence, but we all knew Jordy did something. Anyway, Jordy liked this girl, Brianna, on the street. Pretty blonde with blue eyes, and she wanted nothing to do with him. One day, Brianna's younger brother heard Jordy talking smack about her. Ian talked smack right back, which wasn't smart since he was half Jordy's size. In a flash, they were on the ground with Jordy whaling on Ian. I jumped in, knocked him off, and we tussled."

"And you beat some sense into him?"

"I wish. I held my own, though."

"You were the hero. Did you get to date the blonde?"

"We were like fourteen. We 'went together,' just holding hands and first kisses and stuff," he admitted with a bashful grin.

"Ah, ha."

"I didn't help her brother to impress her if that's what you're thinking. Besides, she dumped me when she went to high school a month later. But Jordy quit messing with us after that."

"You liked the feeling of being a protector?" She'd seen the same quality in Eric and other Rangers she'd known.

Mack waggled his head. "I'd been thinking about the military, and when my friends were applying to colleges, the idea of four more years in classes sounded like torture. You talked about the freedom that comes with flying, me, I wanted to be outside. Hiking, hunting, camping, fishing." He motioned to the woods around them, and his relaxed posture and confident smile embodied his complete contentment with his surroundings. "The Army seemed like a good fit, so I signed up. Guess I started thinking about Special Forces about three weeks into boot camp."

"It took that long?" she teased. It didn't surprise her. A large percentage of guys dreamed about serving in Special Forces, though few made the cut.

He laughed. "I played baseball and ran cross-country in high school. I was in shape, so basic training wasn't a big deal for me. Quitting's never been an option. Push me, and I keep going. What?" he asked when she chuckled.

"Oh, nothing. Just sounds like standard alpha-male syndrome."

"Very funny."

She laughed again when he rolled his eyes at her, but he didn't deny it. Instead, he wrapped their joined hands around to her back and pulled her body against his. With his free hand, he tipped her face up to his. He stroked his thumb across her cheek. His hand slid around to the small of her back. Their mouths met and opened. His tongue stroked hers.

The earlier kisses made her weak in the knees, but now a pleading murmur outed her need. Their hips met, and the solid length of his arousal pressed enticingly against her. Her pelvic muscles constricted in pleasure. It'd been so long since she'd felt this way. Disappointment crashed through her when he put space between them again.

"Mmm, hmm," was the only response she could muster.

"Yeah." He cut his gaze in the direction of other voices, then released a drawn-out breath before nodding.

They hiked further down to the base of Raven Rock. They slowed to study and take pictures of the other-worldly intertwining roots that snaked out from the tree bases before disappearing into the earth. They passed boulders and heard the river before it came into view.

They followed the path alongside the Cape Fear River, enjoying that part of the trail before they headed to the stairs. The overlook was about a hundred and fifty feet above the river and gave a sweeping view of the forest's variegated shades of green. A hawk drifted on the air currents.

"Let's get a picture together." He positioned them by a circle rock wall that kept visitors away from the edge of the cliff. With their backs to the river, he snapped a few pictures.

He turned the phone to show her a picture. A full smile played across Mack's face. A slightly more subtle one on hers as well. What if? The possibility of this working out between them rose another notch.

When a pair of hikers approached, Mack and Kristie moved on and tracked back down to the trail close to the river's shore.

"My turn to ask you a personal question," she said.

"Size eleven."

"What?"

"My boot size." He gave a playful grin.

"That's so not what I was going to ask." But she got what he was implying.

"No? I figured it might be more personal, so thought I'd lead with humor."

Nice plan. She liked that about him. "Why did you and your ex-wife divorce?"

Mack sighed and gave her hand a squeeze, but didn't let go. "After years of deployments, Rochelle was fed up with the Army life. She wanted me to get out, not just out of Spec Ops, but the Army. My old team leader left for the private sector and later Jarrod tried to recruit me to join him. Because they offer a recruiting bonus for operators, he resorted to having his wife talk to Rochelle about it—promising better money, a more regular schedule versus me disappearing for a mission with no idea where, how long, or when I'd be back. She was all on board, except I don't see the honor in protecting companies and their assets."

Eric had felt the same way. He didn't serve for the money, but to make a difference for the better.

"Eventually, she gave me an ultimatum: the Army or her. I didn't think she was serious. I thought we could make it work a few more years. This far in, it didn't make financial sense to not stay in until I hit my twenty for full retirement benefits. Only Rochelle filed for legal separation right after I left on the next deployment." His words came out slowly, his tone low and filled with regret.

"I'm sorry." Not many women had what it took to be the wife of an operator. She once thought she did. Stephanie thought Kristie still did, but she wasn't so sure.

"I tried to get her to go for counseling when I got back,

but, well, she'd been to Georgia to visit her folks and ran into a guy who dated her best friend in high school. They'd started chatting and had this long-distance thing going."

Kristie bit her tongue to refrain from bashing his ex. Stephanie's comment made more sense now. It was bad enough to start down the road to divorce when her husband was out serving their country, but to start a new relationship? She kind of hated Rochelle without having met her.

"She was done. Wouldn't give an inch. Refused to even go to counseling. Said it was too little, too late. That's when I admitted it was over. I don't quit on things," he stated, "but it takes two to make a marriage work. That's my side of things. She'd probably spin it differently."

"I appreciate you telling me." Lord knows it couldn't be easy for a guy like him to open up about his marriage failing. "And for what it's worth, you seem to be doing a great job with the girls."

"I'm trying. Probably doing a better job spending time with them now. They're why I kept trying to make it work with Rochelle and why I'd do it over again. Just —differently."

"We all have things we'd like a do-over for."

Mack tugged on her hand, pulling her closer as he stopped. He stared into her eyes. "Kinda glad we got that out of the way. I haven't dated much since the divorce, so I haven't had to share that, but no more talking about my ex today."

She nodded in agreement.

"Wanna eat?"

"Sounds good." They ambled over to the picnic table perched amid a flat expanse offering an unobstructed view of the river.

Mack unloaded the food from his pack and took a seat

facing the woods, affording her a view of the river with light glittering off the slow-moving water. A beautiful backdrop to his handsome face.

The scratch on his cheek had faded to a faint, thin line. The sun overhead played up the auburn hue of his hair. His blue T-shirt made his eyes look bluer. As they talked, she kept getting distracted—by his eyes and those strong arms that she longed to run her hands over again. She had an overwhelming urge to trace a finger over the freckle on his lip.

"You might want to get up on the table."

His unexpected statement jarred her back to reality. "Excuse me?"

His gaze didn't deviate from looking past her. "There's a snake right behind—"

"What!" She wrenched her head around and spied a long, black snake a few yards away, slithering right toward her feet. She scrambled onto the table, nearly sitting on the remainder of her sandwich.

Mack didn't disguise his amusement. "I figured you might not like snakes." He took another bite of his sub, staring over the tabletop as the snake continued closer. "Looks like it's a rat snake. It won't hurt us."

Despite his calm demeanor, she was not reassured. "Can it climb up here?"

"They're good climbers, though my guess is he's looking for mice. Under a picnic table is a prime snacking spot."

"You're just going to sit there?" Her body trembled as the snake neared the table.

"You want me to grab him and relocate him?"

"No! Don't touch it."

She felt foolish sitting atop the table, but there was no way she was getting down with the snake below. She gave Mack a pleading pout, motioning him to join her.

He pushed his meal aside and complied, perching on the edge of the table. He gave a nod of his head, so she scooted over to sit beside him. After verifying the snake wasn't climbing up the side of the table—yet—she lowered her feet to the bench. Trusting Mack would warn her if the snake was about to wrap itself around her leg or worse, she managed to carry on a conversation and eat the rest of her lunch while keeping an eye out.

"You ready to hike some more?" he asked, wadding up the sandwich wrappers and chip bags.

"Is the snake still there?"

He leaned forward and peered under the table. "Yup. All coiled up like he's sleeping. Hard to tell, though." He smirked slightly. "You planning to wait until he moves?"

"Nooo …"

"Do I need to carry you?"

She hesitated, unsure what to say. That's what Eric would have done. He would have scooped her up in his arms or tossed her over his shoulder, despite her protests, and carried her to safety. She'd always felt safe and protected with him. Mack made her feel the same way.

"I'll get down first," he volunteered, "if you'll give me a kiss before I act as a human shield for you."

She raised an eyebrow at him. "Really? You just said to call if I needed rescuing, and now it comes with a price—and I have to pay in advance."

"No, I wasn't. I …" He backpedaled with a sheepish smile.

Good thing for him, he was a good kisser. Though his actions, interest, patience, and addictive kisses were overcoming her strategy to take things slow and keep her emotions and thoughts in check. If she wasn't careful, she'd let her guard down too far, but damn, it felt good.

They hiked a shorter trail, then Mack picked the path back to the parking lot.

"You don't want to do another trail?" It'd taken half their time together to let go of her worries about someone seeing them, and now the idea of leaving unleashed a deluge of rain on her parade.

"Wanted to get you back by four. That'll give you a few hours to nap or rest, then shower and change out of your hiking clothes before your dinner date tonight."

"Dinner date …?" After the park outing, she wanted to trust he had a safe option, but her heart rate accelerated enough to make her limbs tingle.

"We have reservations at Hanlon's Pub. The time's flexible. The menu is limited, but the food's good."

She broke into a smile as his intent—and intentions— became clear. If she gave him leeway on what counted as a date, and gave him credit for two dates today, they were awfully close to that magic number. "Sounds like my kind of place."

It could be a very promising night.

TWENTY-FOUR

MACK SCANNED THE KITCHEN. Flowers on the table. Check. Candles on either side. Check. Hopefully, it was enough to impress Kristie and show her she meant something to him. Especially since Spec Ops guys had a reputation—a fairly warranted one—about only being interested in sex. This wasn't just about sex, and after today in the park, he hoped they had the same plan for tonight.

When he heard a knock, he hurried to the door.

"Welcome to Hanlon's Pub. And may I say, wow!" He ushered her inside, closed the door, then held her at arm's length, admiring her pink top that showed enough cleavage to fuel his imagination. "Thank you." Her smile indicated she probably intended to have that effect on him. "I like this shirt on you." She hooked a finger in the opening over the top button, drawing him closer and making his blood pressure spike.

Stick with the mission plan. Don't rush her.

"I'll have to wear it more often," he said in what he hoped was a low, seductive tone. She smiled while he moved in for a kiss. Her fingers curled into his hair, and her lips parted, giving him a taste of her sweetness mixed with mint. His heart beat a hard, rapid tempo. It took extreme effort not to back her against the door, skip steps A through C of tonight's mission plan, and charge into action. With eyes closed, he put a few inches between them and slowed himself down. "Would you like a glass of wine?"

She cocked her head, pausing before answering. "Sounds good. Can I help with anything?"

"I'm good." He led her to the kitchen. "Salads are in the fridge. Bread and potatoes are in the oven on warm. I just need to put on the steaks. Hope you're hungry." He retrieved the bottle of wine and a corkscrew, even though he wanted his hands free and touching every part of her body.

"Yes. No. I—Mack …"

The desperation on her face shot white-hot heat through every inch of his body. He assumed she expected flowers, candles, dinner—the whole shebang. Then— hopefully—sex. But if he read her right, he liked her actual expectations better. He set the wine on the counter, then swaggered toward her, his eyes devouring her body.

"I take it, you can wait to eat?" she asked with a sultry smile.

Oh, yeah. That's what I'm talking about. "I can go days."

Her seductive chortle pushed him to the limit. He reached for her, and their mouths joined in a deep, probing kiss. Their tongues met and teased. He couldn't get enough of her. He took hold of her top and pulled it up, off, and tossed it aside. The pale-pink, lace bra underneath increased his urgency.

He'd had a hundred and three fantasies about making love to her. Now his eyes locked on hers, and he returned her smile. She was better than any fantasy. "You're sure about this?"

"It's been two years, Mack. Do not make me wait."

Two years? No. No more waiting. Before he could reach for the bra's front clasp, she slid his shirt up and over his head —which totally worked for him, too. Her gentle push on his chest directed him out of the kitchen.

Yeah, the kitchen counter or table probably weren't the best options for the first time they made love. But, damn, it was a long way to the bedroom. He slowed his backward trek long enough to undo the button on her pants and had the zipper down in seconds.

She kicked off her sandals and shimmied out of her pants, leaving them on the living room floor. She was sexy as hell in only a bra and matching panties—and a belly button ring. The sight made him harder, if that was even possible. She edged past him while he unbuttoned his own jeans, and he nearly tripped following her before he got them off.

He caught her by the waist and pulled her back against him. Holding her there, he nuzzled her neck, breathing in her sweet, floral scent. Sliding one hand up and over her smooth, taut stomach, he stopped when his fingers found the bra's clasp, then flicked it open. Pushing aside the lacy cups, he fondled one perfect breast, his fingertips circling her hard, pert nipple. His other hand worked its way under the lace of her panties.

She murmured with pleasure when his fingers stroked between her damp folds. Damp and wanting. Her body arched, and she braced her forearm on the hallway wall, steadying herself as she rocked against his hand. He slid a finger inside her. The sensation of her muscles tightening drew him closer to his own nirvana.

His thumb stroked her, back and forth, gradually applying more pressure. Her bottom pressed back, nestling his erection.

Man, it's been too damn long.

He wasn't going to last long if she kept this up—not that he wanted her to stop, either. And as enticing as those panties were, he wanted them out of his way and his lucky boxers off.

Kristie reached down and gripped his hand. "Not yet," she said, her breathing labored. She nodded to the bedroom a few feet away.

He got the message. If that's what she wanted, the bedroom it was. He'd give her anything, do anything she wanted.

She led the way, then stopped at the edge of the bed and turned to face him. As if reading his mind, she dropped his hand and skimmed the skimpy panties down her legs.

He watched her every move, barely refraining from tossing her onto the bed. Then he saw her expectant gaze—which focused on his boxers. Before she could blink, he'd wrestled them over the bulge, and they hit the floor. She gave a light laugh as he closed the distance between them. She sank onto the bed, pulling him down with her.

He fought to restrain the desire overpowering him. While he wanted to be inside her so bad he could hardly catch his breath, he didn't want to rush it now. He wanted to touch her. Taste her. Make sure he left her with no regrets.

His tongue swept into her warm mouth, and the kiss they shared was fierce and possessive. His hands roamed, relishing the freedom to touch and explore. He filled one palm with the soft flesh of her breast, squeezing and gently pinching her nipple. She moaned his name, increasing his need. His left hand cupped her bottom, holding her firmly to him.

Her nails raked across his shoulders and his back, down to his butt. His muscles constricted, and a strangled groan mixed with his breath.

"Hurry."

The lone whispered word was a symphony to his ears.

Oh, yeah. So close to paradise. He shifted, lowering his head and running his tongue over her breast, suckling and savoring her reaction. Her arm curved around his head, her fingertips running through his hair, encouraging him with the pressure. He moved to her other breast, lavishing it with equal attention. Her hips rose and pressed against his chest.

"Please, Mack." She pulled on his arms, dragging him upward when he was about to go lower. But …

He propped up on one elbow and reached for the condoms in the nightstand. Using his teeth to hold them, he tore one from the strip.

"Three, huh?" Her sultry voice was a definite turn-on.

"I'm an optimist."

Rolling to his back, he tried not to lose control when she kissed his nipple as he worked to get the condom on. His mission accomplished, he flipped her to her back and reclaimed her mouth. He kissed her thoroughly, taunting them both with slow strokes of his body. Then, poised above her, he waited for her to open her eyes and look back at him.

She sighed blissfully when he entered her. He eased in, then out at first. Her arms tightened around him as he increased the rhythm and depth of his thrusts. She let out the most delicious moans, raising her hips to meet his, again and again, as he went harder and deeper, taking him right to the edge.

Her cries came more rapidly and loudly as he got lost inside her. Sharp nails dug into his flesh, giving exquisite pain, as she shattered, her body shuddering and tightening once, twice, then a third time. He thrust deeper inside, and his own release came with the intensity of a shock wave. Another long cry of pleasure escaped her, then she pressed hot kisses to his neck and cheek.

"Sorry. I couldn't—hold out any longer. Promise me— we'll do this again," she said between ragged breaths.

"Can you give me ten minutes?" He'd love to help her make up for lost time.

———

THE ONLY SOUND was their still-labored breathing as Kristie lay beside Mack. The gentle waves of bliss ebbed, leaving her feeling as though she was floating in the ocean—her body and limbs weighted as the endorphin rush faded. Admiring his profile triggered ripples of lust to surge through her again.

She eased onto her side, reaching her hand up to stroke his chest. He gripped her hand when her fingers circled his nipple.

"That tickles." He kissed her knuckle, settling their joined hands on his solid chest.

She froze, her heart skipped a beat, and her breath caught. Eric had been ticklish there after they'd made love, too. Almost as quickly as the memory constricted her lungs, it released, allowing her to breathe normally. Eric was gone, and he was never coming back. Being with Mack didn't mean she had stopped loving Eric. Or that she'd forgotten what they'd shared.

He wanted her to move on. She didn't have to live in the past anymore. The stab of guilt faded as she lay naked with Mack, wanting to make love with him again. And again.

She traced a finger over the scar on his cheek, then trailed it across his smooth skin—mmm, he'd shaved for her—to that sexy freckle on his bottom lip. He caught her fingertip between his teeth and held it. His tongue swirled around her finger, his eyes telegraphing clear messages.

He slid his hand under her side, and with firm pressure on the small of her back, rolled her on top of him.

"Mmm," was all she managed to say as Mack pushed his hips off the bed, his arousal distracting her. Was ten minutes up? Because he was making her crazy with need. She reached down between them. His eyes closed, and his head lolled back as she stroked him. He was smooth and hard and eager.

The low growl that emitted from deep in his throat ramped up her desire another notch. Burying her face in his neck, she kissed him, her nose rubbing his chin. She inhaled the spicy scent of his shave cream, the male scent of his body, and the smoky smell of … Smoke?

She reared her head back and sniffed the air.

"Don't stop," he pleaded, running his hand up her back and tangling his fingers in her hair. Tugging her back to him.

"Do you smell something burning?"

"Burn—Oh, shit! The rolls!" He rolled her off him and leaped from the bed.

She chuckled at the sight of his lily-white butt dashing from the room. The clatter of metal hitting the stovetop was followed by mild profanities. When she heard a door open, she abandoned her plan to wait for him to return and scooted off the bed.

After slipping into her panties, she retrieved his boxers with their Jack Daniel motif from the floor and rolled her eyes. How Mack. When she spotted the back door propped open to clear the air, she picked up his shirt and pulled it on.

He noticed her after he removed the potatoes from the oven, setting the crusted dish on the cutting board. "Sorry. The rolls are, well, toast." He nodded to the trash can. "And I don't know if we can salvage these. At least there's steaks and salad."

He bit his lower lip while his gaze roamed over her bare

legs and the shirt that hung to her thighs. "Though it'll take a few minutes to start the grill." He stepped toward her. "Then I have to cook the steaks. Seven minutes on one side. Then flip." He gripped her hips, pinning her against the counter. "Seven minutes on the other. That's a lot of interruptions." His voice was husky. He batted the door closed before he lifted her to sit on the countertop, his hands sliding up her thighs.

She wanted him inside her again. Now. She draped her arms over his shoulders and scooted her bottom forward until her crotch pressed against his waist.

"We could skip the steaks. We have the salads and left-over pizza from last night."

Staring into his mesmerizing blue eyes, she nodded. "I wasn't in the mood for steak anyway."

She took in his amazing biceps and forearms, the sparse hair and faint freckles on his hard-muscled chest. The way he made her feel like the most desirable woman on the planet melted her defenses.

If only he weren't Special Forces through to his core … Still, she couldn't resist him, kissing him, tasting him as his lips parted and welcomed her tongue. After two years—years —without sex, Mack had stoked her fire, and she needed to kiss him, with her legs wrapped around his waist, and experience the soul-shattering sensations of climaxing with him again.

"Do you have whipped cream?"

"What?" he sputtered and coughed.

She downplayed it with a shrug, even though her skin heated, and she imagined she must be a blotchy shade of red.

His face lit up. "Don't think so. Might have chocolate syrup, though." His Adam's apple bobbed as he swallowed. "Let me check the fridge. Stay right here."

Good lord, she'd really suggested dirty sex. It hadn't fazed him, either. The heat from her cheeks traveled low, making her muscles constrict in anticipation at the thoughts of where he might start.

With no self-consciousness about being naked, he made his way around the kitchen island.

When Mack's phone vibrated on the adjacent counter, she jolted. He halted, and his smile disappeared into a grim line. She eyed the phone warily. What were the chances this would be a good interruption? Slim to none. She kept her perch on the counter, praying it would stop or be a telemarketing call or a wrong number.

Mack muttered a profanity as he checked the caller ID. "I have to take this." He punched the button, then raised the phone to his ear. "Hanlon."

Her own mood plummeted, watching his head hang, then his shoulders sag. He pinched the bridge of his nose while he listened.

"When? Roger that." Once he hung up, he pounded his fist into his bare thigh and cursed under his breath.

Kristie slid off the counter and wound her way over to him. "Let me guess. They need you to go save the world?"

"Not the whole world, but the team's going out."

She tried to silence the voice that immediately whispered he might not come back. "I see."

He wore a guarded expression as if he expected her to get angry. Not like she was thrilled, but after their mission in Colombia had given her an up-close glimpse of what they did, she couldn't beg him to stay. They needed the whole team. He couldn't control being called out on a mission any more than she could. She wrapped a leg around his and pressed against his chest, running one hand up his bicep to his neck.

"I planned to give you an encore performance and hoped for a standing ovation …"

Oh, lordy. "How long do we have?" This would stop any negative thoughts from taking hold.

He peered past her at the clock on the microwave. "Wheels up in thirty-two minutes. Twelve minutes tops before I need to be on the road. Missed a few calls while we were, uh, otherwise engaged."

Talk about short call. This would take some getting used to. Twelve minutes. And he needed to get dressed, grab his kit bag, probably pack some clothes … She dragged his face down for another deep kiss.

Pounding on the front door made her jump back, and Mack startled.

"Ray!" They laughed in unison.

"Be right back."

"Um, Mack." She plucked his boxers from the kitchen chair, wadded them up, and threw them at him.

He stepped into the boxers while Ray banged again.

She hid in the kitchen when Mack went to the door. She picked up the package of steaks on the counter and put them in the freezer. As she put the wine in the fridge, she overheard Mack telling Ray he'd called in, assuring him he'd be ready to go in time.

"You, uh, you might want to put on a shirt and pants before you show up. Sorry for the interruption, Kristie." Ray's amused voice resonated clear into the kitchen.

Though Ray was smart enough to know what they were up to, she wasn't going to say hello wearing Mack's shirt. Where was her shirt anyway? She found it on the countertop. Since she still needed her bra and pants, she waited until hearing the door close before emerging. Oh, awesome. Her pants were on the floor behind Mack. As if they needed to be more obvious. She gathered up her sandals and pants and met Mack's sorrowful gaze. Ten minutes left.

He slid an arm around her waist. "I am so freakin' glad you weren't hungry." He hugged her to his chest as they laughed. "I'll make this up to you," he promised.

TWENTY-FIVE

TWO APACHE HELICOPTERS flew low across the highway as Kristie drove toward the airfield. Even though she'd been flying several years and saw a variety of aircraft daily, the magic never dulled. She had the coolest job ever. She'd miss it when she couldn't fly anymore, but hopefully, that would be years down the road since there wasn't a mandatory retirement age for aviators.

The past few days with Mack being gone, she missed him more than she'd expected. She snatched up her phone at every incoming text or call, and each time it wasn't him, the resulting implosion sucked away the adrenaline hit of hope. He couldn't contact her, she got that, and had no idea when he'd be back.

It was too soon to make long-term and life-changing decisions, especially considering they weren't exactly a couple. They'd made love one time. Though if he hadn't been called out when he had …

The Apaches disappeared, leaving her with two equally strong desires: flying and family. Currently, a forbidden relationship stood between them. A relationship that would more likely cost her one of those things than bridge them together. Yet, she couldn't walk away and leave herself full of what-ifs.

She adjusted the rearview mirror. *Don't do anything stupid, Donovan,* she warned the eyes staring back in the mirror. Eyes that looked less empty than they had a few weeks ago. She sighed, then shifted the mirror back into position.

Wait. She looked again. The truck behind her blocked her view, but she swore a black SUV had pulled out onto the highway from the cross street. No need to panic. There were dozens of SUVs on the road. Sheehan should be at work since maintenance worked an eight-to-four schedule. She could be wrong on that. Though he wouldn't know her schedule nor that she was flying nights this week. Could he have found out somehow?

Calm down. She didn't know if it was Sheehan, and he had made himself scarce after her confrontation. It could be anyone, and they hadn't done anything to indicate they were following her. She took the off-ramp for the airfield, keeping an eye on the mirror. Both the truck and SUV exited, too. Great. She needed to quit being overdramatic and get a look at the driver. Which she couldn't do with the truck between them.

Coming to the intersection with Honeycutt Drive, she straddled the line between turn lanes. When the truck went to the right, she drifted left. The SUV took a few moments to commit to the right lane, maintaining a good distance behind the truck.

She shifted in her seat to get a visual, but with the tint of the windshield, she could only make out the hand resting atop the steering wheel. Tanned skin disappeared under a camouflaged sleeve. The truck next to her made the turn, and she waited for the SUV to pull up. It didn't move. A chill raced up her arms. *Come on.*

She put her hand around the gearshift, ready to back up if necessary to get a look, when another car came up the off-ramp, forcing the SUV to move into her line of sight. Instead of Sheehan's blond hair and ruddy cheeks over pale skin, the driver had a darker complexion with shaggy black hair. There was a second soldier in the SUV, who wasn't Sheehan, either. A bit older than the driver, he looked straight at her and nodded before they turned.

Feeling somewhat relieved, she turned left. After the Hwy 210 underpass, she swung around to head toward the airfield. Coming to the intersection again, a black SUV passed her on the other side of the median. She couldn't see the driver, but the manufacturer's emblem on the front grille was the same. Was it the same SUV and they U-turned as well? Or a different one? Damn, she should have tried to get a look at the license plate.

Had her paranoia kicked into overdrive? Put her in an aircraft, and she was fearless. It didn't hurt that her bird was armed with a .50 cal machine gun or mini-gun capable of firing four thousand rounds per minute. But those men were U.S. soldiers. Surely, Sheehan wouldn't get buddies to follow her. They were supposed to be on her side. She'd do a flyover of the area around the airfield after takeoff and before landing. If she didn't see an SUV hanging around, then she'd know it was her imagination running wild.

"YOU WANT TO COME IN?" Ray offered as Mack retrieved his bags from the back of Ray's SUV.

Tempting, but Kristie's car wasn't in the driveway. "Naw.

I better get some sleep." He'd call her. He owed her dinner, at the least, after running out for this mission. But not tonight.

He dragged himself across the street. Once inside his quiet house, he said a prayer for the young boy they'd found in the terrorist training camp the team took out. The idea of a suicide bomber using the toddler to deflect attention before they … He shuddered, and it took several deep breaths to let his anger abate.

The whole mission reminded him of how much he took for granted. He longed to hold Darcy and Amber in his arms and tell them he loved them and would protect them at all costs.

After he dumped his dirty clothes in the washing machine, he peered through the blinds. No sign of Kristie's car yet. He called and got her voicemail. "Hey. Don't know if you're flying tonight. Thought I'd check in and let you know we're back. I'm gonna hit the rack. Talk to you soon."

He wouldn't mind waking up with her, but he wasn't sure she'd want to be around him right now. Missions like this didn't make him good company. A shower would cleanse his body, but it wouldn't wash away the melancholy—or the doubt hiding in the dark recesses of his mind. He went to the refrigerator and grabbed a beer. He twisted off the cap and downed it in a few long gulps, hoping to clear his mind so he could sleep. He tossed the bottle in the recycling bin and went to the bathroom.

In the mirror, he studied his reflection. Did he look different? Older and harder after this mission? The memory of holding the crying toddler on the flight back to base left him disengaged. He assumed the boy would be sent to a local orphanage. How much better would that be? He rubbed his forehead to relieve the pain from the dull headache, then downed a couple of aspirin before heading to bed.

MACK WOKE to the morning light that streamed through the cracks in the blinds. His stiff muscles ached, and his shoulder popped when he stretched. A glance at the clock showed he'd managed to sleep nearly ten hours. The time zone changes and previous lack of sleep still drugged his body and mind.

Part of him wanted to hide out for a day or two to process everything. But while the coffee brewed, he realized what—who—he wanted more than solitude.

Several hours later, when Kristie pulled into the restaurant's parking lot, Mack stayed put, leaning against his truck. After she parked, she made her way to him. She'd hesitated when he asked her to meet him for lunch, agreeing *after* he suggested a small, out-of-the-way location where they'd unlikely run into anyone they knew.

He attempted to smile. Without a word, she came to him, slipped her arms around him, and rested her head against his shoulder. He wrapped his arms around her and held tight, drawing comfort from the contact.

She finally pulled back and studied him. "Everyone okay?"

"Yeah."

"Rough one, though?"

Unable to speak, he nodded. He couldn't disclose details and wouldn't burden her with the darkness anyway. She'd picked up on his mood with a single glance and given him the touch he needed. The warmth she imparted melted the cold detachment clinging to him. He'd been right about her ability to support him in what he did. She didn't complain, nor did she ask more questions.

Over lunch, Kristie upheld the conversation, drawing him out with questions about Amber and Darcy.

"Hey, did you find out if Sheehan also has a black SUV?" Kristie asked him out of the blue.

"I went by one time. There was a black sedan in the drive. No SUV."

Kristie's eyes widened for a moment. "Okay."

"I think it was a Nissan Maxima. Why? Did you see him?"

"No. Thank goodness. I think confronting him at the hangar did the job."

Something didn't feel authentic about her answer. "I need to go by and check again; eventually retrieve the tracker from his truck, too."

Kristie nodded in agreement.

"Sorry," he continued. "I slacked off after you kicked me out."

"I didn't kick you out. I—"

"No. You kicked me in the—"

"Hey!" she cut him off, finishing with a bashful yet alluring smile.

He reached for her hand. "I'm just glad you changed your mind."

"Me, too." She slid her hand in his and squeezed back, her wary expression melting into a contented one.

The waitress appeared and refilled their water glasses. "Can I get you anything else?"

"I'm good," he answered. Definitely better than an hour ago.

"I'd like a chocolate sundae. Heavy on the sprinkles, and we'll need two spoons." Kristie winked at him. "Ice cream always makes things better."

"Sprinkles, though?" He shook his head, although the impish grin she shot him lifted his mood. "Will you come over tonight?"

"I'm flying afternoons this week, so it'd be a late dinner."

"That's fine. I've got the girls this weekend, and I'd rather not wait another three days to, uh, make up for that dinner I owe you."

Her eyes danced left and right before settling on him. The smile that lit up her face jump-started his lungs.

"If you're sure ..."

He leaned forward. "I. Am. Positive. Whatever time."

"Okay. Dinner at your place. Then, maybe tomorrow, you could bring the girls out to the airfield for the tour I promised them."

"I'll ask Ray about getting off early to get them from school, and we'll head over." Best idea of the week. Though he knew better than to start thinking of them as a couple, he liked seeing how she interacted with his daughters and wanted to gauge how they reacted to her.

The server delivered the sundae, dripping with whipped cream, sprinkles, and topped with two long-stemmed cherries. The whipped cream brought to mind where they'd left things last week. He needed to pick up a can.

Kristie snorted lightly.

"What's so funny?"

"Long story." She gave a sheepish smile.

Her blush amped his curiosity. "Tell."

She shook her head, but he persisted. "Come on."

She glanced at the neighboring tables, then leaned forward. "Halfway through my last deployment, they opened a Baskin-Robbins on base. One of the guys I flew with a lot, was bummed they didn't have cherries for the sundaes. In his next care package, William's wife sent him three jars of maraschinos. It was kind of a joke, but imagine a bunch of bored, competitive, horny guys with an overabundance of cherries—with stems."

"Really? Who won?"

She merely rolled her eyes and dug her spoon into the sundae.

"Did *you* win?" he pressed, getting hard thinking about it.

"No! I let Ty and Big Norm battle it out. Being the champ of tying knots in cherry stems with my tongue was not the reputation I wanted to have." She took another bite of ice cream, her chest and neck flushing further.

"But you can do it?" he asked. The coy expression on her face aroused him further. "Show me. *Please*," he added when she shook her head.

"You aren't going to let this go, are you?"

"No. It was a really bad week," he cajoled her. "I'll owe you."

Kristie gave a resigned sigh. She shifted her eyes to study the people seated around them. Deliberately, she picked up the cherry and bit it off.

Next, the stem disappeared into her mouth.

Her jaw moved back and forth and up and down. In seconds, he had a killer hard-on. He twisted on the booth's bench, before popping the other cherry into his mouth.

He narrowed his eyes when she pulled the stem from her mouth and showed it to him, tied in a loose knot. "Not bad. Though we might need to work on your technique." He raised his eyebrows and winked. He removed his stem, also in a knot. "I'm happy to give you some tips."

"Smug brat," she retorted, with a smile so big, so warm it erased the dark memories of the past few days. "Is there anything you can't do?"

"Nothing that comes to mind. Oh, wait. I can't fly a Black Hawk—very well."

Laughing, he instinctively threw up a hand to deflect the cherry stem she tossed at him.

And in that moment, he was certain that he was falling in love with Kristie.

TWENTY-SIX

MACK GOT the steaks from the fridge in preparation for his do-over with Kristie. Damn, he'd meant to get flowers again. Too late now. It wasn't the end of the world, and he already had to push back their dinner after Rochelle texted requesting they meet tonight to discuss the summer custody schedule. Though Kristie deserved better than his agitated mood, he couldn't cancel on her after the way she'd made him feel over lunch today and getting called away last week.

Her knock at the door a few minutes later revived his sagging spirits. When he opened the door, she breezed in carrying two grocery bags.

"Is there anything else to bring in?"

"Nope. This is it." She set the bags on the island, and his gaze dropped, raked over her, then worked slowly back up.

"I need a can opener, a bowl, and knife, please," she said, blushing under his scrutiny while she unloaded the bags.

He retrieved the requested items, not releasing the can opener until she kissed him.

She opened a variety of canned beans while he lit the grill.

"What can I do to help?"

"If you'll drain the beans, I'll do the chopping." She placed plum tomatoes and a cucumber on the cutting board. "It's also going to need a little kick. Got some hot sauce?"

"What kind of soldier would I be if I didn't have hot sauce?" he quipped, opening a cupboard door. "Do you want hot, extra hot, or made-for-an-MRE hot?"

"Just hot for me. You can add more to yours."

He and Kristie worked side by side. He emptied beans into the bowl while she diced the tomatoes. It felt good. Comfortable.

"Everything go okay with your meeting with Rochelle?"

The way Kristie studied him, knife poised over the cucumber, made him decide to get her input. "I thought we were going to hammer out the summer custody schedule, but she proposed taking the girls to Georgia for most of the summer so she can spend time with this guy, Grayson."

"As in you wouldn't get to see the girls?" Her pitch rose.

"Not the way I'm supposed to. Sorry if I'm distracted. I thought it was over with him, and she'd date someone local. Finding out she's still involved with someone back home, where she has family, and he has a business …"

"Would she be able to move out of state with the girls?" she asked, immediately picking up on his predicament.

"She can't under the current custody agreement. But, if she remarried, who knows."

Would Grayson be willing to rebuild his business from scratch here? The idea of Rochelle fighting to move the girls to Georgia scared the hell out of him.

"She could petition the court to change it. Happened to Shuler with his first wife. His oldest had started running with the wrong crowd and got in some minor legal trouble. His ex used his service and deployments to convince the judge to let her move them back home—to Montana—when she was hoping to remarry. Said her new husband would be a steadier figure for the children."

Georgia wasn't on the other side of the country, but it eliminated their Wednesday night dinners and made their overnights every other weekend impractical. He couldn't make the girls endure that much travel. His stomach cramped at the notion of being a dad who only saw his kids every other holiday and for a few weeks in the summer.

"From what I've seen, you're a great dad, and the girls adore you. I don't think she could make a case against you because of your service." Kristie's much-needed perspective countered all of Rochelle's years of complaining and tearing him down.

"Appreciate you saying that. I shouldn't let this mess with my head."

Kristie scraped the diced cucumber into the bowl. "Losing a spouse to death is hard, but I think in lots of ways, it's harder to go through a divorce. Especially when kids are involved. You're doing the right thing by fighting to stay in their lives."

She didn't bash Rochelle. Instead, she affirmed his decision and showed him respect—as a soldier and a father.

"You're great with the girls yourself," Mack commented.

She'd cheered on Darcy as she'd learned to ride her bike, jumped rope with both girls when it would have been easy to beg off, then offered to show them her Black Hawk. He'd hit the jackpot with her.

He picked up the plate with the steaks to put on the grill. "I'm kinda surprised you and your husband didn't have kids." The words slipped out without thought, but the change that swept over Kristie's face and posture, and the sadness that flashed in her eyes halted him in his tracks.

He set the plate back on the island, wishing he could grab the words and stuff them back down his throat. There was no way to do that, though, and he couldn't walk outside and grill the steaks like he hadn't noticed. Not knowing what to say, he stood there watching her. Waiting.

"We wanted to." She spoke so softly he could barely make out the words, and she didn't quite meet his gaze.

The pain in her voice sliced through him like a .50-caliber round through a paper target. He wanted to say something to comfort her but feared he's say something stupid—again—so he stood there mutely.

"We'd started trying just before Eric got orders to deploy. Then I got orders. We planned to start our family when we got back."

Except Eric hadn't come back. She'd lost her husband and her dream of a family. And yet she'd said she thought *he* had it hard dealing with Rochelle. Maybe, maybe not. He wanted to take Kristie in his arms and say the right words as she had to him.

"I'm sorry," he offered lamely instead. Sorry for what he'd said. Sorry she didn't have the child she so obviously longed for. Sorry she'd lost the man she loved. He wanted to offer her hope that she could still have those things.

"Not your fault." She breathed in through her nose and blew a long breath out her mouth. "Go put the steaks on and give me a minute."

He didn't want to walk away from her, but she turned her back on him to get the dressing for the bean salad, effectively dismissing him. Picking up the steaks, he retreated, more determined now to find a way they could be together—to take away her pain and show her she could have more than just flying.

MACK PUT the steaks on the grill and came inside after a minute or two. Barely enough time to blow her nose and regain her composure. Most days, Kristie focused on her career without thinking about how much she wanted children.

She studied Mack's back as he washed the plate and tongs. With two older daughters, would he want another child? Being a part-time stepmom would be a blessing, but would that be enough?

The romantic fantasies she'd arrived with tonight had taken a direct hit, but she refused to let his innocent comment spoil the evening. She'd be strong and concentrate on the present. Her grief counseling taught her she couldn't change the past, and she couldn't control the future, so she had to live in the present. And her present included a nice dinner with a man who gave her goosebumps in a myriad of dangerous ways.

Mack came around behind her and placed his hands on her hips.

"Taste?" She offered him a spoonful of the bean salad.

"Not yet." His hand slid along her forearm, returning the spoon to the bowl. His fingers intertwined with hers, then he wrapped their arms around her waist. His face pressed against her hair, and his breath tickled her ear.

They stood there, rocking ever so slightly, with the radio playing an '80s soft rock song in the background. She closed her eyes and let the music carry away her heartbreak. Without words, Mack managed to make her feel less broken. More whole. More hopeful.

"Are you able to bring the girls to the airfield tomorrow afternoon?"

"Yeah. We'll come after I pick them up from school. Just

gonna be hard to keep my hands off you," he added in a husky, meaningful way.

She tilted her head to see him out of the corner of her eye. Why did this have to be so hard with so many obstacles in the way? The heart-stopping dangers of his Spec Ops job. The career-ending complications of her rank. Her head didn't have the answers, and her heart wouldn't listen to any warning signals. She pushed them aside to enjoy the here and now.

THE CLOSING of the dresser drawer roused Kristie from sleep. Turning over, she spotted Mack in the dim light from the ajar bathroom door.

"Didn't mean to wake you."

"What time is it?" She looked from the closed blinds to the nightstand.

He made his way to the edge of the bed. "A little after five."

She groaned, laying her head back down on the pillow.

"You aviators have it easy." He chuckled. "What time do you go in?"

"Not until this afternoon."

He leaned over to kiss her. "Stay as long as you want. Or I could call in sick. Stay here with you."

Tempting. The mood during dinner last night had been more subdued than their prior meals together, but they'd eventually fallen into easy conversation when planning the visit to the airfield. After cleaning the kitchen, he'd asked her to stay for a movie, which led to her spending the night.

It hadn't been the romantic evening she'd envisioned, but helping each other work through real-life issues boded well for making this relationship work long-term. This morning was a new day. And seeing Mack not fully dressed was enough to put her in the mood. "Ray might suspect the real reason you don't come in."

"I think he'd understand. But the rest of the team might not. So," he drawled, smiling down at her in one of his T-shirts. "I'll see you this afternoon."

TWENTY-SEVEN

"WHERE ARE WE GOING? What's the surprise?" Darcy asked for the fourth time.

"If I tell you, it wouldn't be a surprise," Mack told her —again.

Darcy's face scrunched as she tried to intimidate him into revealing the secret. He fought not to laugh. Keeping focused on the road prevented him from giving in to her.

When a Chinook helicopter flew low overhead, it was Amber who studied him, a smile lighting up her face. She'd probably figured it out, though she didn't say anything, which kept her little sister in suspense. They approached the airfield sign a minute later. Darcy stared outside and tugged on his arm.

"We're going to see helicopters! Aren't we? Is Miss Kristie flying that one?"

"Not that one; hers isn't that big. But she's waiting for us."

Darcy started bouncing on the seat once he confessed. Truth be told, he was nearly as excited as Darcy. Her acceptance of his role as dad made her even more attractive—as if he needed another reason. Kristie wanting children made it easy to picture her loving the girls as her own rather than treating them as an inconvenience or intrusion.

He barely got the truck in park before the girls piled out, pointing at the aircraft visible between the hangars. He directed them to the building that housed the company offices. His pulse thrummed through him. *Professional. Keep it professional.* He better not give her colleagues any reason to suspect this went beyond her showing a neighbor's kids her aircraft.

He opened the door, and Kristie surged upward, a smile brightening her face.

"Hey, girls! Good to see you." She introduced him and the girls to the crew, careful to mention they were neighbors, though Mack figured her crew recognized him from their prior training op and lunch. Kristie grabbed her helmet before they headed out of the office.

"Darcy, stay with us," he warned when she skipped ahead toward the row of Black Hawks on the tarmac. She paused, twirled once, and motioned for them to hurry. Amber even hurried toward the waiting craft instead of doing her typical middle-schooler dawdle.

Kristie walked them around the helicopter, explaining how the two sets of blades controlled the height and direction while flying. The girls didn't get excited about refueling or turbine engines; however, when Kristie asked if they wanted to sit in the cockpit, both piped up with a resounding "Yes!"

He lifted Darcy and plunked her down on the pilot's seat while Kristie helped Amber into the left seat.

The girls' heads rotated as they scanned the complex setup of buttons, switches, and controls.

"What's this thingy?" Darcy pointed to a gauge in front of her. He shrugged, pointing to Kristie.

"Hang on." She peered across the cockpit, then stepped up inside and knelt behind the communications console between the seats. For the next several minutes, she answered Darcy and Amber's questions about the hundreds of instruments and indicators.

"You better not change those, honey," Mack cautioned when Darcy flipped switches.

"It's fine. She won't hurt anything, and she won't be firing any live ammo," Kristie assured them with a wink. Darcy pressed a button on what Kristie explained was the cyclic, or stick, which controlled lift.

Her lilting voice wrapped around him, drawing him in. Her knowledge of all aspects of the aircraft filled him with a deeper sense of awe and respect. He admired her profile as she continued to hit the highlights, laughing when Darcy scooted to the edge of the seat and strained to reach the pedals.

The crew and another pilot appeared a few minutes later to perform the preflight inspection while Kristie continued to indulge the girls.

She handed Amber her helmet. "Here."

"It's heavy." Amber turned it over in her hands.

"That's for protection. The equipment that allows me to talk to headquarters, my crew, and the troops on the ground is built into the helmet, too. Try it on."

"I want a turn!" Darcy exclaimed before Amber got it on.

"Patience, monkey. Give Amber a minute first," Mack said. The girls enjoying the outing and Kristie's comfort level with them was a good sign.

Kristie leaned back. "Powell. Can we borrow your helmet?"

The younger pilot held his helmet out to Mack. It did weigh more than expected. When he helped Darcy put it on, her head bobbed and rolled under the weight. Her small pixie face was dwarfed by the gray Kevlar helmet. She gripped the stick with both hands, pushing it forward. The helmet slid down, partially covering her eyes.

He pulled his phone from his back pocket and took several pictures of the girls in the cockpit, managing to get Kristie in a couple before she climbed out.

"Let me get pictures of you with the girls," she offered.

He posed with Darcy, then walked around to the other side and got some with Amber. Once the girls reluctantly clambered out, he snapped a few more pictures of them posing in front of the Black Hawk. He debated asking a crew member to take one of the four of them together, but that might raise questions.

The girls took off the helmets and climbed back inside the body of the aircraft while the crew finished their inspection.

"Daddy, get a picture," Darcy requested.

He took a picture of them peeking out the door gunner's window. He leaned in past Kristie, looking over her shoulder where the girls settled into seats—right where Judge Vallejo's daughter had sat wedged between his teammates on their flight out of the jungle. A shudder shook his upper body. What would it take to shut Herrera down for good?

"Time to get out and watch Miss Kristie fly," Mack coaxed when Powell retrieved his flight helmet and checked his watch. "Where do you want us?"

"Off the tarmac would be good. Don't want to blow the girls away." She extended a hand to help Darcy hop down.

The way her affectionate smile lingered on Darcy in no way lined up with any images of a wicked stepmother. Yeah, he'd jumped ahead, but everything about Kristie punched the right buttons and flipped the right switches.

"Thanks for the tour," he said.

"No problem. I enjoyed showing off." She shifted her gaze between the girls, then to him. Seconds passed.

Amber cleared her throat, breaking the silence.

"See ya later." He put his hands on the girls' shoulders, giving each a squeeze.

Darcy got the hint. "Thank you, Miss Kristie. This was the best!" Then Amber thanked her, too.

"Fly safe," Mack chimed in.

"Is it dangerous?" Darcy's voice held a hint of panic.

"Flying is safer than driving a car," Kristie assured her.

"Good," Darcy stated authoritatively, her head bobbing.

His daughter's concern for Kristie hit Mack right between the eyes. Even at their young ages, his daughters understood danger. Had friends who'd lost parents during deployments.

Kristie's job was safer than his, but there were no guarantees nothing would happen to her. The reality that something could happen to Kristie struck him like a sucker punch. Gave him a first-hand perspective of how she felt about his job after losing her husband. Of Rochelle's fears. He didn't like the boot being on the other foot.

Minutes later, the blades chopped the air and whipped the girls' hair into a frenzied dance. Even over the noise, he heard Darcy exclaim when the aircraft began a slow ascent. It rotated to face them. Kristie waved, and Darcy enthusiastically waved back. Amber briefly lifted a hand.

"This is so cool." Darcy's body vibrated with excitement as the aircraft rose higher.

"Can we go now?" Amber asked once it had flown into the distance.

"You hungry?"

"Kind of."

Darcy took hold of his hand as they walked back to his truck. "I'm going to fly helicopters when I get big, too."

"Last week, you wanted to be an animal doctor, and before that, a country singer." Amber rolled her eyes.

"Will Huffman said I'd have to be a doctor for snakes and lizards, but I don't want to do that. I can sing when I'm not flying." Ignoring her sister's negativity, Darcy skipped the last few steps to the truck.

"You can be anything you want, monkey. Though you'll probably have to limit it to less than five things at a time." How many could he manage? Operator. Dad. Lover. *Husband?*

TWENTY-EIGHT

KRISTIE CROSSED the street to Mack's front door. Sunday night had been a long time coming. Tonight, eager anticipation, not fear, caused her heart to pound. She enjoyed Mack and the girls' visit to the airfield as much as they appeared to. Memories of Amber and Darcy's smiling faces spread warmth through her chest.

And there was Mack, opening the door even before she reached the stoop.

"About time." His appraisal made that warmth spread to other, more feminine parts of her body.

"Thought you dropped off the girls at twenty hundred."

"It's almost twenty-one hundred." One side of his mouth rose as he closed the front door. "I've been waiting for over half an hour."

She didn't admit she'd waited until dark to reduce the risk of the neighbors seeing her go into his house. "What did the girls say about the Black Hawks?"

"Darcy's starting flight training with you next week." He rested his hands on her hips, pulling her closer. His gaze dropped to her lips, and she swallowed.

"And Amber?"

"She forwarded the pictures I took to all her friends. Was talking about how many 'likes' and comments she hoped they'd get. Guess that's what's important to kids these days."

"She's still got time to decide. She might join the Air Force to fly jets instead."

"I was thinking, after the other day, we could do dinner together next time the girls are here." Something an awful lot like hope played across his face.

"I would love that. Really, I would, but—"

"No. Not but."

It was tempting, but too soon? The girls wouldn't understand why they couldn't say anything. "I'm going down to Savannah to pack up my house then. Figured I'd schedule it when you had the girls."

"O-kay." He sounded somewhat appeased. "We could do a cookout with the Lundgrens. They wouldn't think twice about that."

"*That* sounds like a great plan." She accepted his compromise and slid her right hand over his collarbone and around to his neck, tilting her head in invitation when he pulled her body against his.

Her lips parted, and her tongue met his. Cinnamon toothpaste masked whatever he'd had for dinner. His body was solid, warm, and being molded against him was like heaven. His hips rocked forward, his arousal pressing against her. She leaned into him, sparking the desire consuming her mind and body.

He edged her backward toward the couch. She cradled his head, her mouth never leaving his. Her knees nearly buckled when he tugged her shirt free from her jeans. His hands skimmed her sides as he pulled the shirt up. She lifted her arms, allowing him to ease the shirt over her head. His eyes raked over her body, making her glad she'd splurged on some new—sexier—lingerie this weekend.

She reciprocated, removing his shirt and dropping it to the floor. Mack's hands stroked her arms and roamed over her back. He lowered his mouth to her neck, one of her favorite spots. She wanted more of him—much more.

"Last time we were right about here, weren't we talking about whipped cream?" he said between kisses, his voice husky.

"I don't recall that." Her body temperature shot up. Why had she let that thought slip out?

"Really?" His gruff, sexy chuckle definitely counted as foreplay.

She drew in a ragged breath before nipping his earlobe. He was making her crazy. She loved the feel of skin against skin. Oh, to hell with waiting. She reached for his belt buckle.

Mack sucked in a breath, and with a hint of a grin, lifted his head. He grasped her hands, keeping control of the situation. She stared back, the smoldering in her heart surely reaching her eyes.

He gestured her to the bedroom with a jerk of his head. The covers were turned down, and a can of whipped cream and bottle of chocolate syrup sat on the nightstand. She laughed self-consciously and took a hesitant step back. Oh, geez. What had she been thinking? "We'd make a mess."

Mack maintained a loose hold on her. "I have a washing machine. And a shower."

Did she trust he wanted more than sex from her? Yeah, especially after the other night. In her experience, missionary position tended not to suffice for the living-on-the-edge guys in Mack's line of work. And she certainly had been adventurous in trying things with Eric. Was it too soon, though?

Setting the bar too high? Her brain said slow down, but her body said: oh, hell, yes. Go for it.

She surrendered, giving Mack a slight nod.

His hand slid up to unclasp her bra. He nuzzled her neck as he peeled it off, taking full advantage to fondle both breasts. She touched him, too. Let her hands indulge in the pleasure of his muscled arms and strong back.

His hands glided down her sides at a glacial pace, then he toyed with the button on her shorts, taking forever to undo it and even longer to pull down the zipper. With agonizing slowness, he eased the shorts down her hips. Unable to refrain any longer, her hands gripped his biceps, kneading the solid flesh.

He hauled her body to his and ground his hips against hers.

Mack nibbled her earlobe before moving back to her neck. Now that she was naked, he guided her to lay on the bed. His tongue swirled over her right breast while he teased the other with his free hand. This man knew just how to make her body thrum with delicious need.

He shifted and knelt next to her, picking up the chocolate syrup. He squeezed a few drops on his wrist, then licked it off before running a thin line up his index finger, extending it to her. She closed her lips around his finger, sliding her tongue along the underside and sucking off the chocolate.

"You're killing me—but it's so gonna be worth it," he said.

Killing him? That was hardly her intent.

He stared into her eyes as he dripped syrup onto her breast. "Not too hot?"

She bit on her lower lip. "Perfect." She wanted it hot. Them. Not the syrup.

He took his time tasting and licking her clean before he drizzled more chocolate over her stomach.

"I have to say, I really like the belly button ring." His finger toyed with it.

She sucked in her breath when he added a cold squirt of whipped cream around her navel. The cold quickly changed to heat as he trailed his tongue down her stomach. He left her wanting more after he pressed a kiss at the juncture of her leg and pelvis.

"More," she pleaded with a rise of her hips when, instead, he crossed to her left thigh and worked his way to her knee.

His hands ran up the inside of her thighs, spreading her legs. He picked up a tube from the nightstand and squirted a dab of lotion onto his thumb. As soon as he rubbed it on her, she began to tingle in all the right places. He added a drizzle of chocolate syrup before topping it with whipped cream.

She practically panted with prolonged deprivation. Then his tongue was there. Teasing, taunting, and pleasuring with no hesitation or inhibition. He swirled pressure in just the right spots to make her hips rise higher. Fingers replaced his tongue, going deeper and spreading her in the perfect balance of pain and pleasure.

She sucked in air in rapid gasps, her body trembling on the brink. The sensations came together like a symphony's final crescendo when his tongue returned to deliver the last firm strokes, pushing her into the abyss. Her leg muscles tightened in anticipation, and her body jolted from the intensity.

Her head fell back against the pillow, her body physically spent by the time she stopped clenching from the multiple waves of orgasm.

Mack propped himself on an elbow before he ran a finger

down her side. She shivered and pushed his hand aside when it tickled.

"You have chocolate on your face." And traces of whipped cream.

He grinned. "Mmm, best chocolate sundae ever."

"It was. And you're making me hungry."

He gave a throaty chuckle in response to her innuendo.

"Does that mean I get to reciprocate after I have a minute to recuperate?"

"Take as long as you need," he assured her in an oh-so-gracious, I'm-getting-a-prize way.

Funny how she'd gone two years without sex, and now ten days without Mack had seemed an interminably long time.

TWENTY-NINE

KRISTIE DROVE down her old street in Savannah, waving to the Hincheys as her neighbors worked in their yard. She backed her car in the drive and studied the leggy pansies she'd planted around the mailbox. Maybe the next renters would put in fresh flowers for summer.

She unlocked the front door of her rental house, then slowly pushed it open. Stepping into the house after the past few weeks in Fayetteville was different than coming home after her deployment. It'd felt less alone then since her family had been here with her.

Each footfall of her sandals on the laminate flooring echoed softly on her way to the bedroom to stow her suitcase. She'd lived so many places over the years, moving from base to base with first her dad's career and then her own. Even though she and Eric didn't own this house, it felt more like home than any other place, because it had been theirs together.

She loved Savannah, but it was time to move on. Things with Mack made it easier to let go—not that there were any guarantees with him.

For the next two hours, she packed up irreplaceable items she didn't want going into storage. Then came the hard part—Eric's clothes. She bagged the socks, underwear, and anything worn or stained, then separated what she could donate, setting aside a few things she'd keep. It's not like they had children who might someday want to wear his old uniforms or shirts.

She got her keys to unlock the back door, so she could put the bags in the trash before running to Screamin' Mimi's to get her favorite Stromboli for the last time in the foreseeable future.

When she turned the key in the deadbolt, there was no resistance. No click. She flipped it back and forth, confirming it hadn't been locked.

She retraced her steps. No. She hadn't been out the back door since she'd gotten here a few hours ago. Had she left for Fayetteville in such a hurry that she'd left it unlocked all this time? Maybe. Impossible to remember now, but it didn't feel right.

Even though the knob was locked, after putting the bags in the bins, she looked around the house. Nothing seemed out of place or missing. Not that she had much of value.

The TV was still there. Of course, it would take two people to carry that bad boy out. She checked her jewelry box. Her diamond ring was back at the Lundgrens', and from what she could tell, everything was here. The only thing that made sense was *she* left the deadbolt unlocked. Nothing happened. No big deal.

THE MOVERS SHOWED up right on time the next morning.

Once they started packing, Kristie loaded her car with the boxes she didn't want the movers taking.

A familiar voice called her name at the same time two dogs began barking. She waited as her neighbor Marcela walked her dogs up the street where the occasional palmetto tree graced a front yard, Spanish moss dripped from the live oaks, and the tall pines provided needed shade on warm spring and summer days like today.

"Hey, guys, you know me." Kristie bent to pet Pickles and Charlie. They stopped barking long enough to sniff her before they circled her and resumed barking as usual.

"I'm sad you're leaving." Marcela pouted at the moving truck, then Kristie.

"Military life. You know how it goes with a change of duty stations." She straightened. "I've got to clean out the fridge, but since I'm staying with friends a while longer, I'm not taking anything. If you want some condiments, dressings, and frozen chicken breasts, come on over. I hate to throw them out."

"Since you put it that way, let me put Pickles and Charlie up. They'll go bonkers with the movers in the house. Be over in a minute."

Kristie went back inside and started to unload the refrigerator's contents onto the counter.

"It's me," Marcela sang out and waltzed into the kitchen.

"Take whatever you want. There're bags in the pantry."

"I hope you'll get back down to visit sometime."

"I'll try. I love this area and have lots of friends here." She winked at Marcela.

"And someone special?"

"What do you mean?"

"The flowers. Who's the guy?"

"I have no idea what you're talking about."

"Someone tried to deliver flowers here not long after you went to Fayetteville. A nice-sized arrangement, too."

She couldn't think of a soul who'd send her flowers. Not here. Not then.

"Instead of leaving them at your door, I saw him putting them in the back when I was coming in from walking the dogs, but he left before I could flag him down. Later that evening, Pickles and Charlie were barking longer than usual." Marcela rolled her eyes. "When I looked out the window, the guy was back, trying again. I felt bad he didn't know you weren't here, so I went out to break the news."

"Are you sure he was looking for me?"

"He gave your last name, and he was, uh—" Marcela hesitated as if searching for the right word—"ticked that you weren't here. Anyway, he asked if I had your new address or phone number, but I didn't have my phone on me and figured any guy that had your address surely would have your number. You mean you never got them?"

"No." Could someone have sent them as a good-luck-on-the-new-assignment gesture? "Did the delivery van have the florist's name on it?"

"No. Which is why I thought they were from him at first. Until I got a look and saw he wasn't your type. He was too old and not even close to swoon-worthy. Sorry. Now I feel bad you didn't get them."

"Don't." But Kristie's nerves jangled. Maybe it was legit, or perhaps someone noticed her place was unoccupied and attempted to break in. It wouldn't be the first time lowlifes targeted military members who were away. "In fact, if he or anyone comes around looking for me, don't give them my contact information, but ask for theirs. You can tell them you'll forward it to me, and I'll get in touch."

Even though she tried to sound casual, Marcela eyed her with a hint of wariness.

"Sure, though I'm really curious now. And disappointed it wasn't some wonderful guy sending you flowers and falling for you."

Kristie smiled but didn't divulge any details on dating Mack. Marcela was a sweetheart, but she lived with her military-officer boyfriend. Best to keep mum on the subject of her complicated love life, so she shifted the conversation to safer topics while they cleared out the rest of her fridge.

"I'd better run and get ready for work. I'll miss you." Marcela hugged her, then picked up the bags of food. "Thanks for the groceries."

"Do you need help with those?"

"I've got them. I'll let you get back to work. Good luck with everything. I'll let you know if any more mysterious flower deliveries show up."

"Please do." In a few hours, she and her possessions would be gone if anyone had nefarious intentions.

KRISTIE LOCKED the knob and deadbolted the front door—she'd already tripled-checked the back door.

After she loaded the cleaning supplies in her car, she stood staring at the house. It didn't look right without the American flag mounted by the front door. She couldn't remember a time when it hadn't flown there. Half her neighbors flew their flag daily. After Eric's death, even the neighbors who didn't usually display the flag except for holidays had small flags lining their curb.

Goodbye, house.

It wasn't as hard to leave now that it was empty. She had

her memories, some packed in the boxes that the movers had driven off with two hours ago, and she would leave behind the sad ones with the questions Marcela had raised. Her life was moving forward in a new direction.

Once she got to know the area, she'd find a permanent home in Fayetteville. Though being across the street from Mack did have advantages, like making it easy for her to see him most nights, she needed to line up an apartment soon and get out from underfoot at the Lundgrens'.

First, she had a few hard goodbyes to say to friends here.

THIRTY

MACK CRACKED open Amber's bedroom door and peeked in. The bedside lamp was off, her book lay on the nightstand, and the displaced covers assured him she wasn't faking sleep this time.

Next, he checked on Darcy. She didn't stir when he stepped into the room to pick Bun-Bun off the floor. He tucked Darcy's favorite stuffed rabbit in beside her.

He studied her long lashes and the freckles dusting her nose. Today, when she'd asked if Kristie might help her and Amber practice jumping rope, it boosted his hopes of them having a future together. His girls had to accept any woman he brought into his life—because it meant she'd be in their lives. Their acceptance was vital, so today was a good sign.

He closed the door and turned out the hall light. Though he ached to tell Kristie about Darcy wanting to see her, they still had to work out how she'd spend time with him and the girls so that it wouldn't raise red flags. Before he flicked on his bedroom light, the message-indicator light on his phone blinked from the nightstand where he'd plugged it in.

Swiping on the screen, there was a voicemail and missed

call notification from Kristie. Even though she was having dinner with friends from her old unit and staying with one tonight, she'd made an effort to call him. Another good sign.

He dialed in for the voicemail. Sitting on the edge of the bed, he caught a glimpse of his enthusiastic smile in the mirror. This is the way a relationship was supposed to be. When you missed the other person even when they were only gone a day or two. When the mere idea of hearing their voice gave you an endorphin rush that pushed problems out of your mind.

"Mack, I'm on my way back from Savannah. I know you have the girls, but I need to talk to you. Tonight. I'm about, uh, thirty minutes out. I'll text you when I get there."

The breathless edge to her voice negated the brief jump in his pulse at hearing she was on her way back early and wanted to see him. He touched the screen to play the message again and listened closely.

Definitely an *oh-shit* call.

She'd be back in ten to fifteen minutes. Better to wait and talk face-to-face rather than call her while she was driving since she sounded rattled.

While he brushed his teeth, different scenarios ran through his mind—none of them good—though most were as likely as the French winning a war on their own. How could anyone in Savannah know about them? What were the chances a MEDEVAC slot suddenly opened up, and she was staying? Or going? Would she do that? Leave for her dream job rather than stick around and give them a shot?

By the time he saw the headlights swing in, followed by the brake lights, he'd backed away from the ledge. He gave her a chance to cut the engine before he ambled across the street. When she opened the car door, the interior light showed boxes in the back seat, quickly dispelling his she's-not-staying-at-Bragg scenario.

She looked right at him when she got out.

"Need help with those boxes?"

"Just leave them." She closed the door but didn't move toward him.

"Want to come over to my house to—"

"No. I need to talk to Ray, too. Come on."

Without giving him a chance to give her a hug or a kiss or ask what was up, she headed to the front door. Mack followed, an uneasy feeling seeping out of his bones and into his limbs.

Both Ray and Stephanie greeted them inside. Their wary expressions told him they'd gotten a call, too.

"I need to use the bathroom." Kristie dropped her purse on the sofa. In the brightly lit room, her skin was nearly the color of the light-gray walls.

"We'll be in the kitchen. Take your time," Stephanie said.

Mack locked eyes with Ray. "Any idea what's up?" he asked once Kristie was out of earshot.

"No," Stephanie answered. "She called about half an hour ago, saying she was on her way and needed to talk to Ray when she got in, then hung up."

Droplets of water glistened on Kristie's face and along her hairline when she joined them and plopped onto a chair at the table. Her color was a little better. For a second, the possibility she was pregnant flashed across his mind. Only they'd stayed careful, used protection. Besides, if that were the case, she wouldn't be telling Ray about it.

"Anyone want coffee?" Stephanie offered.

"I'll wait." Mack was wired enough already. Besides, a stiff drink might be needed instead.

"Just ice water," Kristie said.

Stephanie inserted a pod into the coffee machine, then set glasses of water on the table.

Kristie's hand trembled when she lifted the glass to her lips and took several small sips, then let out a shaky breath. "After packing up the house, I went over to Paul and Deb Wilson's for dinner with several of the other guys and their wives. While there, William Kerns told Paul to give me the four-one-one on what happened with Josué, the pilot I flew with on *that* mission." Kristie cut her gaze to Stephanie, clearly trying not to give away classified information.

This had to do with Colombia? The hair on Mack's arms stood at attention.

"Not long after we left, Josué went MIA. Didn't show up or answer calls or return messages."

Ray shifted in his seat, leaning in with narrowed eyes.

"Then, about a week ago, the police identified his body."

Mack's *oh-shit* sensation erupted into full-on "Oh, fuck."

"Along with the bodies of his wife and two children." Kristie's voice broke, and she wiped away a tear.

Stephanie gasped and sat up straight, her eyes wide. She placed a hand over Kristie's. "What? How?" she sputtered. "Someone from your unit in Savannah?"

"Colombia," Ray interjected. "They think it was cartel related?"

That was beyond obvious, but he was probably digging for something.

Kristie nodded vigorously. "In addition to the gunshots to the head, there were signs Josué was tortured."

Stephanie shivered. Despite all his years of service and the horrors he'd seen, even Mack shuddered at what he envisioned the family had been through—before being executed.

"It's not your fault." The twitch in Ray's cheek aligned with the sick feeling in Mack's core. The Colombian pilot and his family were dead because of Bad Karma's mission to rescue the judge's daughter. It was *their* fault. And the sick bastard that Herrera was, he could target everyone on the team *and* their families.

He had to stop himself from bolting across the street to check on his girls and lock the front door. And grab his weapon and several extra magazines.

"Was he involved with the cartel or ...?" Stephanie stopped midsentence and stared at her husband.

"Payback." Ray used the voice no one dared contradict. "Herrera has cops and military on his payroll. No doubt, he could get the Colombian pilot's name."

Stephanie retrieved the mug filled with tea, setting it and the sugar bowl in front of Kristie. "Chamomile. It's calming. Drink it."

Kristie wrapped both hands around the mug and gripped it tightly. "His report would have my name. Or Josué could have given it. I doubt they could have gotten a copy of my report, but it didn't mention any of your names."

"Yeah, but he's not—"

"I'm not finished," Kristie cut Ray off. "The back-door deadbolt at my house in Savannah wasn't locked. Nothing was missing or out of place, so I told myself I overlooked it in my rush to get up here, but ..." She sighed. "That was before I knew about Josué. But even before that, my neighbor said a flower delivery person was at my house not long after I came here."

The grumble emanating from Ray lasted longer than Mack's. Faking a delivery to divert suspicion—classic move. If Kristie had still been living there, they could have kidnapped or tortured or killed her. Or all three.

"After what I heard from Paul and William tonight, I

called my neighbor. Best she can remember, it would have been shortly after Josué went missing."

The imaginary punch hit Mack harder than a real one.

"I asked her specifics about the delivery guy. The driver was Latino and spoke English with an accent. Late thirties. Average height. On the beefy side. She thinks he drove a dark-gray or black SUV. No name of the florist or delivery company on it. And … she told the guy I'd moved here."

"Shit." Mack hadn't even gotten a second of relief that they'd dodged a bullet because she'd relocated.

"She had no way of knowing not to say anything." Defeat laced Kristie's voice.

"Sounds like it could be the same SUV that followed you that night. But if you haven't seen him since he followed you to the apartment complex, maybe they gave up. Went back to Colombia," Mack offered, though it didn't sound like Herrera's MO.

"There was one time since …"

Mack fought to keep from going ballistic at this bomb drop. "Why didn't you say something?"

"Because it wasn't Sheehan driving. It also happened the day you met Rochelle about the summer schedule, and I didn't want to dump that on you."

"Sorry." He gave a begrudging nod, encouraging her to continue.

"I was flying nights, and on my way in, an SUV pulled out from a side street near the airfield. It was two soldiers. Or at least two men in camouflage."

"What do you mean?" Ray asked, eyebrows furrowed, his battle face on.

"I remember thinking the driver's hair exceeded regulation length. Wrote it off that they might be in a Special Ops unit, but …" She hesitated. "I'd gotten in the left-turn lane, and they went right. I did a U-turn to go toward the airfield, and on the way, I passed what looked like the same SUV. Like they'd done a U-turn, too."

"I don't like it," Ray said, flat out.

Neither did Mack. Why hadn't she told him at some point? Okay, don't obsess about it. It was in the past; they couldn't change it. They had to deal with things now.

"Is the GPS off on your phone?" Ray asked.

"For everything but navigation apps."

"Good. We can't rule out that they planted a tracker or followed you here. We'll take your car to the shop tomorrow and use the bug detector to check it."

"I hooked one up because of Sheehan," Mack reminded Ray.

"I've been careful. Watching out and changing routes, but you're right. I can't stay here and put you at risk. I'm going to check into a hotel."

"Probably best." Ray turned to Stephanie. "Pack an overnight bag for you and Alexis. Go to a hotel with Kristie tonight. Use our credit card in case they found anything with her number on it. Tomorrow you can pack to go to your parents, or better yet, start making college visits until we get ahead of this."

"I'm so sorry. I didn't know …" Kristie said to Stephanie.

"Of course. You couldn't know." Stephanie turned to Ray. "Emergency safety and communication protocols?"

He nodded, and Stephanie calmly got up to tell Alexis to pack.

"We'll need your keys to stash your car someplace for the night, then check it for trackers tomorrow," Mack said.

"Airport?" Ray suggested.

"Perfect. Good mislead if they did plant a tracker." Mack took the keys, Kristie dug out of her purse.

Rochelle would be going ape-shit crazy right now. Considering how close the cartel got to Kristie on more than one occasion, she was holding it together like a pro. Compassionate. Empathetic. Cool under pressure. There was so much to love about this woman. "Hey, you're going to have the whole Bad Karma team on this. These guys don't have a chance."

Kristie's attempt at a smile garnered a score of about a three for effort, not even close to reaching her troubled eyes. "I need to grab a few things."

Mack slipped a hand around her arm before she could leave the kitchen. "We'll get through this," he promised.

She squeezed his hand but didn't say a thing.

THIRTY-ONE

KRISTIE STARTLED at the two solid raps on the hotel room door. Alexis stopped mid-sentence and waited. Two identical raps followed like a code. Stephanie strode to the door, peeking through the peephole before opening the door for Ray.

"Hey, beautiful." He kissed his wife.

"What's the plan?" she asked without preamble.

"I filled in Colonel Mahinis last night. We've got a meeting. Kristie, I want you to come with me. Stephanie, you and Alexis can stay here or do whatever. Steer clear of the house until I learn what Intel digs up."

"Church okay?"

"Yeah. But watch your six."

"Aye, aye, Chief," Stephanie quipped.

"I'll call you when I know more."

Kristie pocketed her hotel key as Ray checked the hallway, then escorted her to the stairway.

"Went by the airport and dropped Mack off to get your car from the long-term lot, and he's taking it to post. We've got equipment to make sure there's no bugs or trackers." He checked the parking lot before opening the door. Ray's untucked polo didn't quite camouflage the bulge created by the gun tucked into the waistband of his jeans.

He kept up the serious security protocol by checking the rearview and side-view mirrors and taking an indirect route. Before yesterday, she would have called it overkill. Today, she skipped chitchat to scan every car and driver.

She had to produce her ID even though Ray vouched for her at the guarded access point to the protected area of the post used by the Special Ops teams. Until today, she'd only seen it from the air.

Ray pulled into the nearly empty lot in front of a nondescript brick building. She didn't see her car, but the black Toyota SUV he parked next to had to be Tony's.

Ray swiped his Common Access Card, then held the door for her. Inside the building, she produced her ID again, and he signed her in at the reception desk.

The wall to the side was filled with the faces and names of fallen operators. It struck her like a chisel, carving off another piece of her heart. Eric's name was on a memorial wall at 1st Ranger Battalion's Headquarters at Hunter Airfield in Savannah. Here, she scanned the most recent additions, swallowing the sorrow the sight inspired. She did not want to see names added that she'd recognize.

Rather than linger, Ray led her through another door into a hallway lined with closed doors bearing the names of senior officers. He stopped at a windowless door marked with a number.

Inside, chairs at three rows of long tables faced a whiteboard. A setup similar to an aviation briefing room, except there were no maps on the walls. Nothing detailing any missions. The sterile vibe pricked at her like hundreds of tiny needles tap-dancing on her arms.

Mack and Tony's voices carried down the hallway. Mack ambled to her side, but Tony beelined to Ray.

"How'd you sleep?" Mack asked.

"Barely."

He gave a sympathetic *humph.* "Same here." He reached to pull her to him, but she drew back, nodding her head in Tony's direction. "He's, uh, already on to us. He's perceptive that way. You don't need to worry about him. I promise," he added in response to her you-didn't look.

She acquiesced and let him pull her against his solid chest. In the safety of his arms, the tension drained from her body as she soaked in his strength for a few precious seconds. Though Ray and Tony ignored them, as far as she knew, she couldn't stay cocooned here forever. She eased back.

"Where are the girls?"

"I dropped them off at the Shuler's this morning. Tammy'll take them to church and keep them until we're through."

"I'm sorry you're missing out on time with them."

"Don't be." His words came out with surprising force. "It's not your fault. This impacts them, too."

Yes, it did, and that reality kept her awake last night. If Herrera killed Josué's family, what would keep him from going after Mack's daughters? After Stephanie and Alexis?

Voices in the hallway stopped her mind from going back to dark places. The Bad Karma team rolled in over the next few minutes. One man literally rolled into the room.

Kristie didn't recognize his face, but his leg was encased in a halo brace and extended out from the wheelchair. The smiles as the men greeted him by name left no doubt that he was their teammate wounded in Colombia. Playing a part in this happy reunion gave her a small sense of satisfaction.

Hunter did a double take from his wheelchair when he noticed her, then spoke discreetly to the team.

"Nobody told you we replaced you with a chick?" Juan said to him.

"What? No way. I heard he might be gay, but ..." Hunter checked her out more thoroughly.

"*I'm* the new medic," Devin informed Hunter, then stared Juan down. "You the one spreading that rumor? Would it make a difference if I was gay?"

"Guess you'd make a good wingman at Jumpy's Place since we wouldn't be competing for the same women."

"You're going to be disappointed then."

Ray rolled his eyes at his team's antics, but their teasing brought the stress level down a notch.

"Staff Sergeant Devin Grant, our new medic." Ray made introductions. "Staff Sergeant Andrew Hunter. And this is Chief Kristie Donovan. She's the Black Hawk pilot who flew the extraction in Colombia."

She stepped forward. "Nice to see you conscious and on your way to recovery." While she was truly thankful that he'd survived, a voice inside her head lamented again that no one had gotten to Eric in time to save him. Life never promised to be fair, but it sure seemed determined to shovel crap at her feet lately.

"Thanks for saving my life," Hunter said.

"Credit for that goes to your team."

"Don't let her downplay it. She flies even better than Hanlon shoots," Tony said. "You missed all the action, being unconscious."

"I would have traded places with you," Hunter said dryly.

A brief silence enveloped the room. It could have been any one of them who took the brunt of the IED and crash. Mack. Ray. If that had been the case, how different would things be today? She studied Mack's profile. The idea of him not being in her life brought on an ache almost equal to the one left by Eric's death.

"Does this meeting have something to do with Operation Sparrow?" Hunter asked.

"We may have fallout, which is why we wanted everyone here who was involved," Ray answered.

"Grant wasn't on the team yet," Hunter said.

"He is now, though. Guilty by association. He's need-to-know." Ray ended that discussion without elaborating. "Colonel texted he's on his way over from the meeting with Intel."

Kristie didn't speak up, either. She didn't want to believe the likes of Baltazar Herrera would be aware of her existence, but the pieces added up to his being very aware of her and her part in rescuing the girl.

A dark-haired man strode in. He studied the gathered personnel with a hawk-like gaze. He appeared to be in his early forties, his tanned skin had the texture of mortar-blasted concrete, and his ramrod posture commanded attention even though he wore civilian clothes. "Everyone here?"

"Liu's out of town. The rest of the team's here, sir," Ray reported. He motioned Kristie over. "Colonel John Mahinis, Chief Kristie Donovan."

The colonel shook her hand. "Thanks for being here, and for giving us the heads-up."

She took a seat at the front table across the aisle from Mack, with Ray by her side.

"We're still collecting data, but it's been difficult getting thorough intel on a Saturday night and Sunday morning, especially from foreign partners. However, thanks to Chief Donovan, we're now aware of threats against the team as a result of Operation Sparrow and have enough intel to determine there is a verifiable threat." Mahinis made eye contact with the men in the room.

"Intel got confirmation from the Colombians after your mission that three wounded locals were brought into the area hospital. One of those men died shortly thereafter. And here's where it gets interesting, none other than Baltazar Herrera showed up at the hospital and identified the KIA as his son, Juan Pablo."

"Please tell me they arrested Herrera," Tony interjected.

"Hospitals there don't have security. Though I'm sure Herrera had his own security team," Ray pointed out.

"Exactly. Someone at the hospital made a call to the authorities. By the time they arrived, Herrera's bodyguards had herded him out." Colonel Mahinis sounded pissed but not surprised. "According to Intel, Herrera lost his shit when he found out his remaining son was dead. Swore vengeance against anyone and everyone responsible in Juan Pablo's death."

"Good luck with that. It's not like Herrera knows who the hell we are. And if he did, does he really think he could deal with Bad Karma?" Walt Shuler sounded cocky, but Kristie realized Juan Pablo's death gave Herrera killer motivation for wanting payback. Made more sense than torturing Josué and his family because they'd rescued the judge's daughter.

"Chief Donovan's name would be in the Colombian pilot's report, which Herrera's sources must have gotten hold of. I did review her report, which only refers to you as 'the package,'" the colonel assured the team.

"I spoke with Kristie after we landed. The co-pilot could have told Herrera's thugs we knew each other." Ray's comment changed the mood to downright oppressive in the room as the men took that in. "Why was this information about the Herreras not passed on to us?"

"Guess our Colombian allies didn't feel it was pertinent." Deep disdain draped the colonel's last word. "If it weren't for Chief Donovan—and I'm sorry you got dragged into this, Chief—but we would be unaware of this threat."

"No apologies required." She couldn't blame them for any of this.

"How the hell did Aviation get information on this threat?" Juan sounded indignant.

"One of the guys in my old unit talked with another of the Colombian pilots we were *training*. He told Paul that my co-pilot that day went MIA. He and his family were found. They'd been tortured—and killed."

"Sonofabitch," someone muttered when she paused.

"Clearly, the cartel," Devin mused. "How do you know it's related, though?"

"We had suspicions Chief Donovan was being followed on more than one occasion after she got here," Ray filled in the team, "but we attributed it to an insubordination issue with a former co-worker she encountered. This weekend, her neighbor in Savannah told her about a delivery attempt made after she transferred to Bragg. Not only was it suspicious, but the timing fit, and the Colombian pilot knew where she was based. After she learned about her co-pilot … easy to connect the dots to Herrera since the neighbor told the delivery guy she'd transferred here."

"Shit!" Tony looked wide-eyed from her to Mack.

"She did get eyes on the two men who followed her the second time," Ray said.

Colonel Mahinis nodded in agreement. "Hunter, your name may be accessible through hospital records. That's why I wanted you here today. Have you noticed anything out of the ordinary?"

"No, but I haven't been out much, other than rehab."

"I want to get you and your family someplace safe until this threat is contained. You have any place to go?"

Hunter paused to think, then shook his head.

"What about Master Sergeant Boswell's fishing cabin? It's close, and no one would think to look for you there," AJ suggested.

"That'd work," Hunter said.

"See if you can set that up." The colonel motioned between them. "Chief Donovan has been staying with you, Chief?"

"I moved into a hotel last night," Kristie clarified.

"I'd like to have you someplace even more secure," the colonel said.

Crap. If they wanted to isolate her to the point she couldn't work, it wasn't going to sit well with Colonel Ball.

"If you're on post that will add another layer of security. I'll arrange for you to get a room at the Landmark Inn. What about your phone and social media?"

She could live with staying on post. "I rechecked everything last night. Privacy settings on my social media were restricted to my friends only. I haven't been tagged in any photos since I got here. No one but me can view my location history. I've now deactivated my accounts." Hopefully, that wasn't too little, too late.

The colonel nodded, seemingly impressed.

"Can you talk to my fiancée and get her to understand the importance of privacy regarding military security?" AJ sounded so serious she turned around and saw his expression matched his tone.

Part of her awareness was Eric's influence, combined with not having an active social life recently—other than Mack, which neither of them was sharing.

"Her phone's"—Mack hesitated—"GPS locator is off as

well. Even if they did get her number, they shouldn't be able to track it."

"I'd rather err on the side of caution. Porter, check it for shadow programs. You'll need to get a new phone and number. Only give that number to the chief, as needed for work, and absolutely necessary family members."

She breathed easier when no one questioned Mack over knowing about her phone.

"What do we know about her being followed?"

"Both times, it was around the airfield, and she was able to lose them." Mack spoke up when Kristie didn't answer right away. "She's been following evasive security protocol, so we don't think they've tracked her to the Chief's or had access to her car, which Vincenti and I dissected already. It's clean."

Scumbag Sheehan following her that day may have saved her life. She might have to send him a thank-you—if she could think of the perfect thanks-for-being-an-asshat gift.

"Herrera is rich enough *and* crazy enough to think he can take out a Spec Ops team, but this isn't Colombia. His men are on our turf. His problem is he's got to find out who you are." The colonel studied the assembled men.

"We can't rule out that they've used another vehicle or that there could be more than the two men she's seen," Ray added.

"We do know they would recognize her vehicle, though," Mack brought up.

"If we want to change out vehicles, she can drive my SUV. I can ride my Harley," Tony offered.

"We could keep switching it up. She can use my car or my Jeep in the rotation," Devin chimed in.

"How many vehicles do you have, Grant?" Juan asked so loudly that everyone looked in Devin's direction.

Devin shrugged, though he dropped his gaze to the table.

"He also rides that sweet Ducati." Tony stared at Devin with narrowed eyes. "Trust fund, or you hit the lottery? Don't make me think you're linked to some cartel."

"I … got a little inheritance," Devin mumbled. "Can we, uh …?"

"Boy Scout, you buy beer for the next team get-together. The good stuff." Ray grinned. "Now, let's get back to business.

"We could take turns being her Uber," Juan suggested. "Different person, different car every day. That'd make it tough to pick her out."

"Even if we put her in a different vehicle, they could recognize her, and it could tip them off we're aware they're following her," Mack countered, playing devil's advocate.

Kristie felt the walls starting to close in on her freedom. Worse, these guys tended to think they were invincible and didn't see the flaw in their plan. "He's right. Having me spotted with any of you will put the entire team at risk."

"You have a point," the colonel agreed. "We don't want to make you a target, but we need to stick to the status quo to have a shot at intercepting Herrera's men."

"I'll install a security camera in her car that's motion-acti-vated," Tony said. "Run it manually while you're driving or if you see anything suspicious. If anyone approaches your car when it's parked, we'll get an automatic notification and pictures to work from. Probably a good idea to put cameras on your street, too, Chief—in case they did follow her there."

Heads bobbed as the plan began to come together.

The colonel fixed his gaze on her. "I want you armed at all times, and it wouldn't hurt to spend time on the shooting range. While you've been through SERE school, it would be a good idea for refreshers with the team. Start with defensive driving. The chief can make a list and come up with a schedule that works with yours."

She didn't see how this would put an end to the threat. "If you do catch them, what then? What's to keep Herrera from sending more people to try to get to me, then get to you?"

"We use them to find out where Herrera is," Ray declared.

These guys were boots on the ground. Used to taking the fight to the enemy. If they were Air Force and could determine the right location to call in an airstrike, that'd be one thing, but Ray meant the team going down to take out Herrera. Despite their skills and training, the lopsided battle sent an unsettling feeling straight through Kristie's body into her bones.

She tried to pull back to view the situation from a different angle. There had to be another way to keep Herrera from getting to her to learn the identities of these men without putting their lives in jeopardy.

THIRTY-TWO

KRISTIE HESITATED. With Colonel Ball's head down, it wasn't too late for her to keep walking past his office. Instead, she raised a leaden arm and knocked on the open door, committing herself.

"Donovan, come on in. Colonel Mahinis brought me up to speed on your situation." He shook his head in a disbelieving manner. "Whatever you need, time off, set your own schedule, you let me know."

His accommodation made this harder. "I'd like to run something past you. Get perspective from someone not personally involved in, um, this mess."

"Of course." He pointed to the chairs across from his desk and assumed an authoritative posture.

"The current plan is for Bravo Team to escort me to and from post to the airfield. Keep me safe until they identify my tails. Then turn the tables on them."

"Mahinis shared that."

"We know Herrera has two men here, but it could easily be more, as well as vehicles that I'm unaware of. These guys pose a risk to *my* team."

"Or *anyone* at the airfield, if they tried something here," Colonel Ball stated in a mundanely matter-of-fact manner.

Her stomach twisted into a tight knot. She'd been fixated on Ray's team. Their families. Herself. But Colonel Ball was right. There was nothing to keep Herrera's men from trying to get to her here. It was the one place they knew she'd be. "If you'd prefer not to take the risk of my reporting for duty, I can use my accrued leave …"

"I've already planned to increase security, but I'll run it past Mahinis. He's confident they can protect you. Now, if you have concerns about your safety, we'll reevaluate, but if we do that, it'll disrupt the Special Ops team's plan. Hopefully, they'll identify and intercept your tail. If their plan works, it could lead them to Herrera."

"I'm concerned the men tailing me might catch on and be able to identify the team—who are their main target. Herrera could send more people." Then came the part she didn't like. "If any of his guys went MIA, it gives Herrera a heads-up they may be coming."

"And he'll have the home-field advantage if our guys go there," the colonel agreed.

"Bravo Team knows they aren't invincible, but this threat extends to their families. They won't play it safe to keep them safe." Which is why she needed someone unbiased to reaffirm her decision. "They're still gathering intel, but right now, it looks like Herrera doesn't know about the injured operator. Which means *I'm* the only connection he can make to them."

"What are you thinking?"

"If I'm not in the equation, Herrera has nothing."

Colonel Ball leaned back in his chair. His brows furrowed as he studied her.

"I'm asking for a transfer."

"But—"

"I know I just got here. If I join a unit that's deployed though, Herrera can't get to me or get any useful information from me."

His eyes widened. "True. It'd be next to impossible to find you or access a base there. You can't stay deployed forever, though."

"No, but it would give us all more time to come up with options for security. Herrera would have to find where I'm based next—since I wouldn't come back here." As hard as she tried to sound committed, her voice quivered.

If only Colonel Ball had detected some fallacy in her plan to keep her, the Special Operations team, and their families safe … Something so she wouldn't have to leave Mack. Instead, he sealed her decision to press on. "If my new unit is based overseas, that'd put a lot of distance between us. Eventually, Herrera's got to give up if he doesn't get what he wants."

It'd be too late for her and Mack by then, but things with them had been a long shot anyway—even for a skilled sniper. The idea of telling him she'd made this decision choked her with dread.

"You'd still face risks that accompany a deployment."

"I'm aware." Those were better odds—for everyone.

He covered his mouth with one crooked finger and nodded. Seconds passed with nothing but silence before he dropped his fist to lightly pound on the desk. "All right. I'll have to find out which units are deployed and contact them. There may not be an opening right now, but that'll change sooner than later. I can't guarantee you'll get a MEDEVAC slot anytime soon."

"There are other ways to save lives." Starting with those personally important to her.

He nodded. "I hate to lose you. Heard how you have a

real knack with the newbies. Taking them beyond the mechanics of flying. I was looking forward to flying with you myself."

Her heart broke even more. She'd managed to both impress and disappoint her tough commanding officer in a matter of weeks. Worse, she was giving up her shot at love again *and* indefinitely postponing her dream job, all because of a drug lord bent on vengeance.

THIRTY-THREE

MACK EXECUTED a complete surveillance pass around the perimeter of the airfield. He wished Kristie had been able to confirm the make and model of her previous tail, but they'd narrowed it down to four models.

Neither of the two black SUVs he'd passed was the right make. He still checked out *every* dark SUV and looked for any car, truck, van, or motorcycle idling on the roads near the airfield or people walking close to the security fence around it.

If Tony was right, Herrera's minions probably bought a vehicle for a few grand at one of the hundred used-car dealers in the area. There were too damn many to check that might have sold a black SUV recently. By now, they could have traded or bought another if they thought she'd picked up on them tailing her.

He texted Kristie to let her know he was in position for tonight's escort across post to their training compound. She texted right back.

He waited until he saw her passing through the security gate, then led her for the first mile. When she pulled alongside him at a stoplight, he ignored her idling next to him. From a safe distance, he followed, constantly scrutinizing the area around them as thoroughly as a mission in Afghanistan. He hadn't spotted any suspicious vehicles when she drove through the gate to post, and it pissed him off. He wanted to end this. To know Kristie was safe. To know his girls were safe.

It'd also help get things back on solid ground with Kristie. It had only been a few days since she'd moved to the inn, but she wouldn't come to his house now. She had a point. It'd be reckless to give Herrera's men any opportunity to link them. He had to put Amber and Darcy's safety over his desires.

But Kristie staying at the Landmark Inn totally sucked since she wouldn't risk that he'd be seen going to her room, either. He would get to spend time with her tonight while he assisted Vincenti with her survival training session, and maybe convince her to hang out afterward—without Vincenti around.

They parked outside the command post and headed in side by side. Unfortunately, there were too many people around for him to do more than act as a bodyguard. No holding hands, kissing, or even asking how she was.

"Is there a place we can talk privately for a few minutes before you leave?" she asked before they got to the building.

Maybe she *was* thinking along the same lines as him. "I'm staying to help with tonight's training. We can, uh, talk afterward."

"That'd be better. Then we won't keep Tony waiting."

"Sounds like a good plan," he said, though the tone of her voice hadn't conveyed the same message as his thoughts. Still, he brushed his fingertips along her back when he held open the door for her.

INSIDE THE COMMAND POST, Mack led her to a different conference room this time. One marked BRAVO TEAM.

Whoa. Most of Mack's team stood around. Good thing she hadn't told him yet about her decision to transfer and deploy. She had to tell him, but he'd need time to process it before she broke the news to Ray and the others. She didn't expect Mack to lay down his arms because she essentially conceded this battle to prevent Herrera from winning the war. Not when their relationship became collateral damage.

"What'd I miss?" Mack asked, glancing around at his team.

"Not much," Ray said. "Only news from Intel is they managed to wipe all information on Hunter from the hospital's records. It doesn't sound like anybody's asked about him there, and even if they had, Hunter is a common enough name that he'd be difficult to track down. Rozanski's calling Hunter to let him know, but the plan is for him and his family to stay at the cabin for now."

While Ray talked, she took in the personal touches in the room, from the few team pictures on the wall to the folded American flags on the shelves with notes tucked in the ends. She paused on a boonie hat with a bullet hole through the brim. A shiver shook her body before she tore her gaze away to rove over other mementos from missions she'd never hear about. Missions no one outside this room would ever hear about.

Juan ambled over to her. "Get to practice any of those evasive driving maneuvers on the way in?"

"Not tonight. Mack was the only one following me."

"I'm telling y'all, she's as badass behind the wheel as she is in the air," Juan announced to the room.

She didn't know how to interpret that. "Thanks, I guess."

"It's definitely a compliment. Looking forward to the defensive part next week."

She didn't want to waste their time. She should tell them about the pending change of station. But it could take weeks. Better to do all she could to stay safe until she knew about a transfer—and tell Mack first.

"You need me to help with whatever you guys are doing tonight?" Juan offered.

"Nooo!" Tony said with a near growl. "She's got enough to deal with without you hitting on her."

"Hey. I haven't done or said—"

"Yet," Tony talked over Juan.

"We know your MO, Dominguez," Porter said, laughing.

"Juan was all business." Kristie knew enough about team dynamics to get that sometimes the men didn't click on a personal level, but they came together to get the job done. Tony and Juan clearly butted heads—a lot like real brothers.

The other night, one-on-one in the car, Juan was professional and focused on imparting safety skills. No wisecracks or come-ons. She'd bet there was more to the guy than the player persona Juan projected.

The room went to total silence before the dubious men erupted in laughter. Mack didn't laugh; instead, he stared hard at her.

She tilted her head at him. *Really?*

He shrugged bashfully before speaking up. "Thanks for offering, but I'm helping Vincenti with tonight's SERE training."

Ray shifted his gaze from Mack to Tony, then over to her. "I told the colonel someone would be here if he got an update. I'll, uh, text him to pass anything on to you.

Dismissed." He gave a wave of the hand and herded the rest of the team from the room.

"Let's get started. Empty your backpack," Tony ordered.

So much for easing into it. Kristie looked to Mack for support.

"Impress him," he said.

She unloaded the contents onto the table.

Tony inspected each item. "Good." He loaded the water bottle and two energy bars back inside. He flipped over the gallon-sized storage baggie. "What's this?"

"T-shirt, shorts, and flops."

A huge grin spread across Tony's face. "Quick change?"

"There's more than one kind of camouflage."

"If you weren't seeing my best friend, I'd so ask you out. *Don't* tell Dominguez I said that. I have something to add." He rummaged inside his own pack, then pulled out a package. "This is a wig. I went with black hair and bangs. Figured it'd be less likely to catch the eyes of the guys following you. You can try it on later." He winked, though she wasn't sure if it was at her or Mack.

"This looks like a regular key fob, but it's actually a GPS tracker." He showed her the small black device. "Range isn't great, though."

"I've got Porter working on something more discreet she can keep on her," Mack interjected.

"Great." Tony picked up her keys to add the tracker and checked the label on her pepper spray. "Keys should be in your hand whenever you're outside. This spray is good, but this one's better." He changed out the canister attached to her keychain. "You know how to use this?"

"Spray it in their face."

"Grip it in your palm and use your thumb to depress the trigger. It's got a range of about ten feet. Aim right for their eyes. There's enough for like twenty sprays, so coat them good then move aside. They won't be able to see clearly for thirty minutes and will have trouble breathing immediately, so get the hell away."

"Yes, sir."

He gave her a side-glance. "Let's get started with the fun stuff." He produced a roll of duct tape from his pack. "Go ahead and take off your boots."

She swallowed. What the hell was coming now?

"You right-handed?"

She nodded, and Tony reached for her left boot once she tugged it off. He proceeded to wrap the duct tape around a razor blade, then took another piece to secure the blade to the arch inside her boot. "That'll cut through rope, plastic ties, and can be used as a weapon. And we have a paracord bracelet—with …" He unfastened it with dramatic flair and pulled a small key from the clasp. "You know what this is?"

What felt like an arctic chill wrapped around her body. "A handcuff key."

"Yup. Just in case. And the paracord can be used if you have to saw through duct tape or plastic flex-cuffs. We'll change out your laces for paracord, too," he said as if this was routine thinking.

Mack took both boots and the tan laces Tony handed him.

"Here. This patch is thermal reflective. We can see heat signatures, but this will identify you as a friendly even from a mile high."

She replaced the current camouflage flag patch on her sleeve with this new one. While aviators used FLIR technology to identify friendlies in all weather conditions, they didn't typically need to be identified in the dark. This role reversal opened her eyes to a more sinister worldview.

Tony gave her a critical once-over. "Turn around." She turned for him. "Let me have your hair-clip thing."

She removed the barrette securing her braid and handed it to him.

"This should work. Grab me some Gorilla glue."

Mack hustled out of the conference room while Tony measured off a piece of glint tape the length of the barrette. He took the tube of glue Mack brought back and coated the top of the barrette, then carefully placed the tape on top of the plastic.

"We'll trim the tape once it's dry, and you'll have a new fashion-accessory identifier like the patch for when you aren't in uniform." He sounded pleased with himself. "Next, we're going to teach you how to get out of tape or flex-cuffs if you don't have access to that razor blade. Mack'll demonstrate." He spun a chair out into the open space. "People don't typically carry around rope, which takes longer to use. Fortunately, most people also don't know how easy duct tape is to get out of."

Mack sat, and Tony wrapped him with tape, first binding his wrists around the chair arms, then his trunk to the back of the chair, and lastly, his ankles. This should be good.

"Jerk your arms up like a gorilla beating on its chest." The tape ripped like it was paper. "Then lean back and give a quick jerk of your torso toward your lap."

Mack did just that, making it look super easy.

"Whoa." Mental note: duct tape worked to fix an aircraft, not to secure a person.

Grinning, Mack wadded the ripped strands of tape into a ball and tossed it at Tony. "For my feet, all I have to do is stand. Put my hands together and then shove them down between my knees. It'll force my legs apart and break the tape. Like this."

With one swift motion, he broke the tape, and his legs were free.

Okay, that was pretty damn hot, especially the way the long-sleeved combat shirt hugged every inch of muscle on his arms and chest. Way sexier than the standard camouflage jacket.

"You want to show her the hands?" he asked Tony.

"Let her try this one." He tossed the roll of tape to Mack. "She's your girlfriend. You can do the honors." Insinuation dripped from Tony's voice as if he'd read her thoughts.

Mack cleared his throat but couldn't keep the suggestive grin off his face as he sauntered over to her. "Vincenti hates having the hairs ripped out of his arms. For your hands, it's a slightly different technique. Hands together. You want to let them make it tight." He tugged her uniform sleeves down before he wrapped the duct tape around her wrists. Then around again and a third time. "And one more time for good measure."

The intensity in his eyes before he finished inspired all kinds of lascivious thoughts.

"You gotta raise your arms above your head as high as you can."

Images of him backing her against a wall filled her mind as she complied. Only instead of moving closer, he backed away. She didn't dare look in Tony's direction.

"Next, you'll jerk your arms down against your ribcage. Hard. Go ahead and try it."

She inhaled, closed her eyes, and pulled her arms down as hard and fast as she could. *Boom!* The tape ripped and hung from her left wrist. "Wow!" That was even more empowering than the evasive-driving lessons with Juan and AJ.

"See? No sweat." Tony beamed. "Next up, flex-cuffs. Flip you for your choice."

"Fine," Mack sighed out.

Tony chuckled and produced a coin. "Call it."

"Heads."

Tony flipped the coin just short of hitting the ceiling, snatched it out of the air, then slapped it onto the back of his left hand. "Tails. *I* get to use the paracord. Look at it as getting to show off for your lady." He slipped his hands into a pair of flex-cuffs.

"Should make you do it from behind your back." Mack crossed his arms over his chest.

"I can." Tony sat in one of the chairs. "But we'll save that for next time. For this, you want to clench your fists when they tighten the cuffs."

Mack did the deed, pulling the plastic tight.

"That'll give you more flexibility to make the friction saw." Tony leaned over to untie one of his combat boots. With his limited range of motion, it took a few minutes to get the paracord lace free from the hooks and eyes and pulled out. "Then, you want to make slipknots on both ends."

Mack handed her a length of paracord and kept one for himself. He walked her through the simple steps of making a slipknot. Easy-peasy. At least with two free hands.

After Tony managed to tie slipknots in both ends, he slipped one over the toe box of his left boot. "Hook one end over, then work the cord through the cuffs." He pulled the loop through with his teeth. "That'll make it easier. Hook the second slipknot over the other boot. Pull your hands up and bicycle your legs."

It took a few seconds for the plastic to snap, freeing his hands. "It'll work on rope, too. Either cut through or loosen it enough to slip your hands free."

Her head began to swim with invincibility.

"We'll wrap up with another way to get out of the flex-cuffs. If time is a factor, this is way faster."

"But more painful." Mack picked up another pair of thick plastic cuffs. "But pain that gains your freedom is worth it."

Tony secured Mack's wrists until he winced. "You want 'em tight as you can get 'em. Do the same maneuver as with the tape. Show her."

Mack took a deep breath. Then a second one as he raised his arms over his head. Her gaze took in every single movement and muscle twitch. His arms moved in a blur of high-speed motion. The cuffs flew to the floor, bouncing a few feet away.

She'd never wanted—no, needed—to be with a man more. This man. Now. Well, not *exactly* now.

Mack rubbed the red marks on his wrists. She took his hands in hers, rubbed her thumb ever so lightly over the welts forming. He stared into her eyes when she raised his hands to touch her lips to one, then the other wrist.

"I'm out of here for tonight. You two can clean up the supplies." Tony picked up his pack, swung it over his shoulder, and headed to the door without looking back.

Mack waited for the door to click shut, then turned his heated gaze to her mouth.

"Did you, uh, want to go somewhere private to—*talk*?"

Talking was *not* what she had in mind anymore. "Does that door lock?"

Mack's rumbling snicker amplified the heat low in her abdomen. "Of course. And Vincenti kinda locked it on his way out."

Good. "You sure he won't say anything?" With all Tony's innuendo, all she needed was him slipping up.

"Trust me, if anyone is a master of situational discretion and can keep a secret, it's Tony Vincenti."

Her slight nod was all it took. His mouth was on hers. Hard. Desperate. Possessive. She kissed him back just as hard. Just as desperate. He gripped her hips and held her body tight against his. Her fingers burrowed into the hair at the back of his head, and her other arm wrapped around his torso to get closer.

The kisses deepened, their tongues delving in to taste and caress. Had it only been days since they'd been together? When his mouth finally left hers, it was for her neck. Totally her weak spot—and he knew it. She ground back against his body, already aching with need.

When he went for the button on her pants, she stopped him. Though she did dangerous, she didn't do stupid. "You sure the door's locked, and everyone's gone?"

"Team is long gone," he assured her, keeping his hands still, waiting for her permission to proceed.

Leaving to go someplace safe to be together would kill the mood. Her conscience accused her of using him for sex by not telling him she'd be leaving soon, but reducing their relationship to sex might make it easier when the time came for them to end things. Oh, hell. She tugged at his shirt, pulling it free.

He helped by unfastening his belt and unbuttoning his pants. "Let me." He crossed his arms and took hold of the snug combat shirt and pulled it off.

If Mack was half dressed, it was only fair if she ditched her uniform top. Velcro ripping apart sounded overly loud. As soon as she shrugged out of the jacket, he pulled her back for another consuming kiss.

His fingers traced down her sides, skimming the curve of her breasts. They slipped under her waistband and gripped her T-shirt, working it free, then up and off.

As if he'd read her mind earlier, he maneuvered her back

until she was flush against the wall. He separated their bodies enough for him to unbutton her pants and work them down her thighs. They dropped, and with her boots already off, she kicked them away. No backing out now.

Gliding his hands up her body, he raised her arms over her head and pinned them there with one hand. She inhaled the woodsy scent of him as he held her against the wall, kissing her senseless while his arousal pressed hard against her. Their bodies were damp from the earlier exertion and the heat building between them.

He slipped a hand inside her panties. His thumb stroked her in exactly the right place, eliciting a needful moan.

"More," she rasped out the plea.

He responded by inserting two fingers, still teasing her with his thumb. She pressed against the wall to ride his hand, already near the brink. "I need you. Inside me," she panted.

Like a good soldier, he followed orders. He tortured her, rubbing his length against her with tantalizing slowness. She raised one leg until her knee rested beside his hip. His tip teased in, then out. Again. And a third time. Her leg wrapped around his bottom, giving him full access and her leverage as she freed a hand and brought it down to cradle his head. She nipped his ear before she kissed him fiercely.

Foreplay was over.

He reached down, locked his arms around the back of her thighs, and lifted her off the ground. She draped both legs over his hips and slid down, moaning as he buried himself inside her, then gasping with each powerful, upward thrust. It wasn't the kind of sex meant to last long. This was going to be fast, hard, hot, and kinda rough and dirty. Which was working for her.

As she got closer, her calf muscles quivered, and her body tightened around him. He was in tune with her and slowed the pace, nearly pulling out and holding for a moment before plunging back inside deep and hard. His arm under her buttocks added to the force. A few more times was all it took. She held him tight as she came. Neither of them could breathe, which heightened the pleasure when he came, too. She didn't count how many times she clenched before her body went limp, and her head dropped to his shoulder.

He cradled her against him, keeping their bodies joined as he kissed her cheek, her temple, then rubbed his cheek against hers. Her labored breathing came easier, and tension returned to her limbs. Her legs slipped from their locked position and slid down his thighs to the floor. He edged his hips back, reluctantly pulling out.

She spotted their clothes strewn around them. "We should probably get dressed."

"We don't let anyone, not even a cleaning crew, come in here. Oh …" He made a face, removed the condom, then looked around the room. Once he got his pants up, he grabbed the torn pieces of duct tape and wrapped them around the used condom. "Problem solved." He dropped it in the trash.

He cast her a hopeful look as they finished dressing. "I was planning to see if you wanted to go somewhere tonight. A hotel or even pitch a tent. I—I want to wake up with you in the morning."

"Can't very well do that here." His sweet words reminded her of all they might have had—and now wouldn't.

She sat to lace her boots with the paracord. It might be one of their last chances to spend the night together. It could also give her the opportunity to break the news. Which would be a buzzkill, and probably not the best idea. Besides, what if they got caught? Like a coward, she went back and forth, unable to commit as he cleaned up the supplies used in tonight's lesson.

"We can pick up something to eat. Where to go is the question. We could leave your—"

The doorknob rattled. Kristie's heart jumped. Mack whipped his head toward the door, to her, then back to the door. Keys jangled on the other side. He turned his hands up in a what-do-we-do gesture like she'd know.

A quick check that clothing was in place, other than her boots and jacket, dialed her pulse back a notch or two as Mack rushed to the door and opened it.

"Oh, you are still here." Colonel Mahinis strode in carrying a file folder and wearing a perplexed expression. "Where's Vincenti?"

"He had to bolt after we finished showing Chief Donovan escape techniques. We were cleanin' up and changing out paracord for her laces. You get some intel?"

Though Mack sounded remarkably casual, she bent over to pull on the boots to avoid eye contact with the colonel.

"Nothing major, but I fly up to D.C. in the morning and wanted to leave this for Chief Lundgren." The colonel handed the file to Mack. "The DEA has an agent undercover in the Cauca area. Buzz there is Herrera's men have significantly kicked up recruiting protection forces, and there's talk of them setting up actual training."

"Training them to use an AK-47 versus handing over a weapon and wishing them luck?"

The way the colonel cocked his head and puckered his mouth made goosebumps break out on Kristie's arms. "You don't think they'd come here, do you?"

"At this point, we don't know what his plans are." His noncommittal tone fed the fear in Kristie's gut. "I assure you we'll do everything in our considerable power to protect you. We're in this for as long as it takes. Herrera may have resources, but he's due for more bad karma. I'll let the chief know if I get more intel from my contact at the DEA."

He moved to the door. "If you're done for the night, I'll walk out with you. I appreciate you sacrificing your time to work with my men. I recognize it's not how you want to spend your time, but it's what we need to keep you, them, and their families safe."

Safe. If only there were a way to ensure they could all be safe from Herrera beside her deploying halfway around the world. What the colonel had shared did absolutely nothing to give her hope.

THIRTY-FOUR

LATE MONDAY AFTERNOON, Mack hung out in the conference room, shooting the bull with Vincenti after a long day of training. He'd refrained, barely, from telling Dominguez he'd drive over to the airfield to serve as Kristie's escort. She'd texted earlier that she needed to talk to him tonight, but it would have to wait until later. His buddies knew him too well, and showing an extra interest in her could raise their suspicions. He wasn't a hundred-percent sure Colonel Mahinis bought their innocent act last week, and he'd only been in the room with them for a couple of minutes.

Their tryst had been on the reckless—yet oh-so-satisfying —side. If the colonel had shown up a few minutes earlier … He didn't want to think of what might have happened.

Fortunately, he hadn't, but his surprise appearance and the intel update had doused the embers still smoking in the conference room. After that, Kristie had claimed not to be hungry and used an excuse about an early schedule to shoot down his plan to spend the night together. Since he had the girls over the weekend, he was dying to lay eyes on her. He could look, even if he couldn't touch, with the entire team also in the room.

It'd been two weeks without any suspicious tailing, but they all knew better than to let their guard down, no matter how badly he wanted this wrapped up so he and Kristie could get back on track. If anything, their separation made him realize how much he wanted a real shot at a relationship with her. The past two nights after the girls went to bed, he'd worked on his Warrant Officer Candidate School application. He'd do whatever the hell it took for them to have a chance at a future together.

The moment the conference room door opened, Mack's gaze shot there. Dominguez walked in, without his usual jabber, Kristie right behind him. It only took a second for her sullen expression and the way her shoulders sagged like she'd been saddled with the weight of the world, to clue Mack in that something was off.

It didn't escape Ray's notice, either. Before Mack caved to the instinctive urge to go to her, Ray pulled Kristie aside.

What could have ... *Dominguez!* He glared at his teammate.

Dominguez froze when he caught Mack's expression. "What?" he mouthed.

Mack jerked his head toward Kristie, steam probably pouring out of his ears. "What'd you say to her?" he mouthed back.

Dominguez's mouth tightened, and he glared back as he stalked over to Mack. "All I asked was if she was ready for some fun driving tonight. She was moody from the minute she got out of her car. She's tough, but this stress could be getting to her."

Damn. Dominguez might be right. The constant prepping

for the worst contingencies had to be draining and gave her no downtime to put Herrera out of her head. As isolated as they were keeping her, she probably needed someone to talk to. Right now, he needed to dial it back a notch and figure out a way to help her deal with all this.

He edged closer to the chief, straining to listen in.

"I can't say yet." Kristie's gaze landed on Mack with a pained expression before darting away.

"If it impacts the safety of my team, then you need to tell me what is going on," Ray pressed.

"What I'm doing is for the safety of your team! And your families." The emotion and desperation in her voice sliced through Mack. "I need—" Her eyes closed, and she gave a defeated huff before her lips disappeared, and she dipped her head. When she opened her eyes, she looked at him, not Ray.

"I've asked Colonel Ball for a transfer to a—"

Transfer? The word penetrated right through his chest wall.

"If you do that, we can't protect you," Ray cut her off.

"You won't have to. I'll be deployed to Afghanistan." Sorrow filled Kristie's eyes.

Stunned silence echoed in the room.

"But what about …" *Us?* Mack swallowed down the word that turned rancid in his mouth.

"Actually, that makes a lot of sense," Tony said. "Even if Herrera's goons find out where you've gone, you're not accessible. They aren't going to hang around waiting until you come back. Or—" He paused, and Mack wanted to tell his friend to shut the fuck up, but the words kept pouring out. "Would you come back?"

Fear crawled up Mack's spine like some insidious insect.

"A unit out of Wiesbaden has a pilot who needs to go

home due to a family emergency. I'll be taking his place. And"—she paused, exhaling audibly—"I will stay with that unit after their tour of duty."

She'd been planning this, yet she hadn't said anything, *anything,* to him? No, she had *tried* to tell him. That's what she'd wanted to talk about. And she made the decision without him. A temporary separation was one thing—hell, it was an expected part of military life—but Germany was halfway around the freaking world. Mack's hope for them to have a future slipped through his fingers like mist.

"This way, you all will be safe. Your wives, your sons, and your daughters will be safe." Kristie scanned the faces as she spoke, landing on Mack as she drove her point home. "Eventually, Herrera has to give up, and I'll be safe."

It made nearly perfect sense. Still, thoughts ricocheted inside his skull as he chased after any alternate way to keep from surrendering her.

"When would you leave?" Ray's voice sounded raw.

"My pre-deployment checklist is pretty short. Nothing's changed since last time. I figure with completing the paperwork and arranging travel, it'll be about a week, maybe ten days, before I ship out."

"Until then, we're going to continue like nothing's changed. We're staying on task with the defensive driving tonight. Time on the range later this week," Ray declared.

Oh, this wasn't a done deal yet. Mack rallied and shifted to battle mode. They couldn't do it here or now, but they would talk this through.

———

TONIGHT'S defensive driving was dangerous yet exhilarating. It helped expel her frustration, but after two hours, Kristie's body was drained of energy, and her stomach was still sick from blindsiding Mack with the news. Somehow, she'd held it together and not broken down into tears at the look on his face.

Both AJ and Juan walked with her to the parking lot. Her feet dragged, and her energy level took another hit when she spied Mack's truck next to her car. Had he been waiting this whole time?

He got out as they approached.

"Thought I was escorting her home," AJ said.

"No. I got this. Need to give her the tracker Porter put together," Mack said, his expression unreadable.

"Thanks, man." AJ gave her a farewell salute and detoured to his car.

Mack blocked her access to the driver-side door; she didn't even attempt to get in. She'd seen this coming.

"We need to talk."

"I know," she responded. "I wanted to tell you first. I tried, bu—"

"How can you make a decision like this without consulting me?"

She went from resigned to defensive in one second flat. "Because you'd have tried to talk me out of it. You're too damn close to the situation. You're looking at it from the perspective that you *have to* go to war with Herrera. This is a battle you *don't* have to fight. Sometimes it's better to walk away and avoid the carnage."

"You're walking away from *us*!"

"Do you think I want to? I don't. But I have to face reality, Mack. Things working out for us was a long shot from the get-go. If something happened to Amber or Darcy because of this, I'd never forgive myself. You'd never forgive yourself. Or me. We'd never be able to overcome that." She took his hand. To hell with it, if anyone saw. This was the end anyway. "This sucks, and it's not fair, but it's the best alternative for everyone." *Everyone else.*

His face scrunched in emotional turmoil, hopefully accepting what had to be. "But what if we get Herrera—?"

"What if you don't? Or someone dies?" She couldn't let him sway her with false hope.

"This doesn't have to be the end. At some point, the law or a competing cartel will bring down Herrera."

She gave an agreeable nod. "Eventually, yes. There'd still be the rank issue, and"—she kept going when he tried to interrupt—"I don't know that I'll ever get over my fears about what you do and what could happen to you. These past two weeks, getting an inside look at what you face with every mission ... I swore I'd never get involved with someone in Special Ops again, but damn if you didn't make me fall for you." Her voice broke along with the dam holding back her tears.

She'd begun to believe they had a chance. Losing Mack and the girls hurt almost as much as losing Eric. It would get worse if she didn't end things now. It wouldn't be fair to any of them to put their lives on hold indefinitely. He could easily find a woman to share his life with. One without her complications, who could commit and wouldn't put his daughters' lives in jeopardy.

He pulled her into his arms. "This feels like getting the shit kicked out of us."

"At least we live to fight another day." The cliché didn't stop her heart from shattering. Part of her didn't want to go on without him. However, this would not kill her; Herrera would. The prolonged torture would fade. Once she deployed, she'd stay too busy to grieve. The distance would give her the perspective to accept they weren't meant to be.

She summoned her resolve and eased out of his hold. The car beeped when she unlocked the doors. "You're still stuck with escort duty."

"To the Landmark Inn? I need to come up with you tonight."

"You can't."

A range of emotions flashed across his face. Anger. Frustration. Resignation. Sadness. Determination.

He took a small box out of his pants pocket. The kind used for jewelry. "Here. This is what I need to give you."

"What is it?" She couldn't take it from him.

He shook his head with a clearly exasperated sigh. "The GPS tracker Porter made for you."

She accepted the box, surprised when a wave of disappointment rocked her. She opened the top. A belly button ring? "Really?"

"It's something no one will see. You can wear it all the time."

"It's a tracker?" The pretty floral design was larger than most she'd seen.

"Yes." He took it from the box, then flipped it over. "Because of the size, it doesn't have a long battery life or huge range, so only turn it on if you need to. You do that by turning the flower part. It'll send a notification of your location."

"To who?"

"Me, but only if you activate it. I won't be stalking you." He held eye contact with her. "I'd appreciate it if you'd put it on tonight to test it. Get familiar with how it works. Guess I won't be there to, uh, show you how."

She dropped her gaze from his hopeful one. If he came to her room, her resolve would collapse like a sandcastle when the tide rolled in. "No, but I will test it out," she promised before getting into her car.

The slump of Mack's shoulders as he walked around to his truck gave her the impression of a soldier coming back from a lost battle. Except there'd been *no* winners in this fight.

THIRTY-FIVE

Kristie pulled behind the line of cars at the security checkpoint to get on base. In her rearview mirror, AJ Rozanski flashed his Mustang's brights and continued on. She waved thanks to tonight's unlucky escort. Once she reached the inn, she followed orders and searched for a spot to park near a working light.

She turned off the engine and sat there. An empty room hardly motivated her to rush. Isolation had already set in. If she wasn't at work, where she got to talk with others, she pretty much lived in her room. Things would be better once she deployed and could interact normally. But she still wouldn't be with Mack. Each heartbeat echoed in her hollow chest.

Over the weekend, she'd met her family for dinner to break the news about her plans to deploy. That meant giving them enough of an explanation to keep them safe without breaking operational security protocols. When would she see them again?

In addition to the rotation of her shift messing with her body clock, being overly cautious all the time was exhausting. Even with her escorts, she was watching her back, checking out cars and faces wherever she went. Each time she caught a glimpse of the tracker she wore or attached to her keyring, it reminded her to be vigilant.

She scanned the lot. When two uniformed soldiers made their way down the aisle of cars to the building's entrance, she got out. Ahead of her, a man in a wheelchair rolled toward the door, too. He muttered when a bag of groceries slid off his lap to the ground, and oranges scattered in different directions. Kristie scooped up the two that wound up in the grass.

"I can get it," he mumbled and clumsily maneuvered the chair when she chased after another orange.

The streak of pain in her lower back came from nowhere. Her knees gave way as pain crashed through her body. A strong arm wrapped around her middle in time to prevent her from collapsing to the ground.

Who? What was happening? Another shock tortured her every nerve.

Instead of a cry, she gurgled out a strangled noise. Somehow she ended up in the wheelchair, and the man previously in it, stood beside her. *How?* He quickly pushed the chair away from the building. Though too disoriented to speak, Kristie comprehended enough to panic, yet her body refused her mental commands.

The side door of the minivan parked in a handicapped spot banged open, revealing a thin, young, dark-haired man waiting inside. She was manhandled out of the chair and into the van before the door slammed closed.

The young guy hunkered into the space between the captain's chairs. Kristie managed to twitch her arm, but he brought her hands together and secured them with a zip tie. Though it took superhuman effort to hold her head up after the shocks from the stun gun, she craned her neck in search of help. The soldiers she was following had disappeared inside the building, and no one else was in sight. She tried to yell again, only *"Help!"* sounded like a low, awkward laugh.

By the time he buckled her in, the heavier of the two had shoved the wheelchair toward the building and climbed into the driver's seat.

How the hell had they gotten on post? Then she saw the base sticker on the windshield. That'd do the trick.

Two crayons lay on the van's floor, and sunshields were over the middle-row windows. An air freshener was clipped to a vent. Had to be a family's van, either stolen to get on base or after the men somehow sneaked in. What were the chances it'd been reported stolen, and they'd get stopped leaving post?

She wanted to kick herself for letting her guard down and falling for their ruse. Mack was going to kill her—if she survived. *Please don't let them blame AJ.*

When she got a good look at the young thug, she recognized him as the driver of the black SUV she'd seen that day near the airfield. Once he had her bound, he emptied her pockets of her keys—with the whistle and pepper spray and wireless key tracker. He said something as he passed them to the driver, who took one look and chucked them out the window.

Patting her down, he took advantage of her limited mobility, his hands touching places that would normally earn him a knee in the groin. Instead, she stared through him rather than give him any satisfaction from dominating her.

She needed to stay strong.

Working his way along her legs, he found her phone in her right thigh pocket. He checked the screen, then tossed the phone onto the other seat. *Please stop now. Please stop there. Please stop. Shit.*

Just above her ankle, his hand froze on the concealed holster Ray and Mack insisted on. He pushed up her pant leg and confiscated what could have been her saving grace. His mouth curled into a victorious smile. She bit down, so she didn't spit in his face. Her chances of escaping dropped like a two-ton bomb.

The man took his seat, and as the van neared the base's exit, she had to try something. Anything.

The guards only checked vehicles coming in. But if she could open the door? Roll out? The guards had M-4s. In a firefight, she could end up dead, but if she didn't escape these two, the possibility she'd die was greater. Slowly. Painfully. And put others at risk. She had to try.

With her arms pressed tight against her body, she strained to reach the seatbelt release discreetly. Her fingers brushed over the buckle. *Almost there. A lit—*

Her body slumped sideways. The shock lasted longer this time. Her teeth gnashed together, and her vision blurred as her eyes teared from the pain. Things came slowly into focus —outside the gate.

Too late. Too late.

To keep from hyperventilating, she lowered her head and drew in slow, deep breaths. *Think.* Her addled brain couldn't lock onto Plan B between the effects of the shocks and choking despair.

Keep it together. Keep it together. Be strong. This isn't over.

Her mind started firing again. All she needed was a few minutes alone to get out of the ties and activate the belly-button-ring tracker. God bless Mack's overprotective heart. But she didn't reach to activate it. No, she'd learned her lesson. Wait for the right time. Keep her wits, and don't give anything away.

The men remained silent, which added to the tension coiled around Kristie. She lost track of their location the farther they drove from base and outside the city. It didn't matter. Once she got a signal out, Mack and the team would find her. Until then, she'd rely on her SERE training and stall as best she could. She'd failed to evade, but she could still survive. Could look for opportunities to escape. And she would sure as hell resist giving them any useful information.

After about twenty minutes, the van turned off at a dark, one-story clapboard house set back from the road. There were a few houses spread out along the rural road, but no one close enough to see them park behind the house, beside the dark SUV that could definitely be the vehicle that followed her. The men hauled her out and dragged her into the house.

She was led into the kitchen. The driver flicked a switch and dim light emitted from the overhead fixture. Empty food containers and take-out boxes filled a garbage bag and spread across the counter, accounting for the rank odor. A mini-fridge sat in the space allotted for a larger one, and there wasn't a table or chairs.

They passed through the kitchen into an open living area, and the young guy flung her onto the sagging sofa.

"What do you want with me?" She managed to get herself upright. "No one is going to pay a ransom. I can get you a thousand from an ATM, but my insurance money is tied up."

Confused expressions preceded a brief exchange between the men. She studied them, and they didn't give a rip that she knew what they looked like. The younger of the two had a neck tattoo, and more down his arms and hands. The driver was built like a bouncer, and a distinctive scar sliced his right eyebrow in two. If they took the bait and used her ATM card, they'd stand out to anyone viewing security footage.

"You were in Colombia," the bouncer said with a noticeable accent.

"Yes, on a training mission for Colombian pilots on the electronic instrument systems in Sikorski UH-60 Black Hawks."

He smirked at her technical description. "You, uh"—he paused and circled a hand as if searching for the right word—"pick up girl and American soldiers."

"Were they Americans?"

Bouncer backhanded her across the right cheek. "You know." He shook a finger for emphasis—as if the slap hadn't made his point.

"We got a call to pick up a group of soldiers. One was injured, so we flew them back to the base. There was a girl with them. I don't know who she was."

"Tell me where to find these soldiers."

"How would I know? I'm in aviation. We picked them up, but we weren't told anything about them or their mission."

Bouncer looked to Tattoo and gave a jerk of his head. Tattoo's blow to the side of her head knocked her sideways. Twinkling stars danced in her field of vision, and she lay there until he pulled her back upright.

"You know one. Give me name!"

"I can't tell you what I don't know." Even though she braced this time, she landed on the floor. Tattoo added a kick to her stomach. Every slap, every punch, every kick fueled her resolve not to tell them anything they could use to hurt anyone she cared about.

She curled into a ball. Her arms and hands still couldn't reach the belly button ring, but it'd serve these bastards right if they accidentally kicked it on. She managed to separate the

Velcro at the bottom of her uniform jacket before they yanked her back up to the couch.

"Tell us soldiers' names," Bouncer demanded again.

"It's over. They don't have the girl."

"They killed Juan Pablo."

"Who?"

"Herrera's son."

"Sorry to hear that." *Not.* "So, he wants revenge? How much is Herrera paying you? Because it won't be enough, and you can't spend it if you're dead. Do you think he cares whether you live or die? There's no way to tell which one killed his son. Do you two really think you can take out a whole Special Ops team? Good luck with that, because you have no idea who you'd be taking on. You might get lucky and get one. Then what? They'll be hunting *you* down. If you want to stay alive, you should take whatever money you've got and disappear. Now."

The two spoke Spanish too rapidly for her to make out more than a word or two, but the minuscule possibility they'd surrender upon realizing their odds gave her a spark of hope. Better yet, the pair stepped away to keep her from hearing.

Twisting her wrists, she went for the tracker. She hooked a thumb under the ACU uniform coat and then worked her hands underneath her T-shirt. The cuffs were so tight she couldn't maneuver her hands to get a grip on the ball end of the ring. Keeping her eyes on the men, she tried again. If she could just trap it between her pinkies and turn … Dammit!

Bouncer spoke into his phone. She slid her hands to her lap when Tattoo stood to face her, eyeing her suspiciously. They'd expect her to try to get free. It might earn her another blow or two, which she could deal with, but she could not risk tipping them off. Be patient.

"Necesito ir al baño." She added a squirm, hoping to convince them she really needed to go.

Tattoo responded to something Bouncer said, then headed to her. He grabbed her arm, jerked her up, and they escorted her to the bathroom.

Bouncer blocked the doorway. "Take uniform off."

"What?"

"Take off," Tattoo repeated. The smirky set of his mouth and hard glint in his eyes took a chunk out of the confidence she clung to.

"I can't." She held up her bound hands, praying this didn't go worst-case.

Tattoo pulled out a knife and sliced through the plastic tie. Neither man made a move to touch her. If they thought taking her clothes would keep her from trying to escape, fine, they could have her clothes. She tugged apart the front closure and shrugged out of the sleeves.

Bouncer held his position, keeping the phone to his ear. She unlaced her boots and worked them off. She unfastened her pants, let them drop, then stepped from them, pulling her T-shirt lower. If they had her strip naked, they'd see the belly button ring. Would they take it and her chance at contacting Mack?

She waited, pleading with her eyes for them to let her pass. Bouncer stared back; Tattoo swayed expectantly.

"Can I pee now?"

Bouncer's head jerked, and he stepped back. *Oh, thank God.* She brushed past him. When she went to close the door, he wedged his foot in the opening. The death glare she shot him had no impact. Stomping barefoot on his brown loafer would likely get her another bruising rather than a moment of privacy. It didn't matter. The single window was only about a foot high and over five feet from the ground, running the length of the shower.

She sank onto the toilet. *This is not over, you sons of bitches.*

The vanity shielded her from view while she twisted the ball of the belly button ring. It clicked into place, keeping her hopes from getting flushed down the virtual toilet. Relief cleared her head.

Was there anything she could use as a weapon? Soap, shampoo, toothbrush. No, no, and no. The shower rod screwed into the wall.

How long could she draw this out? Each minute would bring rescue closer.

Bouncer nudged the door to peek in. At least he was preoccupied on the phone. The rummaging noises from the other room had to be Tattoo.

Were there cleaning supplies under the sink? Doubtful, based on the grunge, but she quickly opened the cabinet to check. Toilet paper. Not helpful.

Why did they want her uniform when she clearly couldn't escape the bathroom? She washed her hands, then wet the dirty hand towel in cold water to apply to her tender and swollen cheek.

The door swung open. Tattoo thrust a pair of gym shorts at her.

Why? These thugs weren't being nice guys by giving her something to wear. No. What was their game plan? Warning sirens went off in her head. She stepped into the shorts, rolling the waistband over so they'd stay up.

When she came out, Bouncer wasn't in sight, but Tattoo took her by the arm, her boots in his other hand. Her oh-shit meter climbed another level when he slung her onto the couch.

He dropped the boots to the floor. "Put on."

The razor blade was there, within reach, but she had to get it out of the duct tape for it to serve as a weapon. Tattoo was not going to stand there while she unwrapped it. She left the blade in place, pulling on the second boot, and didn't even have the laces tightened before he crouched. He grabbed her hands and secured them together with a zip tie, tightening until it bit into flesh already raw.

Bouncer reemerged with her uniform and a black duffel bag. He nodded to Tattoo, who pulled her to her feet and steered her toward the door.

"Where are we going?" Fear forced the question out.

"Colombia." Bouncer tossed her uniform on the couch and dropped her phone atop it. His cool smile mocked her.

She took a step back—right into Tattoo, who shoved her forward.

"You can tell Señor Herrera the names." His voice dripped with confidence and malevolence.

THIRTY-SIX

MACK READ the Warrant Officer Candidate School application's essay question again, debating the safe, expected answer or digging deep. Brutal honesty to "Why I want to be an officer" wouldn't get him very far. He needed to think beyond Kristie Donovan ...

Forget it. He didn't have to finish this tonight. It'd be better to sleep on it. Talk to Ray tomorrow. He pulled up his email to send a message to Colonel Mahinis about getting the necessary endorsement. Wait. What? He clicked back to his inbox. There, in the bold letters of an unread email, was an alert about the activation of Kristie's GPS tracker.

He couldn't click fast enough. The map showed the initial location northwest of base. Even though it could be a false alarm, and despite trying to think rationally, both his heart rate and breathing accelerated. Kristie had flown tonight. Maybe in that area.

During the interminable time it took for the site to load, he snatched up his phone and dialed Kristie's number. *Come on. Come on. Pick up.* It rolled to voicemail.

He typed his password to log into the tracking software to

pinpoint her current location. An error message popped up on the website.

He was seriously about to lose his shit.

He dialed Rozanski, then retyped his password. "You have got to be fucking kidding me!" *Not. Now.* He tried a third time. Slower, thinking through his system. Capitalization, numbers, special characters. Right now, he fucking hated password security protocol.

AJ finally answered. "What's up?"

"Did you escort Kristie Donovan back from the airfield?"

"Dropped her at the gate about twenty-one thirty. Why?"

It was nearly 2330 now. "Her tracker turned on." Mack checked the email. "Almost an hour ago. She didn't clear going anywhere with you?" He switched back to the GPS screen. Thank God he was in, and it was finally loading.

"No." Alarm sounded in AJ's voice. "Where's she at?"

Mack stared at the screen. The blip on the screen showed movement. He zoomed out to place the location. Then zoomed out more and followed Kristie's path since she'd turned on the GPS.

His arms went numb, and his hands tingled. He sucked a deep draw of air and his mouth stayed dry. "Somewhere in— or over—South Carolina."

REGARDLESS OF THE lights being off, Mack pounded on Lundgren's front door. It took a minute before Ray yanked open the door, wearing a scowl that would send a normal person running.

"Herrera's got Kristie."

"What? How?" Ray snapped to full readiness and stepped back to let Mack in.

"Don't know. AJ tailed her to base. About an hour later, her tracker went off. I called, but she didn't answer."

"Could she—?" the chief started when Mack paused for a breath.

"The tracking software showed the point of origin twenty to twenty-five minutes northwest of base. An hour later, she's in South Carolina. At this speed, she's gotta be in a plane."

THIRTY-SEVEN

RAY'S PHONE RANG, cutting through the chatter in the conference room. Mack's gaze shot to the screen. Rozanski. Please let him have good news.

"What'd you find out?" Ray got down to business.

"We viewed the Landmark's surveillance video. It's not good."

Mack's heart crawled into his throat at AJ's statement.

"From what the video shows, a guy in a wheelchair tased her before she got inside. I'm sorry. I should have followed her in—"

"Now's not the time," Ray cut him off. "Continue."

"He wheeled her to a van, where he and another perp loaded her in and drove off. We got a plate number."

Ray wrote down the letters and numbers AJ read off. "Run this." He handed the info to Porter.

By the time Colonel Mahinis entered the command post, Porter had verified the van used to abduct Kristie was reported stolen from a service member's house the night before. The van's base sticker had worked to get the kidnappers on post.

Mack had vowed to keep her safe, and he'd failed. If only
—*if only what?* They couldn't hide her forever. There hadn't
even been a clear threat. Base security wasn't foolproof—
obviously—but how did these assholes know where to
find her?

Seated at his computer, talking excitedly into his phone,
Porter typed, then motioned to Ray and the colonel. Mack
beelined over, and Vincenti took up position on his other side.

"That was the guy who owns and runs a private airstrip
over toward Raeford. A Socata 850 and its pilot have been
hunkered down there for a few weeks. The pilot filed a flight
plan for Miami just tonight and took off about an hour ago.
The owner gave me the tail number, and this was its flight
path." Porter pointed to a line on the blue screen with a map
of the U.S. outlined in a darker blue.

"They still in the air, or did they land in South Carolina?"
The colonel touched where the line ended.

Porter zoomed in on the map, then shook his head. He
leaned back in his seat, huffing a sigh before raising his face.
"Doesn't look like it. No airstrips in the vicinity. My guess is
they turned off their transponder to keep from being tracked."

"These guys are no amateurs," Ray admitted.

Mack's hope they had established a home base in
Savannah and were taking Kristie there nosedived into a
death spiral. The flight path before the transponder went off
could take them to Miami, but he'd bet money that was a
decoy.

"What's the range of that type aircraft?" Mahinis asked.

"According to the manufacturer, around seventeen
hundred miles," Porter stated in under a minute.

"Colombia?" Ray looked at the colonel.

"I'm pretty damned sure of it. Herrera's not going to keep
her here. More importantly, he won't set foot on U.S. soil.

Where exactly in Colombia is the question. He shuffles between several residences. And those are just the ones the DEA knows about. That's a lot of territory."

"Can they make it without refueling?" Ray asked.

Porter talked to himself while checking the distance and calculating. "With standard fuel tanks, they might make it to the northern part of Colombia. But my money is on them needing to refuel somewhere."

"I'll run this up the chain of command to get an alert out to all U.S. airports in the Southeast. If they land to refuel, we might be able to detain them."

Detain them and Kristie could get hurt—or worse—in a confrontation. What if they didn't land? "If we locate it, could we force it down?" Mack hated both scenarios, but they beat trying to ascertain her location in Colombia when the tracker had a limited range.

"Too risky. Especially since a GPS signal doesn't prove Chief Donovan is on that plane." The colonel killed that long shot.

"We need a Plan B, because I never hit big money playing the lottery," Ray stated.

ALL EYES WERE on Colonel Mahinis when he came back into the room. "Fueling centers are on notice. We also have 7th Group assembling a team that will be airborne and headed south, ready to intercept, *if* the plane lands in south Florida or the Keys. We're proceeding with Plan B." He scanned the men's faces before locking on Lundgren's. "However, I have a call in for Alpha team."

"Two teams is a good idea. Herrera wants us to come. Only he won't be expecting us so soon."

Mahinis started talking over Ray. "You're personally involved. I think—"

"Damn right." Ray's composure slipped a notch. "Not just because we know Warrant Officer Donovan. They took her because Herrera wants *us*." He motioned to encompass the men in the room. "He'll go after *our* families."

He spoke Mack's exact thoughts. *Unless we shut him down for good.* Ray might be thinking that, too, but had the good sense not to voice it.

"I'm happy to have Alpha team along, as long as they understand one thing. This. Is. Our. Mission." Ray crossed his arms over his chest, not breaking eye contact.

Colonel Mahinis puffed out his chest, setting his own power position.

Mack stepped next to the chief, mimicking his stance. Vincenti joined them, followed by the rest of the Bad Karma team.

The colonel blinked first.

THIRTY-EIGHT

AFTER SHE HEARD the landing gear go down, Kristie looked out her window. Through a break in the clouds, the rising sun lit the sky with hints of gold and orange. She glimpsed the ocean behind them and the rise of low mountains in the distance.

The men slept a good part of the flight. Apparently, they weren't worried about her bailing out. She'd tried to sleep to store her energy and stay mentally sharp but only managed to nod off for minutes. The earlier blows hurt, and the hours on the jet had given her reprieve from additional beatings.

Bouncer unbuckled and went to a cabinet by the doorway. He came toward her, holding a dark cloth. Her skin turned clammy the moment he pulled the black hood over her head. The fact they carried them on the plane indicated she wasn't the first hostage they'd taken. Her stomach sent its contents creeping up the back of her throat. She swallowed it down and breathed deeply to override her body's instincts. *The hood is not suffocating you. Don't show fear. No weakness.*

The plane touched down minutes later, bouncing on the

runway twice before the tires maintained contact, and they slowed.

Her guesstimate from the time they refueled a few hours ago was that they were in Colombia. She didn't know the range on the tracker Mack had given her, but she'd lost hope after two hours. No way that tiny thing could be tracked over two thousand miles. Right?

Mack, I am so sorry. It was better her than these cocksuckers getting their hands on his girls. Or Stephanie and Alexis.

The plane turned and eventually stopped. She heard the click of seat belts unbuckling, then felt a hand brush over her breast as someone released her belt. "Get up." Bouncer jerked her flex-cuffed hands.

"Watch your step," a different voice warned, touching her elbow when she was led out and down the steps.

The smooth, hard surface under her feet indicated blacktop or concrete rather than a dirt surface, but she doubted this was any real airport. There'd be no one to see her being led off with her head covered. No one to call authorities.

With the engines off, she listened for any sound that might give her a clue on her location. No other planes. No traffic. The damp, heavy air muffled the distant voices of tree frogs.

She needed info. Something that gave her a clue about where she was. When her feet hit dirt, it was time to risk it. Kicking one toe into the ground, she fell forward. Throwing her hands up, she managed to hook her thumbs under the hood and yank it up before landing hard on her right side.

Ignoring the pain, she raised her head and took in the white SUV in front of her and the field of green behind it.

That wasn't helpful. She rolled left, onto her back, and raised to a sitting position. The jet was parked under a large metal canopy. To keep it from being spotted? Salvation also sat under that makeshift hangar.

A helicopter. One half the size of her Black Hawk. Closer to the size of the training aircraft back at Fort Rucker. She didn't have an iota of doubt she could fly that thing—if she could get to it.

Bouncer reached for her, and between him, Tattoo, and the pilot, there was no frigging way she could get to the craft and get it started. If she acted like she hadn't seen it, maybe it wouldn't be the first place they headed to if—no, *when*—she got away.

Pulling the hood back over her head, they shoved her into the SUV's back seat. Kristie squeezed her arms over her chest to avoid getting felt up again. Someone climbed in beside her and buckled her in before both front doors closed.

The asshole pilot must be along for the ride. Pilots typically shared camaraderie over their love of flying. But a pilot who flew for a man like Herrera, one who let a woman be brought aboard in restraints and led off with a hood over her head, made her hope this guy crashed and burned on one of his illegal flights. With Herrera onboard.

Even if she could unbuckle *and* unlock *and* open the door, her chances of rolling out and getting away from three men— with two of them armed—were zero. Zilch. Zip.

Patience. Don't give up.

The damned bag over her head kept her from seeing any landmarks. She couldn't judge their speed over the rough roads, so even if she could memorize the turns and count the seconds between them, it might not do her any good.

After about sixteen minutes over progressively bone-jarring roads, the SUV stopped. A blast of warm air rushed in when the driver spoke, getting a grunt from another in response. She made out a low hum before they drove on for a few more minutes.

The SUV doors opened, and the men piled out. One pulled her from the vehicle. Damn, she wished she could see. Did she dare stage another fall? Before she could decide, whoever gripped her arm, jerked her up a step. The squeak her boots made was the same as when walking on ceramic tile. Definitely not concrete, wood, or even linoleum. An authoritative voice greeted them once they stopped inside a building.

Her head snapped back when the hood was yanked off. She squinted from the sunlight streaming in through the row of windows and, shaking back her hair, took a quick perusal of what appeared to be a living room with couches on her right.

In front of her, a man stood in clean khaki dress pants and a button-down shirt. He had a military bearing and regarded her with a calculating stare, similar to Ray's. A drug lord might employ the same kind of stare down.

When he spoke to the men who'd brought her in, his words flew so fast she only picked out *Herrera* and *arrive*. He nodded in dismissal, then spun on his heel. Okay, this man was probably not Herrera, but maybe his security chief or the lieutenant in charge of his thugs.

Bouncer and Tattoo led her up the stairs off the foyer. The pilot didn't follow—not that his absence improved her odds.

Upstairs, they let her use the bathroom. The room had metal bars over the window and nothing usable for self-defense. Heavy footsteps made the floor creak. Bouncer said something to which new voices replied.

Outnumbered even more, she needed to save the one weapon at her disposal for the right time.

When she came out, Tattoo led her to a bedroom where two men had joined Bouncer. The bedroom had a full-size bed, nightstand, and two wooden chairs—one smack in the middle of the room, and the other next to the door. There weren't chains attached to the wall or bloodstains on the bedding or floor—yet.

Tattoo pushed her down onto the chair rather than nicely motion for her to sit. No surprise there. He knelt and began to unlace her boots.

No, no, no!

He wrestled off the first boot, then the other. Even though she kept her face passive, the tall newcomer squinted suspiciously at her. Maybe she'd get lucky. Instead, he picked up the boots and stuck a hand inside each one. When he pulled out the duct tape, her plan suffered a serious smackdown.

Shit.

The look of disdain and the contempt in the man's tone with whatever he said made Tattoo mutter under his breath. Tattoo wrapped thick zip ties around her ankles to the chair legs, pulling them until they dug into her flesh.

The tall man leaned down and checked that the ties were tight enough for his satisfaction. He eyed her breasts before rising. Were there no women around for these guys? The thought dredged up possibilities she didn't want to imagine. No. She was not out of this fight yet.

Tall Guy set her boots by the wall as the four of them talked. Apparently, the youngest man, in a plaid shirt two sizes too big for him, drew the short straw because he plunked down in the chair, looking pissed off.

Relieved of duty, Bouncer and Tattoo disappeared with

Tall Guy. Good riddance. They left her boots behind—one tiny thing going her way—so she wouldn't have to run through the jungle in socks if—no, be optimistic—*when* she got out of here.

Her new guard didn't seem interested in conversation and played a game on his phone. Better than the alternatives. From the window, all she could see were trees and sky. Mostly trees. She needed to think. Start forming her escape plan. Though if they were going to station a guard on her twenty-four seven, that drastically limited her options.

Nevertheless, she feigned sleep and started evaluating factors. She knew how to get out of the flex-cuffs and zip ties even without the razor blade, but she couldn't do it with company watching. Then what?

She had to be a few miles from the airfield where they landed, but then she'd have to *find* it. There were vehicles here, and though AJ had mentioned to Juan that hot-wiring should be a part of her escape-and-evade training, they hadn't gotten to it. If she got out of this, she'd make AJ or Mack or Ray teach her. They could probably hot-wire a car in under two minutes. Her? No clue.

What were the chances they left the keys in them? Damn, she should have listened for the jingle or tell-tale beep.

She could disable the cars. Remove the batteries or flatten the tires to even the playing field. But those things would take time. Time for them to catch her.

She'd have to make her escape on foot. Could she do that in the dark? In unfamiliar terrain with trees and roots and who knows what kind of wild animals out there? It wasn't an ideal plan. The best time would be right before dawn. Use darkness to get away from the house but have enough light to navigate by.

If she could get to the hangar or find people, would she be able to differentiate who might help from those who'd turn her back over to Herrera? The odds weren't in her favor, but she could figure out patterns, the weakest link, anything to improve her chances. Except how long did she dare wait to try to escape?

THIRTY-NINE

VOICES AND FOOTSTEPS WOKE KRISTIE. She'd managed to get some sleep, but now her plaid-clad guard jerked upright and slipped his phone into his chest pocket.

The temperature shot up when two men entered the room —as if making it comfortable for the devil himself. The man she pegged as Herrera's security chief moved in as stealthily as a cat and gave her the same indifferent stare.

The man with him was older with a sprinkling of gray in his hair, mustache, and short beard. Shy of six feet, a bit pudgy, and wearing cream slacks and a pale-blue, short-sleeved shirt, he didn't appear intimidating—until she looked into the soulless eyes as he studied her with his superior air.

"You know who I am?" His English wasn't half bad.

She didn't answer with the profane words that came to mind, or give him the satisfaction or power of hearing his name, but gave an affirmative nod.

"Good." He responded with a smarmy smile all the same. "When I read—" He turned to the security man and spoke in Spanish, calling the man *Hugo*, if she'd heard right.

"Josué Varga," Hugo replied.

Herrera flipped a hand as if shooing away an insect. "His report say he fly with a American *woman*. I picture someone not so pretty." He shrugged.

Had Josué been working for Herrera? She doubted it and didn't ask. Remorse ripped through her. Josué and his family were dead, tortured, not because of her, but because of this man. His greed and thinking he was above the law.

Herrera raised a brow as if waiting for her to respond. When she didn't, he ran a knuckle along her bruised cheek.

She flinched—and it wasn't due to pain. The man oozed arrogance and egotism. The way people responded showed his lethal power. He may have the vast majority of the power, but she had information he wanted—making her valuable.

"You know what I want from you?" he asked when she kept silent.

"Flying lessons?"

Herrera's throaty, ominous chuckle stopped suddenly. "From a woman? No. The men you pick up, they took something of mine."

Did he honestly think kidnapping made the girl his? "I'm sure they don't have your property anymore."

The disdain that came through in her tone made him smirk. "No. But I don't need—it—anymore. It was"—he sighed—"to keep my son out of jail. He made mistake, but the *policía*, they want to, uh, make him pay for things they say I do."

She bit her bottom lip to keep from laughing at his understated description. He clearly thought laws didn't apply to him.

"Because your soldiers come, my son is dead. They must pay for that." His tone went cold and flat.

She returned his silent gaze, trying to measure how far this man would go. How close he was to the edge. Eric's tragic death taught her what grief could do to a person. She could not let this man inflict his wrath on innocent people. Ones she cared about. The lengths he'd already gone to get to her and bring her here showed he wouldn't give up this vendetta. Ever. He had her, but no one else needed to die.

"Varga not know who they are. He say you know. You will tell me names. Where to find these men."

She wanted the hell out of here, but telling Herrera their names would not make that happen. It'd just speed up her death. "Can't help you there. They're from a different unit. One that does classified missions. They don't mix with us aviators." She prayed he didn't know the particulars with her and Mack. "You can call the Army and ask."

Herrera took a step closer. His mouth tightened, and his arm flexed.

Even the guard, who didn't appear to speak English, read his boss's body language. The wary look on his face cemented her assumption Herrera wasn't afraid to get his own hands bloodied. No point in implementing humanization tactics, not when her captor was a merciless brute. The Geneva Convention guidelines didn't apply here.

"No lie to me!" he growled.

"Varga say you knew one," Hugo said in an unnervingly calm manner. "A big man with yellow hair."

Fuck. Josué had talked. If she stalled, he'd know she was lying. "What are you going to do if I tell you? Send your men to take on one of the most elite U.S. Army Special Forces soldiers and his team? Are you willing to sacrifice the lives of more of your men? It won't bring your son back."

Herrera's nostrils flared, and his mouth twitched with

emotion. His gaze moved from her to the guards in the room as he weighed her words. "I am not going to send my men after them. I will send message—that I have you. And when they come, this time, I be ready. I have more men. Many more."

Shit. Of course, he wanted them on his turf. That's why he brought her here. Bait. Kristie's confidence imploded. She could not lead Mack and Ray into an ambush. No. No. No.

Maybe Mack didn't know she'd activated the tracker yet. She had to turn it off. But how, without them finding it?

"I need to go to the bathroom." It worked before.

Herrera shook his head. "Until you give me names, you do not eat. You do not sleep. You do not use bathroom. You tell me." He spat the words at her. With a confident jerk of his head, he signaled to Hugo, and the two stepped away.

Denying her food and sleep and use of a toilet hardly counted as torture, especially from a man with Herrera's reputation. What was up with that? SERE training stressed that every human had a breaking point. How long could she hold out under real torture?

She had to figure out a way to outwit Herrera. If she couldn't, and couldn't get away, she'd need a plan to make sure they'd never get the information they wanted—at least not from her.

Listening to Herrera give orders to Hugo and the guard, she understood a few words, but couldn't translate enough to figure out what they were planning before they left.

Her guard plunked back down onto his chair.

"Necesito ir al baño," she tried again.

"No." He stuck to orders.

Time for Plan B, and hopefully, useful intel. *"Tú no importante a Herrera. ¿Quieres vivir o"*—she couldn't remember the word for die—*"muerte?"*

She probably sounded stupid using the Spanish words she knew but, based on the way the guard stared at her, she managed to make enough sense to get her point across. *Think that over.* It didn't matter how much Herrera pays if you're too dead to spend it. With the right psychological warfare, maybe she could persuade his men to desert their posts. *"¿Cuál es tú nombre?"*

He didn't respond.

"Fine. I'll call you Héctor."

He squinted angrily at her. *"Silencio."*

"Don't like Héctor? How about Pedro?" For some reason, that made her think of a dog. Rather fitting. *"Los soldados americanos práctica todo el día to ..."* She didn't know enough to finish. "Practice all day to kill men like you," she repeated in English. "Bang, bang. *Tú.*" She pointed her cuffed hands at him, then faked death.

Pedro gave an unbelieving laugh. Probably at her child-like attempts to communicate.

"Herrera tiene cien hombres viniendo aquí. Mataremos a los soldados Americanos," he told her.

"¿Cien? No comprende."

"Mucho. Mas hombres."

That she understood. A lot of men. Coming. *"¿Mataremos?"*

"Tus soldados mueren. Muerto." He sat back with the smuggest smile on his face.

If she interpreted everything, or almost everything, correctly, it made sense why Herrera wasn't beating the crap out of her. Yet. He needed to get his other men here before he sent the message to their targets that he had her. Herrera figured he had time to get the names and needed to keep her alive until then.

Guess what, cooperation was not her middle name.

The odds were stacked against her and getting worse. She'd have to make a break for it at her first opportunity. With that many men coming, she needed to get the tracker turned off to avoid leading Mack, Ray, and their team into an ambush. It would up to her to escape—or die trying.

FORTY

"No!"

Despite Kristie's scream, the girl took Herrera's hand and walked away from Mack's body.

"No!" When the girl still didn't turn around, Kristie ran after her, but couldn't get any closer.

A loud voice woke Kristie from her nightmare. *It wasn't real. It wasn't real.*

Ricardo, as she'd taken to calling the second guard, stared grumpily at her. She must have yelled out in her sleep, waking him.

"Bad dream," she managed between gasps for breath.

She hung her head to try and slow her breathing. The dream flooded back.

There'd been a girl, but Kristie didn't know who. Amber? Darcy? Alexis? She shook it off. She didn't want to know. Or remember the dream. Maybe it would fade away if she didn't think about it. It was just her here. Mack, Darcy, Amber, the Lundgrens, they were all alive in North Carolina. Still safe.

Ricardo checked the ties binding her to the chair. Satisfied she wasn't sweating from trying to escape, he grunted and straightened.

Outside her dungeon window, dense fog reflected the moonlight. It made the night eerily bright and gave her no clue how long she had before dawn.

Kristie listened but didn't hear sounds of anyone moving about in the house. It'd be a perfect time—if she could get out there before the sun came up.

Rather than laying back down, Ricardo lumbered to the door. She held her breath, waiting to see if he'd sit on the chair by the door. *Please don't.* He stepped out. Really? Her heart beat faster. Yes!

Whether he went looking for a quiet place to sleep, to smoke, or because nature called, she didn't give a damn. The moment the door closed, she leaned the chair onto its back legs as far as she dared. It took about half a minute to work the zip tie down far enough to free her leg. Her other leg was free in seconds.

Now the fun part. She raised her arms, took a deep breath, then jerked her arms down like Mack had demonstrated.

Damn, that hurt. And didn't work. She tried again. Tears sprung to her eyes from the pain, but she refused to cry out. Shit. One more time. *Please work. Please.* She couldn't risk the time it'd take to get her boots and undo the paracord bracelet to saw through the plastic.

Pop! The plastic snapped and flew off. She lowered her head and let the exhilaration of freedom chase away the pain and stars dotting her vision.

Reaching under her shirt, she didn't waste any time turning off the tracker. Mixed emotions erupted as a sharp half sob. Though she'd cut off any chance of Mack and his team finding her, keeping them safe was the right thing. She was on her own now. Utterly alone.

And she needed to move. She scooped up her boots and locked the door Ricardo had left cracked before she pulled it closed behind her. It might buy her a few seconds. She needed every one she could get.

She sprinted down the hallway. Light peeked under the bathroom door. Ricardo was peeing, which hopefully drowned out the sound when the floor creaked. She didn't stop but kept to the edge of the staircase.

Her heart pounded in her ears as she checked the downstairs area. Clear. She dashed to the door and turned the knob. It didn't open. *No, no, no!* If all the doors were deadbolted—

Kristie's gaze landed on a bowl holding keys on the side table. Oh, my God. Thank you!

She snatched up a set. In addition to the key fob for a car, the ring held two keys. The first fit in the deadbolt. Her lungs refused to release until she heard the satisfying click. She eased the door open. No squeaks. No alarm. Hallelujah! And parked on the gravel, just yards away, were two vehicles. Yes!

She couldn't make out the insignia on the key in the limited light. Rather than waste time, she went ahead and hit the unlock button since it was going to beep regardless.

The taillights on the boxy, white SUV flashed. She raced to the driver's side. She had the door halfway open when a bare foot kicked it, ripping the handle from her grip. The door slammed shut as a hand twisted into her hair, nearly yanking her off her feet.

She flailed with both arms to stay upright. One of her boots flew from her hand and hit her captor in the face. Her elbow struck his abdomen. His arm wrapped around her, pinning hers to her body and restricting her reach. She kicked, trying to trip him up, but he flung her to the ground.

Hugo. How the hell …? He kicked her square in the gut.

Curling into a protective position, she waited for the next

blow. Instead, he forced her onto her belly. With his knee in her back, he twisted her arms behind her and pried the keys from her hand.

"I can't kill you, but Baltazar won't mind if I hurt you." He dragged her face across the ground in his effort to get her upright.

Stones cut into her cheek; dirt clung to her lips and invaded her mouth. "Go ahead. You're going to kill me. Do it already."

"We still need you. And Baltazar would be disappointed if I deprived him the pleasure."

His words and menacing tone didn't frighten her. She knew—without any doubt—they *would* kill her. That's what made doing it herself a contingency she had to plan for. Her instincts screamed not to let him get her back inside. When she refused to walk on her own, Hugo cursed and wrenched her arm to maneuver her toward the house.

Patience wasn't exactly her strong suit, but her only shot at surviving came from not giving up and changing her strategy to get further the next time she escaped.

Inside, Ricardo skidded to a stop. His eyes went wider than a scared jackrabbit at seeing Hugo lead her in. She didn't catch the clipped words Hugo barked, but the meaning came through—loud and very clear. From the death glare Ricardo skewered her with, she'd moved to the top of his shit list.

Ricardo trailed behind as Hugo marched her upstairs. After manhandling her into the chair, Hugo scanned the room. He picked up the snapped cuffs, then came over and grabbed her left wrist. His expression gave her the sense he was impressed, though that wasn't necessarily a good thing. Especially when he unfastened her paracord bracelet and slipped it into his pocket.

Tension bounced off the walls as the two men exchanged

words. Hugo stalked out of the room, but Ricardo stayed behind. He leaned over, making her gag on his rancid breath when he spat words in her face. She knew what his words meant, or at least close enough.

Sorry, asshole. Part of my job. *Survive. Evade. Resist. Escape.*

Her original guard, Pedro, shuffled into the room, apparently just awakened. Hugo appeared with zip ties and slapped them into Ricardo's hand, who zealously secured her arms behind her back as Hugo instructed. He then wrapped ties around her legs and over the crossbar so that she couldn't slip them from the legs again.

Hugo smirked and motioned for Ricardo to follow him, then spun on his heel and left. Before Ricardo followed, he backhanded her across the face.

Damn. She shook her head, pursing her lips and staring back in defiance. *Bring it, asshole.* Takes a real tough guy to smack a woman who's tied up.

She definitely made the naughty list because Pedro refused to speak to her. Outside, the fog began to burn off as the sun rose and lit the sky. Inside her, every idea she evaluated for escape sank into a dark abyss. Lack of sleep made it increasingly difficult to concentrate and come up with a workable plan to get out of the ties.

If she'd put her boots on, she'd still have them. Too late for the woulda, coulda, shoulda. Hugo had left them where they'd fallen, and she doubted she'd see them again.

A soft knock roused her from the shallow sleep she'd slipped into. When Pedro opened the door, a woman spoke. He accepted a plate loaded with food and a glass filled with a thick, pink drink.

Kristie's stomach rumbled when she smelled the sausage and eggs. Slices of brightly colored melon adorned the plate and made her mouth water despite the dehydration.

Pedro eyed her while forking food into his mouth, enjoying the chance to taunt her. When he continued to make a show of eating, she closed her eyes and focused on what she'd learned from her escape attempt.

Next time, she'd bet she wouldn't find keys by the door. No. She needed a fresh idea.

Maybe she could pry the bars off the window. How did the Black Widow get free when she was bound to a chair and interrogated? Kristie sure didn't possess the same ninja-like superpowers.

She had nothing. Nothing but dreams of Mack and his team storming the compound. Bullets flying. Bodies falling. Blood flowing. Some of those casualties would be her friends. With the number of men Pedro said Herrera was bringing in, the entire team could be wiped out. She would not let that happen.

Turning off the tracker was the right thing to do. She'd do it again.

———

PEDRO HAD long since finished his breakfast, without sharing, when he jumped to his feet. Company must be coming.

Hugo opened the door but allowed Herrera to enter first.

He tsk-tsked. "I would be disappointed if you not try to escape." He took in the cuts and dirt on her face. "How far she get?"

Since Hugo answered in Spanish, he could have told Herrera anything.

"You steal my car, then you go through gate and get

away." Herrera bent, putting his face near hers. "How do it feel to be *so* close?"

She clamped her mouth shut, refusing to participate in his cat-and-mouse game.

"People in Colombia do not dare take from me. You Americans need to learn." He straightened and spoke to Pedro, who then scurried from the room.

She wished they'd say things in Spanish she understood. Not knowing what they said made her imagine the worst.

"Tell me who led your soldiers."

"Go to hell."

He stiffened. "I say prayers every night."

A laugh burst out. Oh, she'd pay for that, but seriously? He might ask for forgiveness, but clearly, he did not get the concept of repentance.

Something about the cruel grin that spread across Herrera's face when Pedro returned made her turn to look. He held a long-handled sledgehammer.

"You will tell me." Herrera accepted the tool from Pedro. "Now or later. But you *will* tell me." He raised the heavy hammer.

She closed her eyes when Hugo gripped the back of her chair to keep it steady. Every nerve ending burned in expectation of when the blow would come—and where.

Herrera's grunt signaled the incoming strike. Crushing pain shot from her left foot up her leg. Her agonized shout helped expel a fraction of the pain. But pain was good in that it meant her foot was still there.

When she opened her eyes, she found Herrera's arrogant face inches from her own.

"The question is same. Tell me his name."

Pain and panic merged when he lifted the sledgehammer again. She couldn't refrain from whimpering.

The red circle on the top of her foot was swelling grotesquely. He'd probably broken bones, and it hurt like hell. If he crippled her, she couldn't escape. How long could she hold out? What if he resorted to drugging her to get her to talk? She had to do something while she had some degree of lucidity.

"Stop! I'll tell you."

Herrera hesitated before the heavy end thudded against the wooden floor. "So soon?" Suspicion narrowed his eyes.

"They dragged me and m—" Her wince was from pain, but it stopped her before bringing up the rest of her crew that day. "Dragged me into this with a fake training mission. I didn't ask for any of this." That much was true—even though she didn't blame them for doing so. "Pierce. His name is Ben Pierce. Major Ben Pierce."

Though no one called him Ben. Always Hawkeye or Benjamin Franklin Pierce. And Hawkeye deserved a promotion from captain with all his years on *M*A*S*H*. Hopefully, they weren't fans of the show.

Hugo wrote in a small notebook.

"His telephone number," Herrera demanded.

Getting greedy now. First, it was a name, now the full 411. Pain, sleep deprivation, and refusing to capitulate were making her punchy. She'd better stay on top of her game despite the constant throb in her foot.

"I don't know it. It's stored in my phone." Which his dumbasses left at the house in North Carolina. Screwed yourselves there, didn't ya?

"Email will work," Hugo said.

"You'd have to let me sign into my account to get his personal one." She rolled the dice. This could totally backfire, but she bet on them not trusting her.

Hugo shook his head at Herrera, whose eyes narrowed and grip on the sledgehammer shifted.

"You can try Ben dot Pierce at US dot Army dot m-i-l."

Hugo started scribbling, but she didn't offer to repeat it.

"Though he probably uses a middle initial. Whatever that is."

A threatening growl rumbled from one of them. Maybe both.

"Where does he live?" Hugo pressed.

She tried to come up with something on the adrenaline-infused fly. "After his divorce, I think he moved into an apartment off post." Please let that big-assed lie help protect Stephanie and Alexis.

"Where?" Hugo snarled.

She gave the name of the biggest apartment complex she remembered looking at. "I don't know the unit number."

"What type of vehicle he drive?"

"A big gray truck." She described Sheehan's. He wasn't near Ray's size but had blond hair. "Look, that's all I've got. Unless you want to take me back to Fort Bragg …" she dared them. If they believed her, they might kill her now. In their line of work, neither were the kind of men to trust anyone.

The two stepped away and conferred in low voices. She rocked in pain, managing to pick out a few words. City. Pierce. Picture. Truth. Here. Now. She didn't understand enough to make sense, but it looked like she'd bought some time, especially when Hugo took a picture of her with his phone.

"No more escape." Herrera gripped the sledgehammer with both hands.

No promises.

Rather than handing the instrument of torture to Pedro, he swung it back like a golf club. This time she saw it coming.

But couldn't react.

The impact above her ankle nearly toppled the chair. She heard the crunch of bone.

Bright spots of light exploded in her eyes, clouding her vision.

The pain triggered intense nausea, and she gagged on the bile her stomach expelled. Hanging her head might keep her from passing out, but as the world darkened and sounds muted, she only wanted relief from this torture.

WAS SHE DREAMING? No. Same room.

Same nightmare.

Except someone had the humanity to cut the ties and lay her on the bed. Her head, her foot, and her ankle throbbed. And not even in unison. Raising up on her elbows, she grimaced at her swollen foot and the unnatural angle of her ankle.

She was alone in the room. Apparently, if she couldn't stand or walk, they didn't want to waste the manpower guarding her. A faint aroma grew stronger when she inhaled. She sniffed again, craning her neck until she found the source —a plastic bowl of food and cup of water sat on the nightstand.

Pain ripped through her leg as she twisted to reach for the water, but she powered through, grabbing her prize. Her hand trembled so hard that water sloshed onto to her hand she lifted the cup to her lips. She swished the liquid around her mouth to rinse away the dirt and blood, then swallowed it down rather than waste any precious drops.

The eggs were cold and rubbery, but after a few bites, her stomach stopped cramping. Should she save some? Who knew when they'd give her more, but she didn't entirely trust it wasn't laced with drugs.

Giving Herrera a name must have eased up his moratorium on food, and based on the sun's position, she must have slept a few hours after blacking out. It wasn't enough that she was going to buy into the notion he had any redeeming qualities. Besides, when he found out that she'd lied …

Yeah.

If she crawled—dragging her foot?—she'd get caught before making it down the stairs. If she didn't pass out before then. If she could make a splint to immobilize her foot, maybe she could bear some weight. Minimally, it'd reduce the agony whenever her leg moved.

What to use? The only thing in the room other than the bed was the bedside table. Its spindle-type legs were longer than the length from her ankle to her knee, but it was all she had to work with.

FORTY-ONE

THROUGH NIGHT-VISION GOGGLES, Mack studied the flat field below. He pulled the right handle to steer his chute closer to the tree line. Seconds later, he tugged both handles to slow his rapid descent.

His boots touched down, and with two slight steps forward, he stopped, his chute settling to the ground with a ruffled whisper.

Several of Bravo team drifted silently the last few hundred feet through an inky sky. Within minutes, the men had disengaged and gathered up their chutes from the high-altitude jump.

They took refuge under cover of the jungle where they shoved the chutes into camouflaged kit bags. They tucked them around the base of a low palm. Mack drew out his knife and cut off fronds to further hide the stash of chutes. Maybe they'd recover them. It was hardly a priority. But Herrera's men finding them could blow this mission and risk lives. Theirs and Kristie's.

The tip of his knife nicked Mack's pinkie when he sliced through the stem of a palm leaf. *Shit. Focus.*

Plan A had been a total washout since Herrera's plane hadn't landed on U.S. soil to refuel. They were operating on a roughed-out Plan B—get to Colombia, then wing it.

If the drone hadn't picked up Kristie's tracker last night, they wouldn't have a target location at all. But they'd lost the signal around 0500.

What the hell did that mean? Had they discovered it? Turned it off? Destroyed it? Moved her? If so, she could be anywhere by now. Every one of those possibilities conjured up images that ate away at him like gangrene.

What if their target location really did belong to the Colombian coffee grower listed as property owner? They'd be back to square one if Kristie wasn't in the compound mere miles from here. They had a few hours of darkness left to surround the house and begin surveillance.

Unlike the rescue of the judge's daughter, Herrera would expect them this time. He'd be lying in wait, with a trap set. And Kristie as bait. The upside of that meant he'd keep her alive. Mack put several more fronds over the packs as his team started the trek up the hillside.

———

THE ELECTRIFIED CHAIN-LINK fence was eight feet tall and topped with razor wire. Shuler rested a long strip of a leaf against it, waiting to give the signal the moment the power went out.

Shuler had the easy job—as long as he kept his hand back from the metal. Maybe the second easiest since Ray just held his phone, waiting for the text notification from the DEA's inside guy at the power plant. The rest of the Bad Karma team waited with wire cutters ready to go. Based on the "experimental" outage earlier, they'd have no more than three seconds before Herrera's back-up generator kicked in.

The team had surveyed the area around Herrera's compound, but they'd learned little in the past few hours. Mack knew in his gut Kristie was in the house. A coffee grower didn't need miles of electrified fence and armed guards to keep people out. The team needed to breach the perimeter, get closer, get proof, and get her the hell out.

"Going down in thirty," Ray said.

The men crowded into position. Mack crouched, his cutters poised over his first spray-painted mark. His teammates did the same. The muscles in his arms tensed as Ray counted down.

"Four, three, two, one, zero."

"Clear!" Shuler shouted.

Mack cut, repositioned, cut, repositioned, cut.

"Aaah, shit!" Grant cried out. He fell to his ass after making his last cut.

"You okay?" Ray asked.

"Yeah." Grant didn't sound convincing. He shook his arms. "I wasn't going to be the reason we had to wait or risk shutting down the power grid for a third time. Think I pissed myself a little."

"You aren't supposed to admit that." Vincenti gave him a hand up. Once Grant was out of the way, Vincenti bowled his rucksack at the fence where they'd cut. A segment over two feet square fell to the ground.

Success. Grant would shake off the shock in a minute or two. A small price to pay for the mission. Mack tossed his ruck through the hole, then handed his rifle to Vincenti before dropping to the ground and wiggling through on his back. One by one, his buddies passed their rucks and crawled through. Ray squeezed through last, his shoulders barely clearing the opening.

They were inside Baltazar Herrera's inner sanctum. Time to split up, do thorough reconnaissance, then make their plan to start living up to their bad karma name.

MACK POLISHED off his MRE and a bottle of water while waiting for Porter and Shuler to get to the rendezvous point to the east of Herrera's mountainside hacienda. The house itself wasn't all that impressive in size and hardly appeared to be a fortress. Getting through the fence hadn't taken a rocket scientist, just a bribe to a guy at the power company. Periodic outages were a common occurrence in Colombia. Didn't even have to be weather-related.

None of the Bad Karma team expected this to be a cake-walk, though. They'd spotted the bunkhouse outside the security perimeter. It could probably accommodate a good twenty men. Mack liked their chances with the current numbers, but Herrera's hired men had set up two enclosed tents and were constructing two outhouses. That could double the number of men here.

When Porter and Shuler finally showed up, Ray made the call to Alpha team's leader. He put his phone on speaker, and the men crowded around to hear the intel update.

"Got all kinds of news for you," Simpson said. "We flew the drone over. I'm sending you footage. Got thermal read-outs on the house's occupants, and on the bunkhouse and who's there, too. We owe this DEA agent big. Not only were they on target with getting the power shut down, but Machuca is now in the employ of Baltazar Herrera."

"That fast?" Ray asked.

"Using the story Vincenti came up with and paired with our new DEA pal, the guy Herrera's got recruiting fresh muscle talked to Machuca for a few minutes, asked if he knew how to handle a weapon, then told him where to report in the morning for training. Gave him minimal info, but"— Simpson did his signature dramatic pause—"our DEA agent picked up enough bits of conversation to learn that Herrera wants everyone in place by day after tomorrow."

"How solid is that?" Mack asked. They wanted to launch their rescue as soon as possible, but having time to establish patterns and determine the best time to strike upped the chances of a successful extraction.

"The DEA agent wouldn't bet her life on it, but in a way she is. So is Machuca, and he'd appreciate you not shooting him if the recruits roll in before the op goes down."

"We plan to have the package and be long gone by then," Ray stated. "Keep me updated."

After reviewing the footage from the drone video feed, they had a good idea where Kristie was being held—the room where a prone figure barely moved. At least she moved. But they didn't know for certain it was her. Mack wanting it to be her didn't make it so. As much as he hated her being captive, the idea of having this wrong, of having no idea where she was, scared him even more.

The numbers they were up against were not even close to overwhelming at this point. But if the buzz the DEA agent heard was accurate, Herrera had another twenty or thirty men coming. They might be raw recruits, but you put a powerful weapon in their hands, aim them in the right direction, and a few were bound to hit something or someone. It could be anyone on the team or Kristie.

"Too many unknowns," Ray muttered after an interminable silence. "Rozanski, get the parabolic mics up. I want to *know* Kristie Donovan is in there. I want to know if Herrera is there or gives an order that impacts our mission. I want to know if someone so much as scratches their ass inside that house."

"Got it, Chief," Rozanski assured him.

"You determine an overwatch position?" Ray used his I'm-your-boss voice and looked Mack dead in the eye, shooting down his hopes of kicking in the door and being the first to lay eyes on Kristie.

"If that's where she is, there's a location with good elevation, adequate cover, and clear view where I should be able to cover that room and the front entrance to the house."

Ray nodded, sealing Mack's spot. "We'll use the Landcruiser and the Chevy truck at the house for exfil. Dominguez, have them ready to load and roll."

"Got it, boss."

"Gates?" Ray asked Porter.

"Guards there have remotes to open it. Plan is to clone the wireless signal whenever someone comes or goes."

"If not …?"

"We have to blow it." Porter patted his pack with an eager smile. "Rig it to activate remotely is Plan B. Or, Plan C, we fire a rocket on approach. May have to do both depending on timing."

"Thermal imaging showed about fifteen targets around the bunkhouse. Two guards at the gate. One each at the front and back door of the house. What kind of weapons?"

"All of 'em are armed with Skorpions, AKs, and ARs that we've seen," Mack said, with Dominguez echoing confirmation.

"Herrera is too much of a wild card to take at face value. I want everyone in position. Now. We'll continue surveillance and plan to strike at oh-oh-forty-two. But be ready to execute at any minute."

MACK SHOOK the water from the brim of his boonie hat. None of the team complained about the steady rain coming down for the past hour. Not when they knew for certain Kristie was in there. They'd heard her voice. Mostly cursing and some whimpers, but it was her.

The rain didn't totally keep the locals inside, but nobody came tromping around checking the perimeter, and the showers reduced visibility. Those worked in the team's favor, but the two-thousand-percent humidity fogged Mack's scope to the point he'd already had to use an anti-fogging wipe. Not being able to see his target at the crucial moment was a sniper's worst nightmare.

"We've got an incoming vehicle," Shuler updated the team from his post. "Black Mercedes. Looks like one occupant. Window tint is too dark to get a picture of the driver or see in the back seat."

"Captured the wireless signal for the gate," Porter crowed softly.

"Got eyes on the vehicle," Ray said minutes later.

The guard at the front of the house stood straighter when the car came into view. Prickles broke out on Mack's arms.

"I have a visual on the driver. He's solo. Not Herrera. Sending images to command to identify," Ray updated the team.

Through his scope, Mack tracked the man who exited the vehicle and strode to the house with a determined, military bearing. He bypassed the guard without saying a word.

"Rozanski," Ray rumbled.

"On it, Chief."

The team went silent. Listening. First, it sounded like footsteps, then knocking. Mack upped the volume a notch. His Spanish was good enough to follow most of the conversation, although Dominguez gave a loose translation that confirmed men were being trained and brought here. Like a day or two of shooting practice compared to their years of training and experience.

"Must be Herrera asking about the soldier whose name she gave them," Dominguez said.

What had they done to her to make her talk? Drugs? Torture? Part of Mack's soul died. Whose name had she given Herrera? His? Ray's? Another?

Then one of them said, "Ben Pierce." Mack couldn't keep from grunting out a laugh. God love her. But, man, did Herrera sound pissed.

"Our new arrival is Hugo Saavedra. Herrera's right-hand man. Former Colombian military," Ray cut in.

That was fast intel. Of course, they didn't have to look far into Herrera's known associates.

"What was the last thing he said?" Ray asked.

"He called her a bitch. Said she'll pay for lying. And for Diego to bring him something. Or someone."

Shit. This was not sounding good. Ray was the team leader, but—

"We may need to move. Stand by," Ray declared as if he'd read Mack's mind.

FORTY-TWO

LOUD VOICES STOPPED Kristie's unsuccessful attempt to rip the sheet into strips to brace her foot. She slid the table leg under her pillow. The other pieces she'd broken apart were under the bed, and she prayed they didn't notice the table was MIA.

Based on Herrera's angry tone, the real nightmare was about to begin. Heavy feet stomped on the wooden staircase.

The door slammed open. Herrera stormed in first, his eyes dark and mouth contorted with rage. His security chief followed, equally pissed off.

Herrera loomed in front of her. "You think you can lie to me, and I not find out?" He lowered his face to inches from hers and forced her to meet his gaze.

"I don't know what you're talking about."

"You tell me man I want is Ben Pierce. He is fucking television character. You will tell me real name!" he screamed.

"No. I won't." *Ever. I'll die first.* "Those soldiers you're after, they didn't kill your son. I did."

Herrera scoffed. "Pilots fly. It was soldiers. No woman."

Oh, fuck you, you bastard.

She'd pushed that day out of her memory, but now the scene played out in slow motion. "There were three men firing at us from the cover of a black SUV. I grabbed my weapon and fired back. I hit the passenger. Was Juan Pablo wearing dark pants and a light-colored shirt?"

Herrera's head jerked back, and his mouth hung open. She'd just signed her own death sentence. If it kept him from going after the men of the Bad Karma team and their families, it was worth the gamble—because it had been her. "If you want vengeance, a life for a life, then all you have to do is kill me."

Herrera's arm twitched, and she could almost feel his hands around her throat, crushing her airway and squeezing the life out of her. Only he didn't move.

He took in every inch of her. His expression changed from hatred to something more evil. More crazed. More frightening. "A life for a life." He repeated the phrase in Spanish. "*Vaya,* Hugo."

"*Pero*—" Hugo began to question the command.

"*¡Ahora!*" Herrera shouted, pushing him out of the room.

Hugo stumbled backward before following orders to go. Herrera closed and locked the door. Then he turned, slowly, fixing a barely lucid smile on her. "You took my son." He unbuckled his belt and started to unfasten his pants. "You will give me another—before I kill you."

Oh, hell, no.

He shoved her onto her back. He grabbed her shorts, tugging at them, and wrenching her injured leg.

Screeching, she fought through the pain to reach under the pillow for the only weapon at her disposal. Her fingers made contact and dragged the table leg free. She swung with everything she had, and it made solid contact with the side of his head.

His hands released her shorts, but the blow didn't stop him completely. Getting a better grip on the makeshift club using her other hand, she took another swing. This time, it caught him under the chin. Falling backward, he managed to seize the hunk of wood.

Herrera struggled to his feet. He swayed at the side of the bed as he loomed over her, blood dripping from his chin. His arm went up, but before he could strike her, she kicked him in the knee with her good leg. He stumbled back toward the center of the room.

A faint crack came from her right. Herrera's head snapped to the side before he crumpled to the floor. His snarling mouth went slack, and a shocked stare replaced the demented hatred in his eyes. Had her blow somehow done that?

Blood seeped from above his ear. What? Wait! "Oh, my God."

She tore her gaze away to survey the room. The door was still closed. She twisted her head toward the window where a round hole was surrounded by a web of shattered glass. Someone was coming to save her. It had to be Mack and the team. They'd found her despite her turning off the tracker. How?

Mack had to be able to see her, or her outline, with his scope. She raised her hand to first give a thumbs-up, then, in sign language, an "I Love You."

Her surge of relief raced right into panic. Someone would find Herrera's body. Maybe in minutes. How many men would hunt for her friends without the darkness for cover?

She held her breath to listen. Other than her pounding heart, all she could make out was the background chatter of frogs and birds, and rain falling on the roof tiles and running down to plink on the window ledge inches from her head. No shouts or gunfire, but no one was going to waltz in the house unopposed.

Herrera had locked the bedroom door. How long would that keep the guards or Hugo out?

Pain shot through her leg as she grabbed the dirty blanket and tossed it over Herrera's body. It might buy her and the team a few precious seconds when someone came to check on them, plus she could avoid his creepy death stare. "For you, karma's a red-headed hunk with a sniper rifle, and you got off easy, you murderous bastard."

"I HAD TO TAKE HERRERA OUT," Mack relayed to the team.

"We're not in position yet," Ray growled.

"Couldn't wait."

The sonofabitch had clearly lost his shit. Through the thermal scope, Mack hadn't been able to tell with a hundred-percent certainty, but everything added up to the sonofabitch raping her. She was fighting him off, but no fucking way was he watching that happen.

If saving Kristie from Herrera before he'd been cleared to fire got him kicked off the team, he'd accept that. That'd make two less obstacles standing in the way of having a future together.

"Shit. Can you take out the front guard?"

"Roger that," Mack told Ray. He switched his focus to protecting his team—who he'd just put in greater jeopardy.

"Rozanski, Dominguez, get in position to get those vehicles ready to go once we take out the guard at the front door," Ray ordered.

FORTY-THREE

THE URGENT KNOCKING on the door interrupted Kristie's prayers for her rescuers. She cried out, then groaned in the hope of buying time.

The knob rattled, followed by shouted Spanish, but so rapid-fire she couldn't make out a single word. With a crash, the door burst open.

Hugo stepped inside—then froze mid-sentence. His calculating gaze ran over the puddle of blood on the floor and the feet that stuck out from the blanket. His hand gripped his pistol at his side.

She had begged Herrera to kill her. Taunted him to do it to protect Mack and the team. Now, Herrera was dead, and she *wanted* to live. Wanted to laugh with Mack and his girls. Wanted to love.

Her body jerked at the crack of gunfire. The pain from moving her leg shot through her.

It was Hugo who squawked. Instead of raising his arm to fire, he spun out of the room as another bullet impacted the wall. He barked commands, his voice growing distant. Within seconds, voices merged with pounding feet—then gunfire.

The rapid *tat-tat-tat* of a fully automatic weapon cutting loose was interspersed with the softer *pops* of controlled fire.

It ended abruptly.

She rolled from the bed, on top of Herrera, then off him to her side. Clenching her teeth to get through the agony of dragging her broken leg, she grabbed the table leg and commando-crawled toward the door. *You will not pass out,* she ordered herself as she hid the door while more gunfire erupted.

Glass shattered. Men shouted. Furniture crashed—all adding to the chaos she pictured happening on the floor below. It became eerily quiet, then the stairs creaked without the clumping of heavy footsteps. Her limbs tingled in anticipation, and she clutched the table leg like a bat, ready to strike.

"Clear!"

"Clear!"

The familiar voices set off fireworks in her head. "Here. I'm in here," she called out and stuck her good foot out for them to see.

The barrel of an M-4 poked in first, sweeping the room. "Clear!" Ray's voice boomed.

The camouflage uniforms and faces smeared with greasepaint were the most beautiful sights of her life. Tony peeled the blanket off Herrera's face. He removed his glove with his teeth, checked for a pulse, and gave a satisfied grunt.

Ray knelt beside her. "Hope you don't mind us crashing the party. Sorry we couldn't get here sooner."

She squeezed his hand, unable to speak over the emotions choking her.

He studied the way her foot flopped to the side. "How bad?"

"Broken above the ankle. Herrera slammed it with a

sledgehammer after I tried to escape." She had no clue how many bones he'd smashed, but they could cut her foot off for all she cared.

Ray's malevolent glare might have killed Herrera if he weren't already dead. Tony kicked him in the head anyway. "Bastard," he muttered. He took a position near the window and surveyed the area outside.

Ray keyed his comms mic. "Grant, we need a litter. Second room on the right."

Ray closed the door when Devin entered to give them access to her. Devin produced the rolled-up litter affixed to the top of his pack, and she winced as he and Ray slid her onto it.

"We need to get the heck out of Dodge, so morphine will have to wait," Ray apologized.

"Just get us the hell out of here."

"As you wish." He keyed his mic. "How we doin' on the vehicles?" His eyes squinted at Herrera. "Be advised, we're bringin' out an extra body. Have doors open, and be ready to roll." He nodded to Tony.

"You've *got* to be kidding me," Kristie blurted out. Devin paused while strapping her onto the stretcher, his eyes wide, too.

Tony shot her a sly grin as he dropped to a knee next to Herrera. "His men are less likely to shoot me in the back if their boss is on it." He cuffed the corpse's hands together. "Better yet, they see he's dead, they might go have lunch rather than mess with us—'cuz they aren't getting any more paychecks."

It made sense, but she wanted as much distance between her and Herrera as possible, even dead.

"Comin' down now." Ray and Devin lifted the stretcher holding her.

Tony's face telegraphed his distaste as he slung their dead enemy over his shoulder and shoved to his feet.

In seconds, they were downstairs and outside, where AJ and Juan stood guard by the vehicles.

Raindrops wet her face, but she was free.

AJ motioned Ray to the white SUV she'd nearly escaped in. "Here. Steel plates and bulletproof glass."

"Thought we only found keys for this and the truck," Ray said to Rozanski as they slid the stretcher into the back. More of the team appeared. Still no sign of Mack.

"Hot-wired Saavedra's. Insurance we won't be followed, and if we lose a vehicle ..."

"Take lead with our other passenger."

"Great," AJ said when Ray waved a hand to Tony, who loaded Herrera in the passenger seat of the mid-size black sedan.

"Guard at the back took off into the jungle. Lost him," Kyle said.

Ray's mouth tightened, and a growl rumbled out. "Can't do anything about that. What about Saavedra and the woman?"

"The woman wasn't armed. We secured her in the kitchen," Kyle said.

"Saavedra locked himself in some kind of safe room—and he's gonna be there a while. Rigged a grenade to the door," Walt boasted.

Ray nodded. "How's it look, Punisher Six? Radio our ride to be on the ground, ready to load and roll. Plan on a hot exfil." He waved his arm in a circle. "Gotta go! Gotta go! Quick reaction force is on its way."

"Mack!" Kristie exclaimed.

"We don't leave without him," Ray promised, climbing into the front passenger seat.

Juan and Devin slammed their doors.

She trusted Ray Lundgren more than anyone else. As the vehicles pulled away from the hacienda, she had to trust him now—with her life *and* her future.

They didn't get far before gunfire rang out. A bullet tore through metal. The team in the commandeered truck returned fire. It was like déjà vu of her first time in Colombia. Except the roles were reversed.

Devin lowered his window and aimed his weapon toward the low palms ringing the compound. Josué's warning about Herrera's powerful weaponry played through her mind. This time Herrera had expected the men to come. He'd been gearing up, but so far, there were only automatic weapons.

"Where're you guys at?" Ray impatiently studied the dense curtain of green as the vehicles stopped short of the clearing around the compound. From the way he shook his head, he clearly didn't get the answer he wanted.

Fear crept in. This couldn't happen. Life couldn't be that cruel. *Come on, Mack. Please. Please.*

"I've got a plan to buy us time, Chief," AJ shouted. "Meet you at the split." He revved the engine and tires spun in the mud as he peeled out.

"Ray?" Her voice wobbled.

He didn't turn, but she knew damn well he'd heard her.

"Here they come." Finally, he looked at her.

She strained against the stretcher bindings to lift her head. Mack was there, in one magnificent piece, sprinting with Porter from the rainforest to the truck. Tears flooded her eyes, making the pair a blur as they hurdled up and rolled into the bed of the truck.

Juan floored it, and their vehicle lurched forward. Devin rocked sideways, gripping the handhold with his left hand

and his M-4 with the other, as they sped away from the compound.

MACK BUMPED around the back of the truck as Shuler sped over the rutted road through the jungle. He finally got a grip on the side and pulled up to his knees. Though he couldn't see her, Kristie was alive. Herrera was dead. Bad Karma team: two; Herrera: zero.

Simpson, Alpha team's leader, reported there were two aggressor vehicles with ten or so men headed up the hill from the bunkhouse. Ten *armed* combatants. They were just getting into the woods, nowhere near out of them. If he never had to come back to this fuckin' country, it'd be too soon.

Tony tapped him on the shoulder and pointed ahead to where the two roads merged. The truck slowed. What the …? Rozanski, on foot, booked toward them at max speed. Behind him, a black sedan with its doors open blocked the narrow road. Was someone still in it? He gave a satisfied grunt when the pieces clicked together. *Special delivery. One dead cartel boss.*

Armed men ran around the sedan, firing wildly.

Rozanski dove into the back of the truck. "Son of a bitch! That hurts!"

Mack shot the gunman leading the pack. The kid, who probably hadn't hit his twenties, went down, but more were coming.

"You hit?" Vincenti asked.

"Bashed my head," Rozanski complained.

"Stay down a minute. You done good." Vincenti gave him a fist bump to the leg.

The thick canopy of trees blocked Mack's view but didn't

drown out the noise of a low-flying plane. Salvation. They just had to get to the airfield first. What were the chances Herrera's thugs would suddenly get smart enough to quit?

"Bad Karma, this is Punisher Six. Be advised, QRF is past your obstacle."

Damn, that answered that question.

He hung on as the truck barreled down the hillside, turn after turn after turn, occasionally sliding in the mud. They would not hit an IED. This was almost over. They'd be on the plane. He'd get home to Amber and Darcy. They'd be safe. He'd be with Kristie. God, he hoped they'd have a chance. Despite the thoughts bombarding him, his eyes watched their six.

Alpha team continued to feed them updates from the drone. They had a three-minute advantage, at best.

The incline grew less steep. The trees thinned out, and the rain picked up. The world shifted to slow motion the closer they got to the runway. Two trucks came into view as their own vehicles careened to a halt yards away from the aircraft.

While every molecule in Mack's body longed to jump out and get to Kristie, he couldn't abandon his post. He had the weapon with the longest range.

He fired a round into the front tire of Herrera's jet, not that he expected them to give chase, but why chance it. He couldn't bring himself to shoot up the expensive craft, though. A .50-caliber round through Herrera's skull, his own vehicles, and airstrip used for their escape amounted to almost as much bad karma as the cartel head deserved.

Behind Mack, the teamed boarded and loaded Kristie faster than any commercial flight in history. Through his rifle's scope, he counted the number of combatants in the lead vehicle while he waited for his team's signal.

His blood went cold when he spotted the rocket launcher pointed in their direction.

"Load up, Mack!" the chief called over the plane's engines.

Shit. Shit! SHIT!

No can do.

He didn't have time to calculate their speed and trajectory or account for wind resistance to map out his shot. His body operated on instinct and years of training. He drew in a deep breath and exhaled, slowly and steadily, with his eyes locked on his target. His finger squeezed the trigger.

And missed the mark. *Fuck!*

He blinked away the failure, took another steadying breath, and set up his next shot.

His targets ducked when the Raven drone dive-bombed them.

"How do ya like that?" Simpson cackled with glee at his interference.

Aw, screw it. Mack switched the Barrett to semi-automatic and fired repeatedly. The front tire exploded, making the truck swerve. The rocket launched—up and away from their position. One last shot took out the shooter before Mack raced to the plane.

The aircraft taxied as Ray pulled up the steps behind Mack. He grabbed a seatback to keep from landing on his ass or Kristie, where her stretcher filled the space on the floor at the rear of the plane.

He could finally lay eyes on her. The way she smiled at him made his racing heart skip a beat or two, maybe three, before he plopped into the empty seat by her head and buckled up. The tension in his limbs de-escalated the further and faster the jet hurtled down the runway.

The craft lifted off and rose sharply.

"Hoo-ah!" Ray broke the silence.

A chorus of replies followed, including Grant's "Hot damn, Hoo-ah!"

Newbie.

As soon as the plane leveled out, Grant slipped out of his seat. He knelt next to Kristie and opened his medical pack. "I'm going to start an IV and get you meds that'll make you more comfortable."

Mack leaned over to unfasten the straps binding Kristie to the stretcher.

"Other hand, please," she requested, drawing her right hand free and offering her left to Grant.

Though difficult to reach her, he complied with her wishes, working efficiently in the cramped space. When he moved down to her feet to examine her, she extended her right hand to Mack.

Finally, he got to touch her—*really* touch her. The surge of emotions that accompanied her grip on his hand choked him so tightly he couldn't speak. He squeezed back with a shaky hand, trying to keep his shit together in front of his team.

"I've got a pulse in her foot. That's good."

Mack winced, getting a good look at her swollen and bruised leg, her foot flopping unnaturally.

"Can you feel this?" Grant tapped each of her toes.

"Yes."

"They'll have to do x-rays, but I'm thinking you're going to need surgery to get you fixed up." He snapped a cold pack to activate it and carefully secured it to her leg.

She whimpered when he moved her foot.

"Sorry. Almost done."

Mack leaned close. "You know, with your injuries, you can't deploy." She focused on him, and he continued, "With

Herrera dead"—*Satan, torture his soul*—"you won't need to transfer at all."

"Actually, I do need to transfer."

What! "But—"

"To the Guard," she cut him off before panic got its hooks in him. "Then I can date any badass operator I want."

Dominguez whipped around. "Say what?"

"She ain't talking about you, Dominguez," Tony scoffed.

"I think the morphine is kicking in." Mack still gave Dominguez a look that said: *You lose, buddy.*

"Not yet. I don't care who knows. About us."

"Thought you had rules against dating Special Operations guys." If she transferred, he wouldn't have to get through WOCS. They could date, then if she wanted him to leave the team, he'd do what it took.

"I did. But I fell in love with one. Again. I can't seem to help myself."

Blurting this out in front of his team? Maybe the morphine was kicking in. But she'd said that she'd fallen in love with him. "I love you, too."

"I know. And having to let you go, hurt more than this. I'm willing to take the chance." She kissed his hand.

He returned the gesture since he couldn't exactly take her into his arms and kiss the hell out of her. "What about flying MEDEVAC? That's your dream." And he couldn't ask her to give it up. They could find another way.

"*One* of my dreams. Family is a bigger one." Tears made her eyes shine.

Another huge step forward. Her lids were getting heavy, blinking sleepily. They were so close. Did she have to go to sleep now?

But after the hell she'd been through, willing to sacrifice

herself to protect him, his girls, his teammates, she deserved sleep and sweet dreams.

"Go ahead and sleep. We got you. I'll be here when you wake up."

And if he had his way, there'd be a lot of waking up together in their future.

FORTY-FOUR

"HEY. Everything's okay. I'm here. I'm here."

Kristie woke to Mack's voice and gentle touch on her arm.

"Can you pinch me?" She needed to make sure she wasn't dreaming, or that Herrera hadn't doped her up and she was hallucinating.

God, she loved that sexy chuckle. It did things to her insides and—

"You have company."

"Hmm." She managed to open her eyes. Would he have brought the girls? Oops. "Colonel Ball. Hi."

Mack cleared his throat. "I can step out."

"No. Stay." She extended a hand, but Mack had stepped out of reach. Why? Ohh …

The colonel's eyebrows scrunched together. "Glad to have you back, Donovan. How're you doing?"

"Been better. But I've also been worse." She tried to shake off the vestiges of anesthesia. "My leg?"

"Broke two of your metatarsal bones and shattered your fibula," Mack said. "They had to put in a plate and some screws. You'll be in a walking boot for at least six weeks. They're keeping you overnight, considering—everything."

"That also means you can't deploy anytime soon. The 214th needs someone sooner, so your transfer is off. From what I hear, it shouldn't be necessary now," Colonel Ball said.

He meant the threat from Herrera. "I'm still requesting a transfer, but to the National Guard."

"The Guard? I'm starting to suspect you don't want to be under my command." The colonel cracked a grin. "Look, I get that you might need time to process everything after what you've been through, and I suggest you speak with a counselor."

A counselor was a good recommendation, but she needed to come clean. "The transfer is because I've been in violation of Regulation 600-20."

"Fraternization." His head bobbed, and his gaze swung to Mack standing at her bedside. "I see."

"She's on painkillers." Mack gave her an out—one she wasn't taking.

"I don't plan to stop seeing him," she continued.

"Sir, it's my fault," Mack started. "I initiated and pushed."

"It takes two," she owned up to her part. She was the senior officer.

The colonel held up a hand to stop them. "You don't … I don't need details."

"If I finish out my required service in the Guard, there'd be another layer of separation, and I thought …"

"You're not in the same chain of command now." Colonel Ball sighed.

"No, but I …"

"You heard I'm a hard-ass about relationships between the ranks?"

She nodded. "Something like that."

"I started that rumor," he said in a conspiratorial manner. "This isn't the first time it's come up in my shop. I inherited Ries, who's married to an officer in 3rd Group. Last year, one of my Apache pilots wanted to marry his pregnant girlfriend, an NCO, also in my shop. Didn't make sense to flush the money we invested in his flight training. I transferred her to a different unit, outside the chain of command, so they could be together."

If her crew chief based his warning on a misinterpretation of the reason for the transfer, maybe things weren't as black or white—career or Mack—as she thought. She could scarcely breathe as the colonel paused, studying them both.

"Other branches stick to the absolutely no fraternization rules, but in the Army, we look at it on a case-by-case basis. If you weren't a stellar soldier, that'd be one thing. You have an outstanding record. Considering you were kidnapped and tortured by a drug cartel and told them you'd die before giving them the names of fellow soldiers—"

"How'd you know that?" *Mack.* A quick glance confirmed he'd overheard and would probably give her hell over it later.

"Yes, he filled me in. I'd be a fool to lose you to the Guard, Donovan."

"We don't want to jeopardize your career, sir." Her relationship with Mack took priority over all else, but the colonel making it sound like she could continue to fly breathed hope into her soul like flowers that bloomed in May.

"Just be glad this isn't the Air Force. Their PT might be a joke, but they enforce rules like warriors." Colonel Ball gave a rueful chuckle. "I've got twenty-two-and-a-half years in, and I still get to fly. I hate the politics part of the job and have no desire to go to the Pentagon. Besides, you SF guys tend to get whatever you want to keep you happy. If I said no and you went to Colonel Mahinis, I'd probably be looking for a new foursome for golf. *That* would be tragic. But I'd appreciate it if you didn't advertise. No showing up in uniform and kissing on the tarmac."

"No problem. Thank you, sir." Mack shook Colonel Ball's hand.

"You're welcome. Thanks for getting her out."

Kristie felt like she'd just found out she had a fairy godfather. "Thank you for coming by, sir."

"If you need anything, let me know. No rush to get back. You need to heal. Physically and mentally. Take good care of her," he said to Mack.

"I will, sir. I will." Mack smiled and took her hand. "I think this calls for a kiss," he said once they were alone. "But—"

"No buts. I've been through a lot." She crooked a finger, begging for a kiss.

"I need to know that you're really okay with me staying on the Bad Karma team. Because if you're not, I'll leave the team. I'll get a job in the training cadre or teaching ROTC."

"You'd hate that."

"But I'd have you. When I thought I was going to lose you," he choked out the last words. "I kinda got a taste of what it feels like on the other side. I already lost a wife who thought I was selfish for not getting her fears and not getting out of Delta. I'm not going to let that happen again."

"Well, I got a different perspective, too. I wouldn't be alive if it weren't for you. What you do. I won't—can't—ask you to give up who you are or what you do. I'm not saying I won't be scared, but I'm not going to let what *could* happen to you make me miss out on loving you—and your girls."

That brought an even bigger smile to his face and eyes that she'd never get tired of looking at. "How about that kiss?"

"I think you've earned it." He winked, leaning over to kiss her.

She'd never been a believer in fairy tales, but today she was claiming her happily-ever-after with her own version of a prince—a hero who wore camouflage and slayed evil beasts with his sniper rifle.

EPILOGUE

Eight months later

DARCY'S red curls bobbed as she bounced on the balls of her feet. In both hands, she clutched the poster with bold blue and red letters proclaiming, "Welcome home!" Stars and about four bottles of glitter decorated the sign.

Her excitement mirrored Kristie's own. She had butterflies in her stomach, and her heart pounded hard enough to feel it. Light glinted off the diamond ring on her left hand. The ring Mack bought for her while home on leave. His leave had been short, but long enough to assure them both they weren't jumping the gun in getting engaged or married.

She exchanged smiles with Stephanie and Alexis Lundgren. Tammy Shuler's older children ran around in a game of chase while her newborn daughter slept in her stroller.

Tony Vincenti's parents were there to welcome him home, and his mom had brought enough cannoli for everyone. AJ Rozanski's fiancée and Linc Porter's girlfriend and mom waited with the other family members and loved ones milling around.

The small group gathered was different from the large homecoming her unit received after her first tour. She had been deployed when Eric's unit came home, which spared her from attending.

Today, Mack *was* coming home. All his team members were coming home healthy and alive. It helped ease the fear that lurked in the back of her mind.

Her stomach rumbled again, and next to her, Amber giggled. "Told you they'd be late, and you should eat something."

"I was too busy. And excited." Later, they'd eat the dinner of Mack's favorite foods the girls had helped prepare —together.

She wrapped an arm around Amber's shoulder and hugged her to her side. When Mack told the girls they were dating, Darcy had been on board; however, Amber had reservations. Kristie hadn't pushed, opting instead to let the girl work through her feelings about her parents moving on with other people. Spending time together in the three months between her rescue and Mack's deployment, Amber had come around, even after Rochelle and her hometown boyfriend ended things.

Before Mack deployed to Afghanistan six months ago, Rochelle agreed to let Kristie see the girls weekly for dinner and video chat sessions with Mack—if his erratic schedule permitted. Maybe because it gave Rochelle a free night, but Kristie happily seized the opportunity to spend time with the girls in preparation for becoming their stepmother.

Already she couldn't picture a future without Mack and the girls in her life. Any minute, Mack would be home with them. The thought they were getting married *this weekend* sent happy shivers dancing through her body.

Walt appeared first. Tammy's daughter squealed and took off running, her younger brother on her heels. They grabbed Walt's hands and pulled him toward his newborn daughter.

Darcy nearly toppled forward, craning for a glimpse of her daddy. "There he is! There he is!" She jumped up and down, pointing to where Mack led the rest of the pack.

"Go on." Tears obscured Kristie's vision. She wiped them away to see Mack's overjoyed smile as his daughters raced to him. Despite her longing, she gave the girls the first precious moments with their dad.

His oversized pack hit the floor and his eyes met hers in that second before Darcy sprung into his arms. He held his daughter against his chest, cradling the back of her head with one hand, pressing his cheek against hers. He wrapped his arm around Amber, bringing her into their family hug. As he kissed both girls, Kristie edged up, noting the stream of tears running down Amber's face.

Darcy slid down his body to stand on her own feet. Mack's eyes once again locked on Kristie's. All the happy reunions around them faded when he opened his arms to her. His solid body met hers in a delicious melding that washed away much of her past pain. Her toes brushed the ground as he held her, and she clung to him, wanting to make up for all their time apart.

He kissed her earlobe, and she turned her face to kiss him. And kiss him. Savoring the feel, the taste of him.

Darcy crushed her slender body against Kristie's leg as she wrapped her arms around them.

"Enough kissing. You're embarrassing me," Amber piped in, though wearing a half smile.

"Deal with it." Mack pulled her into the circle.

Kristie laughed and slipped her arms around the girls' shoulders. She rubbed her nose against the smooth skin of Mack's cheek and pressed another kiss there.

His incredibly sexy smile sent ripples of desire cascading through her. A desire she'd have to wait to act on. She could wait a wee bit longer to be alone with the man she loved—now that they had their future together stretching out ahead of them.

DARCY'S WEIGHT displaced air in the mattress, making it shift enough to stir Mack out of his sated, near-sleep state. "Whatcha doing, monkey?"

"I need to cuddle with you more." She crept through the darkness between his and Kristie's legs on the queen-size air mattress.

"Come on up." Kristie scooted away from him without a hint of complaint. "I'm sorry—"

"This is awesome," he cut off her apology. He inched over, nearly slipping onto the floor. "I get to camp out under the ceiling with my three favorite girls." *With no worries about someone shooting at me.*

He didn't voice that. No point in worrying his wife-to-be. Kristie understood enough not to ask. He could tell her about the school the American forces built, and the medical clinics his team ran to make inroads with the locals—and gather intel.

The rest he couldn't tell her. Like how HQ was impressed with the number of weapon caches they found. Or the dozens of insurgents and Taliban they rounded up. Or how they'd come close, but not close enough, to nab a terrorist on the top ten list.

Darcy settled in, wedged between him and Kristie. Even in the moonlight, Kristie's face radiated a serene, loving smile as he kissed the top of Darcy's head.

He'd made mistakes in his life, especially with Rochelle, but he got Amber and Darcy as a result. Now, he was getting a second shot. He'd learned from his mistakes and wouldn't repeat them with Kristie. Things would be different this time.

He loved Kristie's heart—and her ingenuity. Planning a campout in the living room meant they could all be together without complaints from Rochelle about Kristie spending the night before they were married.

When he leaned forward, Kristie turned her face up until their mouths met.

"You're squishing me," Darcy interrupted their kiss and made him and Kristie laugh. He tickled Darcy, who giggled and squirmed.

How he'd missed that innocent laughter. "Amber, you want to come cuddle, too?"

"I'm good," she answered him in a sleepy voice.

He reached over and grabbed her foot.

"Stop it!" she complained, pulling her foot free.

He settled back, glad to be home. They had eight months before Kristie's unit deployed, and his next overseas deployment would overlap hers. As long as she was okay with it, he'd stay on the Bad Karma team, doing all he could to protect her and the girls, because there was still work for the team to do.

THANK YOU for reading *Deadly Aim*! I hope you loved getting to know Mack and Kristie and seeing Ray and Stephanie from *Desperate Choices* again. You'll get to see more of them in the rest of the series along with the other heroes of the Bad Karma Special Ops team—whose love lives are as dangerous as their missions.

I appreciate your help in spreading the word about my books. Tell a friend. Share on social media. Post a review on Amazon, Goodreads, BookBub, or your favorite book site. Reviews are like hugs to authors, and I love hugs.

Higher numbers of reviews will help other readers find me and know if this book is for them. It doesn't even have to be a five-star review—though those are certainly welcome and what I strive for.

I don't want to disappoint my readers, so I spend time researching and hire editors. We're human though and miss things. So, if you find mistakes and want to tell me in a nice way (not like the perfectionist acquaintance that takes glee in pointing out errors,) email me so I can fix it and I will be grateful!

And I'd love for you to join my newsletter list which is the best way to hear about new releases, sales, giveaways, and receive FREE and EXCLUSIVE content! Including the backstory of how Tony Vincenti and Angela Hoffman first met which is a great bridge between *Deadly Aim* and Tony's book, *A Shot Worth Taking*.

JOIN MY NEWSLETTER LIST HERE.

Next up is *A Shot Worth Taking* and then *In the Wrong Sights*—both Golden Heart Winners. They are stand-alone novels with a common cast of characters, though reading them in order eliminates spoilers. I hope you'll fall in love with the leads in these books as well.

Following is an excerpt from *A Shot Worth Taking*.

Also by Tracy Brody

Available Now!   Coming Spring 2020

For updates on the Bad Karma Special Ops team,
sign up for my newsletter. You'll receive free
exclusive content including the mission where
Tony Vincenti meets Angela Hoffman.

https://www.tracybrody.com/newsletter-signup

A SHOT WORTH TAKING EXCERPT

Kandahar, Afghanistan

"Porter, I'm talking to my mom. Can you keep your shorts on a second?" Tony turned his chair and laptop, so the bunked beds became the background on his Skype session.

The fun factor of "camping out" with eight of even his closest friends only lasted the first month or two, max, of a deployment. Five and a half months into sharing a space barely larger than his folks' living room tested the most patient of souls at times—like right now.

Too late. Yeah, Mom got an eyeful, based on her wide eyes, and then looking at the camera instead of her screen. By now he was oblivious to the constant overexposure of his teammates' junk, but was it too much to ask for ten minutes of privacy a week?

His noise-canceling headphones kept him from making out his teammates' responses. Probably for the best in case Dominguez made another wisecrack about Tony's weekly call to his mom. "Sorry. What were you saying about Mrs. Pesci?"

"That she ran into Carla last week at the market."

Lord, not again. "Carla's married and has kids, and I'm—"

"But she wasn't wearing her wedding ring. Maybe you should get in touch with her."

He worked not to go cross-eyed. Weren't seven grandkids enough, at least for now? "I can handle my own love life. Thanks."

"Really?"

Ouch. Now would be a good time for the shitty internet connection to go out. It didn't. Tony swallowed and shifted on the hard chair, avoiding his mom's convicting stare that didn't lose its impact even traveling a few thousand miles to his computer screen.

Okay, so he didn't have anyone special in his life. Hadn't in, oh, say a decade, but what he and Carla shared years ago had as much chance of being resurrected as the two US troops and nearly a dozen locals killed by a suicide bomber last week.

Sadly, none.

Carla deemed him too dangerous *then*. She might have been the only woman who saw past his exterior, but she wouldn't even recognize the man he'd become since joining the Bad Karma Special Ops team.

Porter stripped off the PT shorts he'd just put on, then pull back on his uniform pants and motioned to him. Something was up based on the sudden spate of activity in the room.

Tony lowered the headphones to his neck as Chief Lundgren closed in on him.

"Eyes on al-Shehri. We're rolling." Lundgren lifted his M-4 from the hook on the wall.

Eyes on! Seriously? Tony's heart pounded against his ribs like the thud of mortar fire. His body went onto autopilot. The laptop rocked on his lap as he began to rise, then sat again. He quickly pulled the headset back on.

"You love kids," his mom continued without missing a beat. "You're both still—"

"Mom, I gotta go."

"You said you weren't going out until tonight. Anthony Salvatore Vincenti, are you trying to get out of this conversation? Because I know how—"

"The team's going out on patrol. I'll talk—"

"What for? Is something wrong?" Her pitch rose and facial features scrunched together in worry.

"It's just a routine patrol." He stared right at the computer screen and lied to his mother.

His mother's eyebrows arched, the left higher than the right in the piercing manner she'd perfected raising four kids.

He didn't flinch or let his gaze deviate from the screen.

She made the sign of the cross, then leaned closer to the screen. "I'm headed to the market. I'll stop by St. Benedict's to light a candle and say a prayer for you."

Busted. He never could fool his mother's bullshit detector. Though she probably caught his reaction when Lundgren passed on the news that could make his week, if not his deployment.

"Thanks." He and his team could use the extra prayers, even to patron saints, about this mission. *Father, forgive me for lying to my mom.* "Give my love to Pop and the family. I'll talk to you next week and see you soon."

That made her smile and the wrinkles on her forehead disappear. "Be safe. Email me later so I know you're okay."

"We'll be fine. I gotta go."

"Routine patrol, huh?" Lincoln Porter grinned at him and pulled on his Kevlar vest.

Tony shook his head. Not exactly routine. If they nabbed

al-Shehri, the guru of recruiting suicide bombers, it would be like getting extra cheese and double meat toppings on a deep-dish pizza. However, there were a lot of things family were better off not knowing.

"How good's the intel on this?" he asked Lundgren.

"A local told a patrol team from the 173rd he saw al-Shehri going into a home this morning. At least that's what they got out of the translation. I wouldn't bet a month's pay on it."

Tony wouldn't either. They were oh-for-three when it came to translators they shared with another unit.

The first translator had actually been good. Good enough to get shot in a drive-by assassination. The second stopped showing up, likely after he was threatened by insurgents. The third "translator" fired off one shot, hitting Rozanski in the vest, before the team took him down.

Lundgren spoke Pashto better than their translators spoke English, and Tony couldn't think of anyone he trusted more. Well, he could think of one linguist he trusted would have their backs, but he doubted Angel—FBI Special Agent Angela Hoffman—knew Pashto. Besides, her being here could be a major distraction to the guys on the team, him most of all.

Time to gear up, load up on ammo, and pray this intel proved reliable and didn't send them into an ambush. Then it'd be time for the strike team to live up to their name and deliver bad karma to deserving jihadists.

Tony held on to the door handle as the caravan of Humvees bumped down a pothole-rutted street. Outside the vehicle, a sandstorm raged. It sounded like rain as it beat against the metal and glass, only instead of water, the wipers swept aside the grains, and an eerie red glow reflected off the blowing sand and distorted the already shitty visibility.

The vehicle braked to a stop in front of the wall of a family compound. Tony's pulse rate jumped as if someone floored his heart's gas pedal.

They'd been down this street on routine patrols at least a handful of times. This evening was different. A thousand mini shocks of electricity danced on the surface of his body at the possibility of nabbing Samir al-Shehri.

He and the team poured out of the vehicles onto the narrow street. The sand swirled to infiltrate his uniform's neck and sleeves. With his gloved hand, he pulled the *shemagh* scarf higher to cover his nose. He never thought a sandstorm would be good for something. But the storm kept the locals hunkered down inside their mud-walled homes.

Still, he scanned what he could see of the residential street. Only flat rooftops peaked over the high walls which protected the homes.

Tony didn't let the forsaken streets lull him into an over-confident state. Not here. Not *ever* in Afghanistan. Just because he didn't see anyone didn't mean an enemy sniper wasn't there watching. Or waiting.

The team fell into place behind an eight-foot-high wall near a locked metal gate. Porter shifted his M4 Carbine rifle to his back. Tony and Lundgren clasped hands on each other's forearms. Porter placed one foot on their arms, and they boosted him up. He peered into the compound before he swung his leg over the ledge. Within seconds, he gave the all-clear signal.

They boosted Juan Dominguez up next. He kept an eye out while Porter dropped to the ground on the other side.

Metal grated against metal when Porter unlocked the gate for the team to enter the compound.

Time to start this party. Two of the team guarded the entrance, another pair took Dita, the team's working dog, and headed toward the back courtyard.

Tony sprinted across the barren space to the side of the residence with Porter, Lundgren, and Dominguez. They edged their way to the main door.

The compound walls decreased the amount of blowing sand enough to improve visibility by a few feet. Dust rolled in waves along the base of the house. It drummed against the surrounding walls, masking most of the noise they made.

The mud house had a metal door. Solid metal, not a sheet of corrugated or scrap metal. Hardly standard Afghan construction. Major red flag. The fight-or-flight instinct hit and pumped adrenaline through his veins. No brainer. Fight.

He'd do his part to stop one more zealot from persuading kids to strap on bombs. Who the hell decided being a martyr got you a shitload of virgins in heaven? *Gimme a freakin' break. Sounds more like hell.* He'd take a woman with experience any day.

Lundgren tried the knob. No go. He nodded to Porter, who opened his ordnance pack.

Porter made a loop of detcord and taped it to the wall near the door. For the tighter quarters, Tony pulled his Kimber .45 from the holster on his protective vest. After Porter inserted a blasting cap into the C4, the team stepped clear of the blast zone.

Tony turned his face away. The vibration rocked his body though the earpieces of his communication headset muffled the explosive *crack* when the charge detonated. A poof of smoke mixed with the sand in the air. They ducked through the large opening into the house, weapons raised.

He tugged the scarf below his chin and pulled his dusty goggles from his face. Sand drifted downward. He licked rough grains from his chapped lips.

The pungent aromas of fresh herbs hung heavy in the air.

Dinnertime. Somebody's home.

Lundgren and Dominguez veered to the right. Tony followed his nose. Porter trailed him through the doorway to their left. A few steps in, a shadow appeared on the floor of the narrow hallway.

His gaze shot upward, and his weapon tracked with his eyes. Dark gray fabric billowed into the hallway. A figure fully covered in a *burqa* emerged. Definitely not al-Sheri, but his heart rate yo-yoed when the woman squawked and came to a complete stop. He held his index finger to his lips and aimed his weapon away from her chest.

She hobbled a step toward them on a crutch carved out of a branch. Her gravelly voice fussed at them in rapid Pashto. He couldn't make out all of what she said, but the tone and the gnarled finger she waved clearly conveyed her *Get-the-hell-out-of-my-home!* message.

He advanced, trying to force the old woman back into the kitchen. Except she refused to budge. "Move," he growled through clenched teeth and resorted to waving his pistol to direct her.

She rattled off a fresh litany of complaints, something about American troops and invasions. Behind him, Porter cleared his throat, probably to keep from laughing at the diminutive menace.

Damn, she reminded him of his Nonna Sofia. Stubborn cuss. Rules of engagement dictated the only way he could touch her was if she was in danger or presented a physical threat. Her smacking the back of his legs with her stick probably didn't qualify. Just as reprisal wasn't an option when

Nonna's cane accompanied a swift reminder to behave like a good Catholic boy.

A noise came from the next room. Tony surged forward. Using his body as a shield, he spun the woman and lifted her out of the potential line of fire.

Her crutch clattered to the floor. Thin arms and legs flailed at him and Porter, who surged past them. A heel smashed him in the shin. He reared his head back to avoid the clawed hand that reached back to scratch out his eyes.

"I'm not going to hurt you!" he said in Pashto. He couldn't protect her and cover Porter, but he didn't dare release her. She didn't weigh half of what he bench-pressed, but holding on to her was like trying to cuddle a feral cat.

Covered head to toe in the *burqa*, she could be hiding something. Something other than the ragged fingernails that raked over his cheek. He didn't need a mirror to know she drew blood.

She jabbered louder while Porter searched the kitchen. People in the house next door probably heard her since she was louder than them blasting a hole in the home's wall.

He shifted her slight figure and held her to his side and backed into the kitchen. With no viable options, other than to flex cuff her, which he couldn't bring himself to do—at least yet—he dragged the kitchen's high wooden worktable to the doorway and deposited her in the hallway. He wedged the table in the doorframe to keep her out while he joined the hunt.

Heat radiated from the brick oven to his right. Loaves of bread sat on a rough-hewn shelf along the wall. Four loaves. The hairs on the edge of his scalp bristled. Porter made eye contact, then nodded to the pair of floor-length, crimson curtains that separated the kitchen from another room, likely the communal dining room.

Porter pointed, then held up one finger.

Please, let it be al-Shehri. Tony would take him dead or alive. Preferably alive to see what information they could garner from him, but ...

He indicated for Porter to go low.

Behind him, the woman yammered away. Her pitch rose higher, making it more difficult to decipher her words. Just as Porter whipped back the curtain, Tony translated her last phrase.

Don't lay a hand on her.

Her?

Oh, shit!

Too late, he realized he was wrong.

His world shifted to slow motion, and he shoved Porter aside as steaming meat and vegetables flew at them. Hot droplets of broth splattered his face. Food bounced off his body to the wooden floor, some landing on his boots.

Great! "Whoa. Whoa. Wh-oa!" he warned a petite figure clad in a blue *burqa.*

The barely teenage girl clutched a pot with its remaining contents, ready to launch a second round.

He shifted out of firing stance and raised both hands in a surrender gesture. He searched for the right words in Pashto. "You should save what's left of your dinner."

In the back corner of the room, a young boy crouched. His patterned *taqiyah* cap slipped to the side of his head as the child pointed at Tony. His other hand covered his mouth while he laughed.

Tony chuckled along. "I look funny, huh?" He waved a hand down the length of his torso where bits of herbs and onion clung to his uniform.

The boy laughed harder when Tony plucked some dark green leaves and strips of onion from his arm. When the girl lowered the pot from side-armed pitching position, Tony snatched it from her hands. Defenseless, she fled around the low dining table to the corner where she huddled next to the boy.

The room had two small windows high in the wall. Wooden flaps covered the openings, but sand still blew in through the cracks. There wasn't another entrance to the room. It made as good a place as any to corral the house's occupants while his team cleared the compound in their search for al-Shehri.

"Watch them while I get the old lady," he ordered Porter.

His mouth watered like Pavlov's dog as he set the pot down next to the brick oven. The food smelled better than anything the cook at their forward operating base had served in the past five months, but he resisted taking even a bite since most of the family's dinner was on the floor. Besides, he'd bet money the old woman watched his every move. Probably gave him the evil eye from behind the veil, too.

The woman stooped over the table. She released her grip and put a hand against the doorframe for support when he grabbed the table by the edge.

Tony pulled the table back into the room. When she didn't move, he edged around her and retrieved the fallen crutch from the floor. An age-spotted hand snatched it away. She tucked the rag-wrapped top under her arm and limped toward the eating area without any prodding.

"Did he touch you?" The woman's voice crackled with angst.

"Yes," the girl replied. A single, soft-spoken word in Pashto. A flat out lie.

"Wait a damn min—"

Whack!

The top of the crutch made direct contact with his nose. He felt the all too familiar pain.

"*Fu—*" he choked back the string of expletives about to pour out of his mouth. White spots of light obscured his vision. Bent over, one hand braced above his knee, he rode out the wave of nausea. He opened his mouth to breathe as blood dripped onto the floor.

Porter grabbed the crutch from the woman before she could strike again.

"Don't do it," he ordered before Porter could snap the confiscated crutch in half. "But keep it out of her reach!"

She wanted to protect the young girl's virtue, but he didn't deserve a broken nose. Well, there were plenty of other things he *might* deserve a beating for, but he hadn't laid a finger on the girl. *Damn.* A low growl rumbled in his throat.

Porter placed the crutch on top of the brick oven, then dug in a side pocket of his pants. Tony took the offered sterile gauze pads. He rolled one up and stuffed it in his nostril to staunch the blood dripping down his face. Over the communications headset, Lundgren requested status updates.

"We've got three non-hostiles contained at our position," Porter reported.

Non-hostiles, my ass. Tony glared at the old woman while he gingerly touched his nose to determine the damage before it swelled more.

He felt the bump left from the first break in a high school football game. The second break came from a hand-to-hand combat exercise after he made it through Selection and into Special Forces. Those were both stories he could live down; they might even enhance his image. But conked in the face by a gimpy old lady? Hell, this was beyond embarrassing.

Minutes later, more of the Bad Karma team crowded into the kitchen.

"What the hell happened to you?" Dominguez was the first to take in the bloody scratches, gauze protruding from his nose, and damp patches on his uniform.

Chief Lundgren's eyebrows rose at his appearance.

"Don't ask." Tony prayed that Porter would keep his mouth shut. His teammates flanked a man in a flowing white *perahan tunban* over black pants. His hands were flex-cuffed behind his back. It made the throbbing pain worthwhile—until the prisoner faced him. The universe sucked his flash of enthusiasm into a black hole.

"No sign of al-Shehri, and he's not talking." Lundgren shifted his gaze back to their prisoner. A muscle in Lundgren's cheek twitched. "Got a teen in the back bedroom. He's not talking either—because he's in no condition to. Chemical burns on his arms, chest, and face. Wounds are infected. Dad here was praying for him but won't let us take the boy to the base for treatment. Grant's cleaning and dressing the burns, but …" The grim set of Lundgren's mouth and shake of his head conveyed paragraphs of information, ending ominously.

Silence settled around them. Tony cast a glance at the shrouded woman, her arms wrapped around the children. He wanted al-Shehri. He wanted people like this family to not live in fear of al-Qaeda *or* American troops. He wanted to go home without losing more buddies in gunfights or to freakin' IEDs or mortar attacks.

Tony dug in his pants pocket and pulled out a pack of candy. He caught Lundgren's eye and jerked his head to the kid. "Let me have the picture." The idea tumbled out. "Translate for me?"

Lundgren handed over a picture of al-Shehri. "You're going to have to get your nose fixed this time." His expression issued a challenge.

Tony gave a resigned nod. He signaled for Dominguez to

keep the prisoner out of sight before he approached the trio in the dining room.

He motioned to the boy, but the old woman held him to her side. Tony pulled off his gloves to unwrap the candy, then popped a purple disk into his mouth.

The boy slipped from the woman's grasp and darted to his side, smiling expectantly. Tony handed the rest of the candy to the bright-eyed boy, who turned and spoke to the *burqa*-clad females, then flashed a gap-toothed grin at the men.

Lundgren snickered. "He told his grandmother not to be scared of you. Thinks you're funny." His gaze roved over Tony's disheveled appearance in concurrence.

While tall, dark, toned, and dangerous drew women to him for one reason, kids saw right through him. They knew they had no reason to be afraid of him. He was Uncle Tony.

He squatted, getting on the kid's level. The boy opened his hand, offering to share the candy. Tony took another piece. The time seemed right, so he showed the picture of al-Shehri to the boy.

The kid's eyes doubled in size. The hand shoveling more candy into his mouth froze.

"He was here?" Lundgren asked in Pashto.

The boy's head bobbed in slow motion.

"He's gone now?"

This time the boy nodded more vigorously, and his features relaxed slightly.

"When did he leave?" Lundgren probed over the chatter of the grandmother. One of his signature stares intimidated her to go silent.

"This morning," the boy answered.

Crap! Anticipation waned, and energy drained from his body.

"Is he coming back?" Lundgren remained calm.

Tony's stomach muscles tightened the same way his fingers gripped his weapon in a gunfight. His trigger finger flexed and released.

This time, the boy only shrugged.

So far, Tony followed the conversation with ease—followed it to another dead end. Even Lundgren's shoulders sagged. So damn close. What next? What were they missing?

"How did he get out of the house?" Tony asked in Pashto.

A grin tugged at the boy's lips. He pointed to the dining table.

Okay, so my Pashto needs work. "Ask him how al-Shehri got out of the house," he asked Lundgren.

"You just did."

Their gazes locked. Both men turned their attention to where the boy had pointed. The low dining table sat atop a deep red rug woven with an intricate pattern

Tony rose to his full height. He ushered the boy to the edge of the room with his grandmother and sister, then handed him another packet of candy. The old woman was strangely quiet now, her head down while she held the girl close.

Together, the men turned the table on its side, setting it against the wall. They peeled the rug back to reveal a hole dug in the center of the room. Lundgren aimed his flashlight into the blackness and let out a whistle. It wasn't just a rat hole. It led to a tunnel.

"Bring in Dita," Lundgren said into his communications mic.

The prior adrenaline rush fizzled out like a firework's show fading to black. Every brain cell told Tony that al-Shehri was gone. Long gone.

WANT TO KNOW WHAT HAPPENS NEXT? You can read the whole story of Tony Vincenti and Angela Hoffman in *A Shot Worth Taking*.

Find *A SHOT WORTH TAKING* here.

And I'd love for you to join my newsletter list which is the best way to hear about new releases, sales, giveaways, and receive FREE and EXCLUSIVE content! Including the mission where Tony Vincenti first meets FBI Special Agent Angela Hoffman.

JOIN MY NEWSLETTER HERE.

ACKNOWLEDGMENTS

This book has been a long time coming. It's not the first book I wrote—that one still needs a complete rewrite after all I've learned—but *Deadly Aim* required multiple rewrites as I learned the craft of writing and strategies of plotting.

Thank you to my critique partners, the BBTs, especially Paula Huffman, who pointed out the need for conflict and tension in early versions and listened to plotline ideas on our writing retreats and beach walks. To JJ Kirkmon, C.S. Smith, Mimi Tsuki, Pennie Leas, and others for all the writing meetups that keep the momentum going.

I appreciate the many people who gave of their time to teach at RWA® conferences, chapter meetings, and online workshops. Thank you to the contest judges who gave their time and expertise to provide helpful feedback. To my betas, Paula, Kathryn Barnsley, Carol Thorton, Karen Long, Becky Eien, and Judy Eien, who read every version of Mack and Kristie's story as it changed time and again. I appreciate you hanging in there and continually cheering for me and their story.

Thanks to Cathy LaMarche for turning me onto Suzanne

Brockmann's *Troubleshooters* series and asking that all-important that made me think beyond Mack's story to a series featuring other members of the Bad Karma Team.

Supporting troops has brought many wonderful friends into my life. A huge shout out to my main go-to guy for military and Special Ops information—MSG Dale Simpson (US Army Ret.) Thank you for all your time, knowledge, suggestions, and telling me what you're wearing. Ha! Any errors or artistic liberties are my own.

Thanks to now-retired Black Hawk pilot Jeremiah Powell for answering flight-related questions over and over due to story changes. I still want to ride in a Black Hawk, but getting input from you is the next best thing.

I made a few platoons of Army pilots and crews smile with care packages filled with cookies, brownies, footballs, books, letters, and goodies, but *I* was blessed to gain many Renegades as friends, along with a few Ghost Riders, Outlaws, Killer Spades, and an Outlaw. Thanks for answering questions and your support as my books deploy.

To my friend and copy editor, LTC Kathryn Barnsley (USAF Retired), thank you for your service. When you offered to do a beta read, I was a little intimidated when I learned your rank, but your experience in editing and your perspective in ensuring I portray my military characters and their families respectfully and accurately is invaluable. I hate I had to cut some of those favorite scenes, too.

Thank you to my developmental editor, Holly Ingraham, for helping me add those final polishes to this story.

Christy Hovland, you did a fabulous job creating another swoon-worthy cover. Thank you for all your input on covers and indie publishing.

To JJ Kirkmon, your super-proofing powers caught missing commas and tightened up my writing. You went above and beyond—again! Your friendship is a huge blessing to me.

Passing on early publishing offers was the right decision. *Deadly Aim* became a better story, and it allowed me to repeat the awesome experience of being a Golden Heart® finalist with other amazing writers. Being a Dragonfly, Mermaid, Rebelle, Persister, and Omega enriched my life and gave me a strong circle of friends and allies. Thanks especially to all my writer friends who've shared their insights, recommendations, and experiences related to indie publishing, so I'm not doing it alone.

Thank you to the friends who've repeatedly asked when this book is coming out and have celebrated my successes along this journey. Not only can you say you knew me when, but you still know me, and if you're reading this, thank you! I hope to see you and give you a hug.

Most of all, THANK YOU to my family. My awesome husband has been supportive of my attending conferences and writing retreats and made time to read *Desperate Choices,* despite his demanding workload. Thanks to my wonderful children, who recognized I had a need beyond folding laundry and preparing several meals a day and rarely complained when I would disappear into my office. I appreciate your patience and cheers for the wins along the way. I love you and pray for your "happily ever after's."

ABOUT THE AUTHOR

Tracy Brody has written a series of single-title romances featuring the Bad Karma Special Ops team whose love lives are as dangerous as their missions. A SHOT WORTH TAKING and IN THE WRONG SIGHTS won the Golden Heart® for romantic suspense in 2015 and 2016. DEADLY AIM was a four-time finalist in the Golden Heart.

She has a background in banking, retired to become a domestic engineer, and aims to supplement her husband's retirement using her overactive imagination. Tracy began writing spec movie and TV scripts, however, when two friends gave her the same feedback on a script, saying that they'd love to see it as a book, she didn't need to be hit over the head with a literal 2" x 4" to get the message. She joined RWA® and developed her craft and is still working on using commas correctly

Tracy and her husband live in North Carolina. She's the proud mother of a son and daughter. She invokes her sense of humor while volunteering at the USO. You may spot her dancing in the grocery story aisles or talking to herself as she plots books and scenes while walking in her neighborhood, the park, or at the beach on retreats with friends.

facebook.com/tracybrodyauthor

twitter.com/TracyBrodyBooks

instagram.com/tracybrodybooks

bookbub.com/authors/tracy-brody

goodreads.com/tracybrodybooks

Made in the USA
Columbia, SC
04 June 2020

10160830R00212